Sister LOST Sister FOUND

Jeanne G'Fellers

Bella BOOKS

2006

Bella Books, Inc.
P.O. Box 10543
Tallahassee, FL 32302

Printed in the United States of America on acid-free paper
First Edition

Editor: Anna Chinappi
Cover designer: Sandy Knowles

ISBN 1-59493-056-2

Archell turned, folding his legs so he could face Rankil. His eyes were clenched shut, contorted with the effort of speaking clear, unrhyming sentences. "They burned them," he sputtered. "They piled wood underneath the wagon and set it ablaze in the middle of the square. No one cried or screamed, not even the babies, just sat curled in each other's arms like they were asleep and burned. The air stunk, smelled like the smokehouse at butchering time. Now see . . . see . . ." His bottom lip quivered.

Rankil grappled for something to say. "Burned them? Babies with the adults? Why, Archell, why? What did they do? What could they have done to deserve burning?"

Archell pointed to her, his answer as senseless as the act he had witnessed. "They called them witches and cannibals. Whitehairs. They died because they were what you are, Rankil Danston. Taelach."

Visit

Bella Books

at

BellaBooks.com

or call our toll-free number

1-800-729-4992

*For my mother, who let me prowl the library shelves as a child
so I might know the value of books.*

Acknowledgments

Sister Lost Sister Found and all the novels in *The Silver Kinship* series derived from my need to escape. While my reasons for escaping have changed throughout the years, the need still remains as does the drive to tell the stories of those I met during my escapes. These women live in a plane I reach simply by closing my eyes. Theirs is a less than perfect existence—perfection must be horribly boring to write about—but it is a world built upon my wildest fantasies and deepest fears, a creation that would not have come about if it hadn't been for those dear to me. My sister Anne G'Fellers is no exception to this. Though we may be far apart in age we are kindred spirits, sister writers who both love to go where our imaginations dare. Her determination as a writer and actress inspires her big sister more than she will ever know.

To everyone at Bella—Linda Hill, Becky Arbogast and, of course, my editor Anna Chinappi, I say thanks again for patiently leading me through the road to publication.

Anna, my love, my dearest, once again I have left you for last but only because it is difficult to put into words the impact you have had on my life. You listen, you appreciate, you care and you're not afraid to tell me when I am full of it—all things a writer needs in her significant other. Without your honesty and assistance I might not have reached where I am today. Thank you.

About the Author

Jeanne G'Fellers, her partner and their children share a half-acre plot with two cats, a three-foot-long water dragon lizard and a dozen pampered Arbor Day trees. When not shuttling children or writing, Jeanne is completing her MA in English at a regional university where she also works as a teaching assistant.

Sister Lost Sister Found is Jeanne's second novel and the second in the *Silver Kinship* series.

Cast of Characters

Taelachs

Clanless

Rankil Kaelan Danston: misplaced sister, daughter of Danston Maraloosh

Easton Outbrook: misplaced sister and resident of The Pit

Serpent Clan

Recca July: clan leader and mate of Ashklara

Ashklara Reccas: Recca's mate and former clan birther

Wikkib Indigo: assistant clan birther

Larkette Jasmine: teacher of youth

Kaelan London: potter and glassblower, mate of Jewel

Jewel Kaelans: clan birther, mate of Kaelan

Myrla Kaelan: daughter of Kaelan and Jewel
Hestralandra (Hestra): infant
Leonor Dakota: aging warrior

Tekkroon Clan
Harlis Davies: clan leader

Grethencliff Colony
Medrabbi: colony mayor and mate of Elreese
Elreese Medrabbi: skin inker and mate of Medrabbi
Larza: apprentice skin inker under Elreese
Jefflynn Lewis: Tekkroon lead well master, twin sister of Serrick Lewis and mate of Dawn
Dawn Jefflynns: sculptor and mate of Jefflynn
Abbyegale Finces: seamstress and widow
Webbic: widow
Healer Augustus: Gretchencliff lead healer
Dee Astrid: Easton Outbrook's attendant

Bowriver Colony
Maestro Lisajohn Marion: lead musician and choral director for Bowriver colony
Commander Andrea Stiles: Powder Barrier officer in charge of recruit indoctrination, mate of Annya
Annyalae Stiles: manager of Bowriver colony stores and mate of Andrea

Adner Colony
Genevic Leed: Powder Barrier trooper and girlfriend of Isabella Langley
Isabella Langley (Bella): medic in isolation caverns and Genevic's girlfriend
Beverlic Redicci: former Powder Barrier Trooper and resident of The Pit

McDougal Colony
Healer Sarah Garrziko: mental healer in charge of The Pit
Shaedra: Burning victim and resident of The Pit

Autlachs

Maraloosh Family: small, two-house farming compound

Danston Maraloosh: head of first house, brother of Tisph

Meelsa Danstons: wife of Danston

Tessa Danston (Tessie): eldest daughter of Danston and Meelsa

Sallnox Danston: eldest son of Danston and Meelsa

Tisph Maraloosh: head of second house, brother of Danston

Quyley Tisphs: wife of Tisph

Tilnor Tisph: eldest son of Tisph and Quyley

Archell Tisph (later becomes Archell Kaelan): second son of Tisph and Quyley

Eloc Tisph: third son of Tisph and Quyley

Granny Terry: great grandmother of Danston and Tisph

Others

Serrick Lewis: Autlach living with Tekkroon clan, brother of Jefflynn Lewis

Longpass: High cleric in the Raskhallak temples

Sharillia Longpass: wife of Longpass

Olitti Longpass: eldest daughter of Longpass

Paylu Longpass: oldest son of Longpass

Flynne Longpass: second son of Longpass

Humans

Captain Tara Conway: pilot of downed spacecraft discovered by Rankil Danston

Preface

When the first human colonists settled on the Saria Two, they didn't intend on being permanent residents. But, as time passed and hope of rescue faded, they began to make homes for themselves among the Autlach, a humanoid species indigenous to Saria Two, the second planet surrounding the yellow star Sixty-One Cygni. The Autlach, a swarthy humanoid species of stocky build, were slow to accept their multiracial human counterparts but eventually allowed them into their lands, villages and, finally, families, creating a hybrid generation whose descendents understood little of their human heritage and the genetics which shaped a select few of their children. These daughters—the Taelach—were pale, blue-eyed, sterile and telepathic—all things the pious Autlach could not and would not accept. Rejected by their families, the Taelach sought acceptance in each other, forming small clans that kept to the mountains far above the Autlach.

These clans survived for centuries relatively untouched,

1

descending into the realm of the Autlach only for trade and to save infant Taelachs from the cruelty of infanticide. This relative peace changed, however, when Longpass, a high cleric in the Autlach deity Raskhallak's temple, claimed to hear the voice of Raskhallak speak against the Taelach. Raskhallak, said Longpass, claimed the Taelach were sinful beings—witches, whores, and half-women whose only hope of redemption was cleansing by fire. The resulting crusade forced the Taelach clans higher into the mountains. In this harsh, barren environment, Taelach numbers dwindled but persisted, maintaining their culture through stories and songs that sought to explain their origins, rationalize their continued struggle, and keep hope alive when little else seemed tangible.

This is the tale of one such sister, a Taelach born between two worlds, one that abhors her very existence, the other that fears what she has become to survive. This is the first tale of Rankil, a sister lost, a sister found, but a sister never to be forgotten.

Introduction

A Creation Story from the Serpent Clan teaching tales

The Mother Maker grew lonely in her singular existence and longed for a family. There being no male she dared leave the heavens for and no magical means by which she could conceive, the Mother Maker began to cry, the tears landing in her hands as glass seeds. She placed each of these seeds in the bodies of Autlach women and from these women and the descendents of these women, Taelachs were born. The Mother Maker delighted in her creations and granted them the gifts of empathy and telepathy. These skills, along with the Taelach's diametric appearance to the Autlach, took their toll, and the Mother Maker soon found her daughters ostracized by their Autlach kin. Taelach infants were slaughtered in the name the Raskhallak deity, and the ones who did survive to adulthood were either enslaved or driven high into the mountains in order to survive. Fearing for her children, the Mother Maker took pity on her delicate, pale-skinned daughters, creating a physically stronger daughter, a broadback daughter to assist and love the gentler form of her creation. But, in return for her gifts, she expected her daughters to obey a single request: They were to respect nature and all things wild, including their enemies. They were to love the barbaric Autlach and try to be at peace with them.

Some things are easier said than done.

Part I
Aware

Chapter One

We lash out at that which we don't understand.

—Taelach wisdom

They named her Rankil, odd enough name but one she rarely heard. More often, they called her Ugly, Stupid, or simply Rank, like her smell offended them. She answered to any of them because they all meant the same. They wanted her to do things no one else would—clean, lift, carry things far heavier than any child should. Of their blood, she served them as a slave and nothing more, the middle child of the family, a mark of sin on their otherwise prominent position within the isolated farming community they called home. She bore their anger, suffered as the vent point for their frustrations. Rankil was light among the dark, too tall and skinny to be one of them, physical evidence of the long-forgotten human influence on their planet—a Taelach child in an Autlach world.

Whack! The sweeper handle landed square on Rankil's lower back, sending her sprawling to the floor.

"Stupid girl. I taught you to brush the floors better than this. You won't be lazy, Rank. Earn your keep if you expect to eat today." Rankil's mother Meelsa raised the sweeper handle for another blow. Fifteen-pass-old Rankil, in a dirty dress and bare feet, cowered, unsure what she had done wrong.

"You see this?" Meelsa pulled her to the front door and shoved her face first into the space behind it. "See the dirt? You sweep *behind* the doors. How many times must I tell you?"

"Too many?" The answer earned Rankil another blow. The question must have been one of the many her mother asked that expected no answer.

"Bite your tongue." Rankil cringed as the handle rose again but, instead of another blow, Meelsa handed the sweeper to her eldest daughter Tessa, who'd been watching her snow-headed sister's abuse with unbridled amusement. "Here, Tessie, do M'ma a favor and brush the floor proper. I've another chore for Rank."

Contempt exuded from Tessa's brown eyes as she narrowed them at Rankil. Tessa's friends routinely teased her for the resemblance she bore to the family's slave and the outgoing Tessa blamed Rankil for the taunts. "Why do I always end up fixing her messes? She forgot the door. Let her sweep!"

Meelsa's graying braid swayed with the rhythm of her shaking head. "I'm sending Rankil to gather cress for tonight's sup. It's high season, and your dah wants some. She'll go, unless you'd rather climb for it." Rankil's heart soared. She loved going cress gathering. No one bothered her in the hills. She could laugh and play, be happy, be Rankil.

"Ugh!" Tessa rolled her eyes at the thought of harvesting the stone-clinging, crevice-growing plant. "I'll tend the floor and then work on my dress. I've all but finished tatting the collar lace. Jin says fancy collars bring out my eyes."

"Jin would," mumbled Meelsa, all too familiar with the ideas driving the young man's flattery. "The dress and Jinwall Mustin can wait. Sweep more and talk less, Tessa. Your dah wants his house clean." Meelsa grabbed a carry sling from the hooks and tossed it to Rankil who nursed her stinging back. "Don't you bring back any over-big leaves. You know what size they need to be. Danston will beat you if his greens are bitter again."

"Yes ma'am." Rankil scrambled to her feet, snagged her wide-brimmed sunshade from the hooks and ran out the door. If she found a good patch, cress gathering wouldn't take more than an hour or two, leaving her time to roam. She could ask for a slice of bread to eat while she worked. Meelsa would probably give her that, but she knew she'd do better foraging in the hills. She should have her fill of cress up there as well. There would be none for her that evening.

So, her stomach twittering, Rankil trotted across the courtyard, past her uncle's family's cottage. Uncle Tisph had eight children of his own, six of them boys, each more inventive than the next in the cruelty they demonstrated for Rankil. As mean as they were, she still preferred them to her uncle. Tisph always looked at her funny. He never acted mean in a hitting way, just the opposite. He would be too nice, his hand quick to pat her behind or run a path across her chest. He'd even kissed her once, a sucking, full-mouth kiss like her father gave her mother. Rankil wouldn't have liked it even if Meelsa hadn't caught them at it. She had been so furious with Rankil that she had beaten her all the way back to the house, swearing something about birthing a white witch with whorish wiles as they went. What were wiles anyway? Rankil knew what a witch was, she'd been called one enough times, and she knew the word whore meant something bad too, but she had never heard the last word before then. The next day she'd asked Tessa to explain, but her sister had said it'd been her own fault Tisph had kissed her. This only furthered Rankil's confusion. No one ever showed her affection, then when someone did it was wrong? She pondered that fact for a while, deciding she would do best just to keep away from Uncle Tisph. His touch made her feel sort of sick inside and besides, she didn't want another beating—there were plenty of those as was. Time made her quite adept at staying clear of him in almost every situation and in the presence of others when she had to be near him.

Keeping close to the garden to avoid attention, Rankil had almost cleared the compound gates when her Aunt Quyley, Tisph's perpetually pregnant, quarrelsome wife shouted to her from beside the garden shed.

"Rankil!" Quyley's voice had become gruff from screaming at her children. "Come here, girl!"

"Yes, ma'am." Rankil took a few more steps before she slowed to a stop, afraid she'd end up gathering for her greedy cousins as well as her own family. "I've been sent picking."

"Good!" bellowed her aunt, pushing the woven shade from her round, sweating face. "Take Archell with you. He's getting on my nerves."

Archell? It could have been worse. If anyone had to tag along, Rankil preferred it be Archell. Everyone else considered him simpleminded, but she knew better. Archell had a unique way of looking at things. He lived in his own version of reality, one far removed from the pain of this one. If Rankil had one friend in the world, it was seventeen-pass-old Archell.

"Yes, ma'am. Where is he?"

Quyley swiped her nose on her blouse cuff. "Are you stupid, ugly, *and* deaf, girl? Can't you hear his singing? He's in the barn combing down them nassies. Swears they like his voice. Go get him and make him help."

The barn!

Rankil began to shake, her knees knocking so loud she knew her aunt could hear them. The barn was her uncle's favorite escape from his noisy family. If she were lucky, he wouldn't be there.

"Yes, ma'am. I'll get him now." Rankil turned toward the building's open bay doors, her feet pushing up little dust clouds as they dragged along the ground. She peeked around the corner then

9

drew back, her whisper almost inaudible above the nassies' greeting shuffles and snorts.

"Archie?"

His answer came as it always did, in song or rhyme. "Oh my my pretty Rankil—too tall girl with the skinny ankles—Archell sees you from nassie Blue's bright stall." Blue's stall stood third on the right. Rankil slid into it and gave the curly-coated gray work nassie a pat of reassurance.

"Want to pick cress with me?"

Archell shook his great unkempt mop of black hair. "Brush, brush nassie Blue—will not quit until I'm through."

Rankil grabbed the brush from his hand and placed it on the top stall board. "Blue looks good enough. Come on. Your m'ma says you can go with me."

Her cousin smiled as she took his stubby hand. He was no taller than her, but stood twice as broad in the shoulder and was capable of strength he wasn't always able to control. "Where to, Rankil dankle?"

"I just told you, silly, cress picking."

Archell's hand dropped faster than his expression, both withdrawing from her with the same hurt reaction. "Archie not silly willy, Rankil dankle." She sometimes forgot he suffered as many insults as she did.

"I'm sorry." Rankil glanced down the stall row. The nassies, with their tri-toed hooves and short tangled fur, were far too quiet for her liking. "I'm just in a hurry. You know I don't like the barn."

With a sullen draw of his lip, Archell turned her face to his. "Archell knows what Rankil fears—dah's big hands will get too near." She'd never told him, but he knew. He always knew what went through her head.

"Yeah, Archie, that's why I hate the barn. Can we go?" She tugged him from the stall and toward the open back entrance.

"Let's run, rangle dangle." Archell stretched his arms and jogged out the breezy rear doors, his run awkward but quick. "Let's go find a redberry tangle."

10

Rankil laughed, threw the carry bag over her shoulder, and skipped after him in one of the few, short-lived happy moments in her life. She'd reached halfway across the barn when a shadow darkened the alleyway behind her. The lively mood halted, as did Rankil.

"Rankil, sweetheart, where you scurrying off to? Come give your Uncle Tisph a hug."

She started running, white hair streaming, skirts billowing at her knees, bare feet scraping across stone, manure squishing between her toes as she slid across the upper paddocks. She kept running, running as hard and as fast as her legs would carry her.

Tisph pursued her to the edge of the barn then stopped. "Get back here now, you damn whore!" His fists tightened around the halter he carried. "Long-legged bitch. I'll catch you sooner or later, just you wait."

Rankil caught up with Archell, and together they ran across the high fields into the foothills where cress grew best. They didn't speak as they gathered the clustering plant from the slopes. It wasn't necessary. Rankil hurt inside and nothing Archell said or sang would change that.

When they had filled the sack, they took it to the nearby sweet brook to rinse the leaves. "Rankil dankle?" Archell's whisper roared in her swimming head. "Dah's big hands, they'll reach again—but Archell's here—he will defend."

Rankil shook the water from her handful of cress and set it beside him so he could trim the leaves. She remained silent for a moment, then smiled. Archell had enough problems without being concerned for her safety, too. "I'll be all right, Archie. I just need to stay out of his way. He don't bother me when I do. Outta sight, outta mind."

Archell pursed his lips. "Run, run you did today—but safe you cannot always stay."

"I know, Archie, I know." *How can someone considered a lack-wit know so much*, thought Rankil as she rinsed another handful. She pinched off a leaf and popped it in her mouth, savoring the delicate flavor. The cress *was* best this time of year, sweet and crisp, just perfect to go with "Redberries!"

"Berry time, Rankil dankle?" Archell grinned at her, revealing the cress between his front teeth. He'd soaked his tunic front as well, but that was typical Archell; he'd never shown much concern over his looks.

"Yep, Archie, berry time." Rankil gave his soggy stomach a teasing slap. "Come on. I'm starved." They found a nearby patch and ate their fill, then lay back in the summer grass, head to head, each resting on the other's shoulder.

"Rankil dankle is good to me—makes me see things as they should be." Archell reached up to pat her head. "Pretty pretty Rankil roo—wish you were not always blue."

"Blue?" Rankil's older cousin's analogy eluded her. "I have a few redberry stains on my hands, but I'm not blue."

Archell cast one of his wise-beyond-his-years looks, his tan face creasing with concern. "Sweeper marks they bruise your back—heart broke in two from dah's attacks. Rankil dankle is blue."

Rankil sat up. "How'd you know about the sweeper? It happened just before I got you."

"Rankil's dress is getting small—welts they show through cloth and all." He touched the lowest mark on her back, drawing back when she cringed. "Rankil hurts, and I do, too—Rankil, Rankil—" He stopped his musical lament to wipe away the tears trapped in the tired hollows below her eyes. "Rankil cry?" As fast as he could rise to her aid, she collapsed against him, shaking hard. "Rankil scared?"

"Why don't they send me away if they hate me so much?" she mumbled into his damp tunic.

"They're scared of Rankil in a way—Whitehairs always are enslaved."

Rankil looked up from the folds of his shirt, her startled face streaked with the dirt that clung to the fabric. "You've seen someone like me before? When? Where? Tell me!"

Archell chewed his bottom lip as if determining just how much information to supply. "Saw a Whitehair once before—That's all I'll say, there is no more."

"Don't dodge me!" Rankil grasped his arm. "Tell me, Archie, please!"

Archell pushed her away and climbed onto a small boulder perched on the brook's edge, mumbling one of his countless songs under his breath as he moved. Rankil recognized the melody as one he sang when he was being beaten, when he hurt the most.

"Come on, Archell, please, I have to know." She drew onto the cooled stone's top and pulled his head up to meet hers. "Please, Archie, for me."

He jerked back. "No, no, Rankil dankle, you'll run away—leave poor Archell all alone—with no friend to call his own."

Rankil scooted behind him and wrapped her arms around his waist, leaning her head against his solid back. "You know I'd never leave you like that. Please tell me. I'd tell you if I ever met some-one with your song voice."

Archell's reply echoed in his chest, vibrating the ear pressing his spine. "Rankil dankle would?"

"Sure would, Archie."

"Okay." He sighed. "Dah took Arch to Rallings once—down on the river shore—for Arch to tote and haul for him—brought two nassies, needed more—went into the market square—Archell found them right in there—cooped up in a wagon cage—the big ones they were shouting rage."

Rankil stopped him. "Big ones? Men?"

"No, no, Rankil dankle. They weren't men, that was plain—Is hard for Archell to explain—five tall women, dirtied up—as tall as Dah and twice as tough—wrapping pretty, long haired ones—pro-tecting them as best they could—shielding small girls from the hurt—of those who taunted throwing dirt." Archell paused to look back at her. "Rankil dankle?"

"Go on, please."

He sighed again then continued. "Babes were caged up, too, my girl—silver heads with pretty curls—sleeping in their parents' arms." He stopped again.

"Archie?"

He turned, folding his legs so he could face her. His eyes were clenched shut, contorted with the effort of speaking clear, un-rhyming sentences. "They burned them," he sputtered. "They piled wood underneath the wagon and set it ablaze in the middle of the square. No one cried or screamed, not even the babies, just sat curled in each other's arms like they were asleep and burned. The air stunk, smelled like the smokehouse at butchering time. Now see . . . see . . ." His bottom lip quivered.

Rankil grappled for something to say. "Burned them? Babies with the adults? Why, Archell, why? What did they do? What could they have done to deserve burning?"

Archell pointed to her, his answer as senseless as the act he had witnessed. "They called them witches and cannibals. Whitehairs. They died because they were what you are, Rankil Danston. Taelach."

Rankil did receive a beating that night, not for the cress being bitter but for being tardy in her return. She and Archell spent the entire afternoon discussing what he had seen in town, Rankil prod-ding him for details until his singsong voice became hoarse. The beating hadn't hurt half as much as usual because now Rankil was angry—angry with those who had let her believe she was alone, furious with them for their being a part of a people who burned her kind for existing.

She took her lashes without tears then crawled to her corner of the main room, her anger feeding into pure loathing as she wrapped her threadbare blanket about her throbbing shoulders. Drawing up in a ball, her arms circling her knees, she pretended to sleep. They always left her alone after a beating. Perhaps they felt guilty. Rankil didn't care as long as she remained undisturbed.

14

"You need to remind the girl of her place before I do, Meelsa." Rankil's father glared at his daughter's curled figure. "She's getting smart-mouthed, questioning her place, Raskhallak's requirements. Why, I even caught her yawning during prayer. Blasphemous witch! Lashes don't seem to teach a thing anymore either. The more I give the quieter she gets. And where have her tears gone? All women have tears when they're beat. It's how I know the stopping point with you and the other girls."

Meelsa paused to bite her lip then refilled his mug from the wine keg. "She's just a child, Danston, and still learning."

Danston's thin mustache twitched in agitation. "Stars, woman, she's fifteen. You'd birthed Tessa by that age. If she don't know by now she never will."

"Yes, Danston." Meelsa set his mug before him then wet a rag in the bucket by the door.

"Someone sick?" asked Danston between chugs.

"Sallnox has a black eye." She took the compress to the children's room and returned a moment later.

"I saw it earlier. The boy's a fool for messing with stud nassie. Lucky it didn't kick his head in."

"Yes." Meelsa's voice trembled. She swallowed hard and took a place on the bench end nearest him. "Yes, he is."

Danston peered at her for a moment, strumming his fingers on the table. "That *is* how Sallnox got his eye black, isn't it? Because if someone is lying to me—" He grabbed Meelsa's arm. "They'd best come clean right now."

Meelsa wilted in his grasp. "Sallnox wouldn't admit to it." She blurted. "He went to whip her for not listening, but she hit him before he could, then outran him and has kept away from him since."

"Rankil hit Sallnox? She put the bruise on his cheek? Why, I otta scoop up the little white witch and—" Danston released his grasp to pound the table. "Damn!"

"I'm sorry." Meelsa dropped her head.

"You should be!" seethed Danston. "This is your fault more

than anyone else's. I told you to keep her under control." He lunged out, knocking Meelsa's empty mug into her lap. "Dammit, woman, now I'm going to have to make one of the stalls into a pen for her."

"But your brother," sobbed Meelsa. "He'll use her."

"We all use her for the heavy work," replied Danston. "Even you."

Meelsa withdrew from the table to refill her mug, putting crucial distance between them before she spoke. "Tisph fancies her in a man's way. Put her in the barn, and she won't be fit to work. He'll use her up."

Rankil let out an involuntary squeak when she heard that, prompting a suspicious glower from her father.

"You sure she's sleeping?" asked Danston around his mug.

Meelsa stopped to gaze into the corner. Rankil curbed her anxiety and held her breath to a sleeper's slow, even pattern. She had a talent for feigning sleep. It let her hear things the other children didn't, keeping her one step ahead of them. "Yes, she's out. Feeling her lashes is all."

"I knocked her good." Danston flexed one of the red, stiffened knuckles on his right hand. "Say, where'd she get the gash on her right calf? Could leave her a cripple if it gets infected."

"Tilnor gave it to her yesterday for working slow." Meelsa remained by the fireside, her arms by her sides. "Rankil swears she hadn't stopped. Said her skirts snagged on a stone. Tilnor struck her with the plow nassies' reins before she could get herself loose. I sewed up the cut. She heals fast so it'll be fine."

"That's what she gets for being clumsy." Danston rubbed his chin. "I shouldn't of let her live. A Taelach witch in the house is bad luck. If you hadn't just miscarried twice—"

"You took pity on me, Danston. I know." Meelsa closed her eyes and bowed her head. "But caging her won't cure the problem with Tisph." She pleaded. "If anything, it'll make things easier for him and harder on her. She won't be fit to work."

Danston's dusty boots tapped the floor in a deliberate fashion. "Tisph might like a pinch or two, but I doubt he'd sink to that."

16

"You know he will." She braced for a violent response to her brashness. "The last hunt left him with a taste for Whitehairs. The barn won't work. There's got to be another answer."

Danston slid forward in his seat. "Like what?"

"How about Granny Terry?"

"No!" Danston's glare set Meelsa's heart to racing. He rose and strode to where she stood, menacing over her. "Where'd you ever get the idea that I'd ever send a Taelach to care for my granddah's m'ma?"

"Please." She placed her finger to her mouth. "The babes are sleeping."

"Your baby is eight passes old," grumbled her husband. "She's not going to Granny Terry's. I told you Tessa's going."

"But—" Meelsa ignored his upheld hand. "Do you think Tessa can look after Granny Terry like Rankil can? Send Tessa, and you'll always be sending one of the boys up to the cottage to split wood and bring in game. Rankil can do it all by herself. She's good at snaring and fishing. Always has been. Send her. That way she can't be trouble and stays clear of your brother."

"Those chores are man's work. Rankil shouldn't be doing them. Besides, Granny Terry doesn't know Rankil is Taelach."

"Rankil does those chores here every day," replied Meelsa in a tone stronger than she usually dared. "And Terry's been blind since long before Rankil was born. She'll never know one way or the other, and she's always been partial to Rankil on her visits. Send her, please. It's the only answer."

Danston lowered his hand. "Won't Tessa be disappointed?"

"Nah." Meelsa sniffed at her eldest daughter's lazy demeanor. "She's dreaded going since you told her."

"Time the girl grew up." Danston swallowed the last of his brew and motioned Meelsa for a refill. "Who's she sweet on these days?"

"Jinwall Mustin."

"That boy?" Danston chuckled. "He's only seventeen, too young to care of a wife proper." Danston ignored the distraught in his wife's eyes. "But I'll visit his dah in a day or two. He's been

17

asking about Tessa since he lost his second wife last moon cycle. He's promised that matched nassie team of his in trade. It'd be a good placing, push us up a notch or two to be known as part of Mustin's family. Tessa will make a good m'ma for those four little ones he's been left with." Danston rambled on, deep in matrimonial plans for his eldest daughter. "Who knows, she might even give him a few more before he gets too old for baby making. Yep, I'm looking forward to seeing that team in the barn." He pushed away from the table and stretched. "It's settled. Rankil goes. Find her clothes that fit. Blasted tree, she is, all limb."

"She's outgrown every dress in the compound." Meelsa's reply couldn't hide her concern over Tessa's future. "Even my castoffs won't fit anymore. I can send her with a set Sallnox has outgrown." She sniffled. "But that's all we've got. If you want her to stay in dresses, you'll have to wait until we weave enough to make some up."

"Don't go wasting new cloth on her. Leggings will do if they're long enough. Granny Terry will never be the wiser. I'll take her at first light."

Rankil snuggled a little more under her blanket. She was going to Granny Terry's! No more beatings. No more names. No more ducking Uncle Tisph. No more—her elation crashed—no more Archell. There'd be no one to listen to his songs. How would he get along without her? He was strong, she assured herself as she drifted off. Archell had advantages she didn't. He was male and Autlach. He'd survive where she couldn't.

Meelsa woke Rankil long before she roused the other children. "Here." She shoved leggings and a tunic at her daughter. "Your dress is too short. Sallnox's old rags are all I've got left."

Rankil rose to her feet, tugged off her dress, and slid on the clothes. She liked the feeling of the leggings and kicked experimentally, enjoying how her strides were longer when free of a skirt's layered weight. The leggings were from the set Sallnox had outgrown several passes back and were just shy of threadbare, but they were long enough, Rankil's slim build so lost in the folds that her mother passed her an old piece of strap for a belt. "You can't travel if your leggings won't stay up."

"Travel?" Rankil managed to sound surprised.

Meelsa dished a bowl of steaming mush from the hearth, poured a generous coating of syrup over it, and set it on the table. "That's right, travel. Can't walk half the morning on an empty stomach either, so get that belt on and sit. Danston is saddling up." Rankil did as told and wolfed down the mush as fast as her mouth could manage the heat. Eating at the table? New clothes? Breakfast served to her? Sweetening when everyone else seldom bothered with it? She'd never been treated this way! Her mother placed a filled carry sling on the table then plopped down beside her.

"Danston is sending you to Granny Terry's. She's always done well by herself but is beginning to lose out on the heavier chores. Help her with what she needs done." She reached to smooth her daughter's knotted hair, looking confused when Rankil cringed away. "Do you hear what I'm saying, daughter?"

Daughter? Rankil had never heard the word applied to her, nor did she remember seeing such a maternal look on Meelsa's face. It seemed misplaced, far too late to be believable, but she answered as not to disturb the gentle mood. "Yes ma'am, I hear."

"You take good care of her. This is the only chance you'll ever get to live outside this compound." Meelsa leaned close as her husband's thick steps sounded on the porch. "Use it to your good. There won't be more chances." She sat back and pushed Rankil to her feet when the door began to creak, and her face tightened to the austere knot she normally presented her lankiest offspring. "Sallnox planted a large garden at the cabin this spring. The vegetables should coming in about now. Dry and store them like you were taught and smoke out as much game as you can snare. It's up to you to make sure there's enough food and wood for winter. I've packed spices enough to see you through until fall and Danston is strapping a nassie with a smoked beast quarter and a sack of black grain."

Danston stepped through the doorway, his angular face speaking beyond words as he drew into the firelight to scrutinize his daughter. Rankil could all but hear the thoughts that darkened his expression. Meelsa had been right. Their middle daughter was beginning to take shape, her slim hips filling, her chest angling into something more than muscle. She'd be almost pretty if she weren't so tall, if she weren't so pale, if she weren't one of *them*. Danston's frown deepened.

"She ready? I haven't got all day. There'll be extra work with her gone."

Meelsa nodded and placed the sling of spices in Rankil's hands. "Danston or Sallnox will be up every moon cycle to check on things." The words sounded like a warning.

Rankil scurried out the door and stood behind the nassies, her usual place when they went into the fields. Danston mounted, took the packer's reins and led the nassies from the compound, Rankil trotting behind. As they passed Tisph's house she could see Archell peeping through the shutter slats.

"Rankil dankle?"

She held up a hand to him as she passed, her voice strong to encourage him. "Sing me a song, Archie." She shouted. "Sing me a sweet one then sing me away."

He rushed to the door, threw it wide and sang her away in the morning haze.

"Rankil girl my heart's own true—I wish that I could go with you—Please tell me you'll come back someday—So in the hills we'll once more play.

"Rankil dankle Rankil roo—Take my songs away with you—Rankil Rankil please don't go—Archell he will miss—you—so . . . Goodbye, Rankil."

Chapter Two

Luck, fortune, or fate—call it what you will, sometimes it's all we have.

—*Taelach Wisdom*

Granny Terry had lived a very long time. How long she couldn't say—old enough to be set in her ways but not so aged she couldn't bend a little every now and again. She was tiny, crouched in the awkward stoop that came from an overburdened back, and fiercely independent, having little use for those who had made her earlier life so complicated. She complained and swore insult when Danston presented her with Rankil but secretly thought it grand to have someone around.

"Well," she told Danston in her warbling croon, "if you have to push someone off on me I'm glad you had sense enough to make it Rankil. She's the only one of my family who doesn't whine and carry on about a little hard work. Never heard more than two words from her."

"Now, Granny Terry," Danston gave the old woman a childlike pat on the head. "Rankil is a hard worker. She should be a big help. You need someone about whether you'll say it or not."

Terry swatted his shin with her cane. "Don't lower me and don't tell me what I need, boy." She turned away and walked toward the nassies' sound and smell, chck-chcking a pleasant greeting to them. "Where is that girl? Come here, Rankil, and let me see you with these old hands of mine."

Danston nodded to his daughter then began to unload the pack animal. Rankil slid from her perch and minded the request, slouching so she wouldn't appear so tall. Terry expected a girl, not a skinny, half-grown Taelach. The old woman grinned up at her, reached a crooked finger to her face, and traced the line of her jaw. "Which one of your parents named you? There's not a thing in the world rank about you. You've grown into a fine young woman. And so tall! How old? Sixteen? Seventeen?"

Rankil ignored her father's hard stare. "I think I'm fifteen, if you please."

"Fifteen?" Granny Terry's toothless grin spread all the wider. "Never knew there was such size in the family, Danston. I believe she's as tall as you. Must come from Meelsa's side." She took Rankil by the arm and led her to the porch, registering the lack of skirt sounds in her grandchild's strides as they walked. "Bring in Rankil's things when you finish unloading that pack mount, boy. My granddaughter and I are going to get reacquainted."

As Danston watched them disappear into the house, his rage became overwhelming. He mumbled, spat and cursed, damning his white witch child and his decision to let her live. Why had he let Meelsa talk him into permitting a Taelach to care for Terry? And Rankil had such a smug look on her face when she'd spoke! Almost superior. She'd best behave if she knew what was good for her. Danston, brooding and still cursing, hung the meat quarter in the smoke shed and tossed the food stuffs onto the porch. He dropped Rankil's only other set of clothes into the dirt, stepping on them as he walked into the one-room house. His ill will rolled into repulsion with what he saw. Rankil sat pretty as you please at the same table as Granny Terry, munching a fresh-baked spice cake while she listened to one of the old woman's countless stories.

"I'm leaving." He cast his daughter a vicious stare that caused her to shrink back. She knew the look—her worst scars were hidden in it. "I need to speak to Rankil before I go."

When they stepped from the porch, Danston snatched her by the hair.

"She told me to sit there—" began Rankil.

"Listen here, you sorry, white-haired beggar," he whispered. "I won't have you thinking you deserve the way Granny Terry treats you." His hand twisted tighter into her hair, bringing her to her knees. "She has no idea how worthless you are. You're to keep that in mind in everything you do." Rankil's spice cake soured as she stared up at him, but she knew better than to cry out. It might bring Granny Terry, and that would ruin everything.

"Yes, sir."

Danston bent down and placed his face against hers, their similar features lining in perfect symmetry. Though she seemed pale against his swarthy skin, their resemblance was undeniable. "You never know when I might show up to check on you. If I see you doing anything other than what you should, I'll drag you back home and give you to your uncle."

Rankil's reply cracked in her dry mouth. "Yes, sir."

He dragged a fistful of hair from her head as he released. "That's my girl," he said in a loud voice. "You be good. I'll be back in a half-cycle to check on you. Goodbye, Granny Terry."

"Goodbye, Danston." Terry appeared in the door with a bundle of spice cakes. "Take these with you and mind you don't eat them all on the way home."

Danston pointed for Rankil to clear her eyes and collect her belongings then he took the lead reins of the pack mount before straddling his own. "Is there anything you need me to do?"

"Go home," said Terry. "You're interrupting my day." She touched her granddaughter's cuff. "I've some darning for you."

Confident of his authority, Danston rode away. He was soon a black smudge against the cresting sun, Rankil's fears decreasing with every fading click of his nassies' iron-shod hooves. When she was certain he was gone, she stared out over the hillside for a bit then turned back to the house. Granny Terry sat in her rocker, patching her worn apron. She turned toward Rankil and patted the hassock by her feet.

"Sit with me, child."

Rankil obeyed, dropping her things by the hassock and reaching for the sewing basket, only to be gently swatted away. "I'd rather talk." Terry set the apron to the side and ran her hand over Rankil's face, pausing at her frowning eyes. "Such a brave young girl and so polite. I don't see how Danston can see fit to be so mean to you."

Rankil stared at her then jerked back. No matter what Granny Terry said she couldn't reveal the truth. "I get what I deserve."

Terry sniffed and brushed the hair from Rankil's face, prompting her to pull back again. "Don't defend him. I know how the family treats you. One of their own! You and Archell both. The two brightest, beaten because you're different."

Rankil's expression grew panicked. "No, ma'am, I'm not diff—"

"Stars, girl." Granny Terry took Rankil's hands in her own and began to stroke the palm, regarding the calluses and scars one by one, allowing there were far too many for such a tender age. "There's nothing wrong with being different. Imagine how boring life would be if we were all the same. Being different is what makes you special. Archell's songs can light the gloomiest of days, and your spirit is like none I've ever known. You're a fighter, a skill I am afraid you've need of." Rankil tried to back away, but Granny Terry held her firm, with strength surprising for one so frail. "I may be blind, but I can see. I knew you were special the first time you crawled into my lap as a babe." Her unseeing eyes regarded Rankil with a curious expression. "What you are is nothing to be ashamed of, Rankil, and nothing worth being flogged over."

24

"I—"

"You what? You thought I didn't know? That this blind old woman doesn't know a Taelach from an Autlach? Would you have me treat you like they do for it?"

Rankil looked toward the door. Terry knew. This changed everything. "I'd know my place."

Granny Terry's sightless eyes stared so hard that Rankil stopped. "Have they run you that far into the ground?" She made a gentle sound with her tongue in way of sympathy. "Ah, but they have, haven't they?" Then, in one fluid movement, Terry pulled Rankil into her lap and began to rock. "I used to do this when you were little, every time I visited at the New Pass feast. Do you remember?"

Rankil stiffened and pushed away, retaking her seat on the hassock. "No, I don't." And she remembered Meelsa's late attempt at nurturing.

"Well, I did, Rankil, and I tried to talk them into letting me take you then." Granny Terry's foot tapped with the chair's rhythm. "Even then they worked you far too hard."

Rankil said nothing.

"I think," continued Terry, "that you're in need of a bit of mothering. I may be old, but I can teach you more than them who dare call themselves your parents. You need me, child, and I you. You're safe, Rankil. No one will harm you here."

"Safe?"

"Safe to be yourself. To be who you are."

Rankil sniffed and looked at the ground. "I'm nobody."

Terry shook her head. "I know otherwise and in time, I hope you'll come to know differently, too. Now, would you do me a favor?"

"Yes, ma'am."

"Go to the large chest in the corner and bring me the measure guides and ribbon-tied pack from the bottom."

Rankil sprinted to the chest and returned quickly. "Here, ma'am."

"Open the pack, child, and tell me what you find."

The ribbon unraveled when Rankil pulled on it and the wrapping cloth fell away in ceremonious fashion. "Cloth, ma'am. Am I to sew you a dress?" She stared at the velvet folds, awed by the material's simple elegance.

"Does the weave suit you?"

Rankil shrank back, her fingers loosening from the fabric she normally wouldn't dared touched. Tessa had a dress of a similar, though not as luxurious, fabric and had once smacked Rankil for touching the hemline. "Oh, no, ma'am, I couldn't! If Danston found out I had such a thing he'd—"

"This is your home now!" The old woman's face drew with frustration. "And I won't have a young person from my house romping about in rags. Worn things are fine for when you're mucking the barn, but the rest of the time"—Terry smiled at her— "I want you smartly dressed. Now hold up the fabric so I can check your length." Rankil held the cloth to her front. It was the perfect shade to complement her pale complexion, the color of trees in high summer, dark and shimmering with morning dew. "Don't worry about your growth." Granny Terry drew the cloth across Rankil's chest. "We can make seams and hems that can be let out as you need them. My, but you're all leg. Now, let me have the measures so I can size your top."

"But, ma'am," whispered Rankil in fear of speaking out of turn. "You can size from the clothes Meelsa sent me with."

"Those clothes are stretched in the belly. They must have been Sallnox's. They'll never fit you right. And they didn't send you with any proper boots either, did they?"

"No, ma'am." Rankil blushed.

"Stars," Terry could feel the heat burning the young girl's cheeks. "What's wrong now? That I noticed or the fact you've never had any?"

"Both, ma'am," she squeaked.

"Quit calling me ma'am. I'm your Grandmother Terry, Granny Terry."

"Yes, ma—yes, Granny Terry."

"Better. The boots are just one of your needs." Terry motioned for Rankil to bend close. "I believe, young lady," she said between feels of Rankil's matted hair, "that you could use a bath and a good cut."

"I try to keep it braided back from my face."

"You've managed a braid of sorts, but your hair is split. I'll need to cut off most of it to get above the breaks."

Rankil gulped. What would happen when her father returned? "Cut my hair? Danston would never let me have short hair! It's not proper."

"Taelachs sometimes do."

The remark confused one unfamiliar with Taelach customs and demanded clarity. Rankil sat on the hassock and looked inquiringly at her grandmother. "You know about the Taelach, Granny Terry?"

Granny Terry's sightless eyes gave her a long, considering stare, first alarmed and then angered. "Nobody ever told you about you own kind?"

"Only Archell, and it wasn't much. He was afraid I would run away." Rankil pulled a handful of snap beans from the sling-full Terry had picked early that morning and began breaking them into edible portions. She had best keep busy lest Terry lose her indulgent mood. "Granny Terry?"

"Yes?"

"You've seen Taelachs before?"

"A few, though not in many passes and never under pleasant conditions. But they're around. They keep to themselves most of the time. Can't say as I blame them, either." Terry brought a cook pot to the table, placed Rankil's beans in it, then took a seat next to Rankil who stared in wonderment as her grandmother began to help. "Now, you know there are men and there are women. You have enough brothers to know that, don't you?"

"Yes." Rankil slowed her work to listen.

"All right, Taelachs are all women. I've heard they pair off just the same as Autlach married couples, but—" Terry's mouth thinned as she considered the best manner to explain. "I don't quite understand it myself, but that's the way things work for them."

"If there's not men then who tells them what to do?"

"Taelachs do it all for themselves," Terry said, with a hint of envy in her voice.

"For themselves?" Rankil delighted at the idea of autonomy. "But Archell said there were short-haired ones with women and children in their arms."

Granny tossed a handful of broken beans in the pot. "Well," she shrugged. "Like I said, some do wear their hair short, broadbacks I believe."

Rankil's confusion ran deeper than her voice could ever register. "But there aren't any Taelach men?"

"Some say broadbacks are somewhere in between, but I don't think it's true. They're just strong—strong women and tall, too, usually a little taller than the long-haired Taelachs, but then again most Taelachs are taller than Autlachs."

Like me, thought Rankil.

"Broadbacks are fighters, warriors even, but they're definitely women." Terry filled the pot with water to keep the beans fresh. "Like I said, Taelachs keep to themselves. I wish I could tell you more. Just keep your eyes open. They do come around on occasion."

Rankil's face brightened at the prospect of seeing one of her own. "They do?" She marveled at how easy their conversation flowed. It felt like talking to Archell when no one else was around. "How do you know?"

Terry set the cutting board on the table and handed Rankil a large slicing knife. "There are round roots in the bottom of the sling. Let's cut them to dry. We'll let them cure today then spread them on the porch tomorrow morning. It gets full sun and will keep them out of the dirt." She took a second knife and began to separate the long white tubers into paper-thin slices. Dried, round root made for hearty winter eating and proved excellent in stew. "Now, to answer your question. How do you think I've gotten along by myself all this time, blind as I am?"

"Danston called you stubborn." Rankil's slices were thin but not as even as her steady-handed elder's.

"Yes." Terry smiled. "I am stubborn, but, whatever your father thinks about me, I've needed help since long before you came. Know who's been helping me?"

Rankil startled and the knife slipped from her hand, just missing her fingertip. "But you said you hadn't seen a Taelach in a long while."

Terry pointed to her shrunken orbits. "No, I haven't *seen* them, but they've been helping me. They leave spices and fresh meat from time to time. That's where I got the cloth. They left it for me as a thank you for some cakes I gave them a while back."

They sliced all the roots and stacked them on the cutting board. Rankil's young mind danced with excitement while they worked. "How often do they visit?"

"Oh," said Granny in an almost teasing fashion, "they ring the smoker shed bell once or twice a moon cycle. That should be any day now." Terry crinkled her nose. "Sure you don't want a bath?"

Rankil's tattered appearance had never been bothersome until now, but then again, she'd never known any other way to be. "Yes. Yes, Granny Terry, I think I do." She took a soapstone and rag Terry offered and rushed for the creek below the house.

The water pool was tepid in the summer heat, and Rankil stripped and waded in, scrubbing from top to bottom, her toes giving an occasional kick to ward off the curious fish. She'd never been given the opportunity to take a real bath and enjoyed the thorough soak, playing among flowering water grasses, floating about in her clean state until her fingers shriveled. Finally swayed by Granny Terry's calls to have her hair trimmed, she emerged from the pool, shook off the worst of the water, and walked back to the house with her clothing in hand. Granny pushed her into a chair so she could loosen the dripping braid Rankil had been unable to remove.

"This is impossible," said Terry between tugs on the messed plait. "It's so matted it'll never come undone. I'm going to have to cut above it, shorter than I wanted." She drew her sharpest knife and held Rankil's head firm. "Don't move. I want the cut to be even."

Rankil winced as Terry removed the braid at the base of her neck. The lifted weight felt strange. Terry trimmed around the sides of her face and ears, using her hands to judge the length. After a few more quick strokes of the blade she stepped back and produced a palm-sized reflecting board from her pocket, which she held out for Rankil's use.

"Take a look."

"No, ma'am."

Terry sat next to her. "Why not?"

"Danston told me never to look cause I'm so ugly I'd break a board."

"Now, Rankil." The old woman was once again angry. Rankil flinched at her tone. "I'm not mad with you. I'm furious with *them* for leading you to believe such a thing. How could you know you might break it if you never try?"

"Boards are hard to come by."

Now the old woman seemed mad at her, too. "Think, girl, can I really make use of one?"

Rankil peered at Terry's face. "I guess not," she whispered.

"Then what does it matter if it breaks? Look!" Terry forced Rankil's face to the reflector. Rankil opened one eye. Nothing shattered or cracked, so she ventured to open the other.

Terry placed the board fully in her hands. "Tell me what you see."

"I . . . I see . . . I see so much, Granny Terry, so very much." Rankil watched the bitter twist of her mouth flatten then curl into a small smile. "I see sky-colored eyes that are shaped like Meelsa's dark ones and the little hump that's in Danston's nose—his pointy chin, too. Why did they call me ugly when I look so much like them?"

"They put down what they didn't understand. Tell me what else you see."

Rankil moved the reflector about until she had viewed her

entire head. "My ears stick out like Sallnox's, and I have Tessa's skinny neck."

Terry shook her head. "Don't tell me the other faces you see. I want to know about Rankil. Tell me something about her. Is she as pleasant looking as I think?"

Rankil bit her lip to keep back the deluge of questions, but they spilled forth anyway, expressing the thousand ideas in her head. "What am I, Granny? What is a Taelach? Do all Taelachs look like I do? Should I wear my hair short? Grow it back long? Where do I fit in?" Rankil stared in the reflecting board again, surprised at the suddenly older face peering back. It wasn't the distorted image she'd seen when drawing water from the compound's central well. There was something behind it, a substance she'd never seen before. She wasn't the stupid waste they said she was. The world was clearer to her now, as clear as the slim-jawed face looking back.

Terry took the reflector and ran her hands over Rankil's face. "Let me tell you what I see. Before me is Rankil, an amazing young woman. She is growing strong and tall. She should be proud of who she is."

Rankil tensed but didn't pull away. "And who is that, Granny Terry?"

Pleased, Terry traced the line of Rankil's small smile then dropped her hand. "Time in general will tell you, as will time with your people."

"*My* people?"

"Yes." Granny Terry's voice became stern. "You're caught between two very different worlds, one which detests the other. You know the Autlach and need to know the Taelach. They'll find you here. They'll teach you, and in the end you will leave here to become one of them."

"But I just got here." Rankil's slender hand clutched Terry, her long fingers easily wrapping the older woman's wrist. "I couldn't possibly go."

Terry broke the grasp and ran the comb through Rankil's layered cut, satisfied when she found it free of knots. "Yes, child, eventually you'll leave. You'll have to for your own safety but, hopefully, that's some time away, and we can enjoy the time in between." She brushed the stray hairs from the table then passed Rankil the rush sweeper. "Clean it up for me. I'd be picking hair for days if you weren't here."

"You'd have no hair to sweep if I weren't here." Rankil tossed the brittle, matted braid out the door.

"I swear I never heard a full sentence out of you before today. You're the sweet little smart mouth when you wish to be." Terry went to the trunk and once again pulled out the piece of rich green fabric. "So, Rankil, you're long overdue for some finery. Today, after we finish working in the garden, we'll begin making you knee skirts and leggings. They're the wear of Taelach youth and what you should have as well, but first things first. Come to the table. It's time for the midday sup." She brought out sweet jam and cheese to accompany the bread already on the table.

"Taelach preserves are the sweetest I've ever tasted. Too sweet for me, but I wager you'll like them."

She placed Rankil at the head of the small dining table, making her the recipient of a precious gift—a belly-filling meal served with a healthy side of attention. Terry cooed over Rankil for the remainder of the day, acknowledging her thoughts, cherishing her presence. They worked outside until the heat became unbearable then retreated to the shade of the porch, deep in conversation as they began assembling Rankil's first new set of clothing. It felt strange to be wanted, like shedding a long-rotted skin. Rankil needn't run anymore and slept safe in her own private loft among the fresh straw, tucked in a soft pallet made just for her. Tisph's hands couldn't reach her. Her father's belt and fist were far away. Rankil was loved, safe, warm and looking forward to someday meeting her own. She'd finally reached a place above the fear and prejudice, a place for learning and exploration of her own identity. Rankil was home.

Chapter Three

Opportunity is chance come knocking. Open the door.

—*Granny Terry*

"Damn!" Kaelan's arrow had barely grazed her quarry's front flank. The deer stumbled then darted away, leaving a droplet trail of blood to show its flight path. Muttering more curses, Kaelan snatched her reins and mounted her skittish nassie. Her adopted daughter Myrla jumped onto her own mount, kicking and whistling until the gentle beast began moving.

"Don't worry." Myrla said as they tracked. "It can't run far bleeding like that. You wait, it'll be on the spit before we know it."

"I'm not concerned." Kaelan shouldered her bow and clicked her tongue for their mounts to quicken their pace. "But you have a lot to learn about hunting, daughter. An animal runs all the farther when wounded. It's running for its life—and toward the foothills.

We'll follow from a distance until it gets tired then I want you to take it down."

"Me?" Myrla's plaits bounced as she rode up beside Kaelan. "You're letting me?"

"You'll be fourteen this fall. That's old enough to hunt. Besides, you've become a fair shot with a bow. Time you were put to the test."

Myrla pulled a little taller on her nassie. How proud she felt, all but fourteen and on her first hunt. Under Kaelan's guidance she took the lead, tracking the deer to a nearby thicket. "Must have hurt it worse than we thought," she whispered as they crept toward the thicket. Arrow in place, bow drawn, she pushed deeper, Kaelan holding back so she could act alone. The clan's evening meal was up to her.

Whisssph—thud. Her arrow landed true, straight in the heart. The deer fell where it had stood, quivering before growing still. Myrla cheered and danced in a circle. Kaelan joined the celebration for a moment then held up a hand for her to cease.

"You know what to do next, don't you?"

Myrla's upper lip curled. "Gut it?"

Kaelan frowned at her. "Before that."

The girl blinked good-naturedly. "Why, Kaelan," she laughed. "You thank the Mother Maker, of course. She's the one who put the deer here to begin with. I knew that." Myrla dropped to one knee and spoke the appropriate prayer.

"Much better." Kaelan tied a rope to the animal's front legs and suspended it from a nearby tree. "Now, in answer to your question. Clan rule. You kill it—you clean it."

"Ugh!" Despite Myrla's objections, she knew she must do the chore. Kaelan showed her how to rig up the deer so it would bleed the best and demonstrated how to open the belly to remove the entrails. "Separate and rinse everything with water from the flask then put it all in the lined sling. Careful not to nick the intestine. It'll ruin the best of the sweetmeats. Good girl! You're quite handy with a knife. Jewel will be proud."

Myrla smiled as she gazed up at her raiser. "We caught this one early. Do we have to go back right now? It's pretty in the lowlands. There're more trees."

"These aren't the lowlands, but I suppose it's lower than you've ever been." Kaelan sliced off a portion of leg meat then hefted the carcass onto one of the nassies. "And, no, we're not going back yet. We've other business."

"What business?"

Kaelan wrapped the meat in cloth, straddled her mount, and pulled her daughter up behind. "Hold this." She passed back the roast. "You'll see soon enough." She steered their nassies through the thick undergrowth and further down the mountain. Myrla sang softly as they trotted along, her off-key melody following Kaelan's low hum. It was a pleasant morning to be out, growing warmer by the minute but clear and dry. They skirted a large clearing, stopping just inside the tree line on the far side.

"All right," Kaelan took the meat pack and leaned back, encouraging her daughter's dismount. Myrla slid down, tied the nassies off, then waited as Kaelan stepped off the animal with long-legged ease. "Come along. We've a delivery to make."

"Delivery?" Myrla trotted to keep up, following Kaelan around a thorny thicket surrounding a small, bubbling spring. They pushed through a stand of trees and on the far side, Kaelan stopped, pulling Myrla low. She pointed down the hillside to a small house and outbuildings nestled against a stream.

"That's where we're going?" Myrla looked dismayed. "But that's an Aut's home!"

Kaelan smiled at the wary sound in her child's voice. "Correct, it is. It's where Blind Grandmother lives. You've heard me speak of her. The roast is for her. We must do our part to help others. Helping deeds are part of the Great Mother's requirements for us."

"But you told me Blind Grandmother knew of us," whispered Myrla. "Why are we hunkered down?"

"Caution is best in all dealings with Auts." Kaelan held her head a little higher, scanning and listening for anything suspicious. "Besides, Grandmother does have the occasional visitor." She edged forward and, after another look about, waved her daughter to follow. The Serpent clan's inking wriggled high on Kaelan's arm when she moved. Myrla admired the strength the simple reptilian pattern represented, but only broadbacks wore inkings in the Serpent clan, and Myrla was old enough to know she didn't want to be one.

"It's clear," Kaelan said. "Let's deliver the bundle."

They made a quiet path to the rear of Granny Terry's smoker shed then opened the heavy wooden box resting against it. "Looks like good eating to go with your deer." Kaelan held up one of the large, juicy vine fruits Terry had provided from her garden. "She left enough for all of us." She took the fruit sack and replaced it with the meat. "Gather a bouquet of those blue hats. They smell nice, and she seems to prefer them."

Myrla hurried up the hillside and gathered an armful of the aromatic wildflowers. "This enough?"

"Plenty. Now lay them on top of the meat and shut the box. It's time we returned home." Kaelan grasped the half-rotted rope dangling from the shed's corner. "Get back to the tree line," she told her daughter. "And keep low." Myrla obeyed, taking position out of plain sight but visible enough to see her raiser ring the rusting bell at the rope's top. Kaelan dashed to her side and pulled both their heads inside their green summer cloaks. "We'll wait and make sure she's around. I wouldn't want the meat spoiling before she finds it."

"The bell!" Rankil jumped so hard root slices scattered across the porch. "Granny Terry, the bell!"

"I heard." Terry rose from the shady front yard bench. "Hope they enjoy the vine fruits. Let's see what, if anything, they've left in return."

Rankil danced along beside her, more excited than she could remember. Maybe, if she were watchful, she'd catch a glimpse of one of them. She followed her grandmother through the garden, unable to contain her joy when they reached the smoker shed. Terry rapped her cane on the box lid. "Take a look."

Rankil took a deep breath, flipped up the lid, and reached inside. "Flowers!" She placed the bouquet in Terry's hands. The old woman took a deep sniff and smiled.

"Blue Hats. My favorite. Bless their kind souls. What else did they send?"

Rankil unwrapped the meat and pushed her finger into the grain. "Deer meat and it's so fresh it's still warm!"

"We'll roast it with garden mushrooms and eat it with our beans. What a feast we'll have tonight!" Granny turned toward the tree line and waved her cane high in thanks. Rankil squinted the same direction but saw nothing.

"How do you know they're up there?"

"Oh, they're up there, and I bet they've seen you." Terry walked toward the house. "Come along. We've work to do."

"But—" Rankil ran her hand over her new, shorter hairstyle and looked to the tree line again. "If they see me, why don't they come talk to me?"

"Give them time, and they will in their own way." Terry shuffled around the edge of the shed and into the garden. "Help me uncover the mushrooms so we can get out of this heat."

Rankil sighed and turned back, slow to retreat though she knew no contact would be made that day. What could she have said anyway? Did the Taelach speak the same language as the Autlach?

"Kaelan, did you see?" Myrla rocked back and forth in her hunkered position. "There's a sister down there around my age! What would she be doing so far away from the clan ranges? Think she's lost?"

Kaelan rubbed her chin, confused as well, but enlightened to the dangers. "No, don't think she's lost. From what I could tell, she seems to be helping Blind Grandmother. I think she's misplaced."

"Misplaced?" Myrla stared at her raiser. "You mean she's been raised Aut? But Taelach babies are killed if they aren't claimed!"

"Occasionally, one is allowed to live, but I've been told it's a horrible existence. They're slaved as children. Worse as they grow."

Myrla began crawling toward the tree line. "Then we have to rescue her!" Kaelan jerked her back to push a stern finger into her round face.

"No, not in this manner. I believe she's safe where she's at for the present. Blind Grandmother seems to care for her. Besides, if she's been raised Aut, she won't know anything of our customs or language. This must be handled delicately." Lowering her finger, Kaelan regarded her daughter in a kinder manner. Myrla had only wanted to help and that sort of blind courage, while foolish, was commendable. "We'll discuss our discovery over the evening fire. Recca must know about this sister in need." Kaelan took a piece of vine fruit from the bag and sliced it.

"Time and patience." She offered half to her daughter. "That's what we need."

"Can I be the one to tell mamma what we found?" Myrla wiped the seeded juice dribbles from her chin.

Kaelan reached back to squeeze Myrla's shoulder before they pushed into the woods. "Fine by me, mighty huntress. You can tell her. She's the one I'd tell first anyway. Let's go home."

The clan's central fire burned high, the air heavy with roast deer and green wood. The children had been fed and put to bed, their raisers returning to the fireside with their ground mats, ready to discuss the day and plan for the next. In reward for her kill, Myrla had been permitted to remain up, an honor seldom bestowed on one below the age of recognition.

"Did a team go out this evening?" Jewel snuggled into Kaelan and wrapped her arms about her neck. Myrla sat on Kaelan's other side, tired, but knowing better than to show it. She unplaitted her hair and stared into the fire, waiting for Kaelan's response.

"One left at dusk." Kaelan fingered the silver wisps that had escaped Jewel's bright headscarf. "There's one close to delivering in a compound west of here."

"They bringing her back tonight?" Jewel loved when a new baby came into the clan, even though it meant enduring the difficulties of the Autlach mother. They were well treated under her care, not that it mattered. Autlach women were always terrified when brought to a Taelach stronghold to give birth, some going as far as suicide to prevent the Taelach from taking one of their own.

"Jewel?" Kaelan's tickling whisper brought her back to the present. "You're a night's ride from here. What's on your mind?"

"Births," she sighed. "Births and babes." The last word led her gaze to Myrla. No matter how big her daughter became she'd always be the tiny newborn Jewel had once cuddled.

Kaelan pulled Jewel's face up to meet her own. "Don't tell me you want another one."

"I'm always giving away the things I help bring into the world. It's natural I feel the urge every now and again." Jewel's eyes almost pleaded. "Do you think we could place our names on the list again?"

"You sure you can bear the wait? Times are dangerous and safe birthing raids are scarce. It may take three of four passes for our turn." Kaelan looked to Myrla. "How do feel about it, young one? Would you like a little sister?"

"Would I!" exclaimed Myrla. "I've wanted one since I can remember." Her elation quieted when the clan leader, Recca, held her arms high for silence.

We'll sign onto the list as soon as the records keeper opens her curtain tomorrow morn. Kaelan's gentle mind phase brought a smile to Jewel's face. She nuzzled into Kaelan all the more and listened to Recca's booming oration. The Serpent clan leader had to be strong, a commanding woman able to keep her people focused when things went well and capable of keeping them in line when things didn't.

"Good day today, all things considered." Recca's pale eyes shone pink from the fire's glow. "The Stores hunters brought in two bandit beasts for smoking and Kaelan's girl downed the doe you're all digesting." Recca cast the youngster an approving nod. "Well done, Myrla."

Myrla squared in her seat. She hadn't known Recca knew her name. The clan leader always seemed too busy to notice the younger clan members, seldom emerging from the caverns when the children were awake.

Recca's leathered face became drawn when she saw Myrla's smug expression. "But, if I may remind the youngest present"—every eye turned on Myrla, deflating her swollen ego to the point she cringed—"there is more to growing up than being skilled with the bow. One's ability with the scroll and stylus is equally important." Recca peered at the rising moon. "Such deeds cannot be achieved by a student who maintains late hours."

Jewel rose from her place to take Myrla's arm. "Come on." Her smile was pert. "It's high time you were in bed." She took a lantern from a lighting hook and ushered her daughter to the small, quiet grotto Kaelan claimed as family quarters. Myrla's bedroll was already spread behind its curtain. Myrla dropped her knee skirts, peeled off her hide leggings, then after kneeling for her prayers, crawled between the fur liner and thin summer blanket, happy Jewel still took time to tuck her in. She wondered if the misplaced girl had such luxuries.

"Sleep tight." Jewel kissed her forehead.

"Mamma?"

"Yes?"

"What will become of the girl I saw today?"

"The adults are discussing it now. I'll give you a full account in the morning. Don't lose sleep over it. Remember, you have a history recitation for Larkette tomorrow."

"I'm ready." Myrla yawned as Jewel pulled the blanket to her chin. "She'll be brought into the clan, won't she?"

"I don't know." Jewel's face flushed. "Misplaced sisters are seldom able to adapt to our ways. They're often damaged from the abuse they've received. We can't take in a potential threat."

Myrla's expression swept into confusion, and she sat up in the blankets. "But she's around my age. How could she be a danger?"

"Now, Myrla," Jewel pushed her back in bed and pulled the

blanket up. "Recca will decide what's best. If she believes there's a chance to save this girl then all attempts will be made." Jewel pulled the curtain. "Good night."

"Good night." Myrla watched the lantern light bob along the ceiling. "Mamma?" The light ceased dancing.

"Yes?"

"She didn't look mad to me."

"I'm sure Kaelan will keep that point in mind." The glow faded as Jewel drew shut the folding partition to their quarters. Raised voices were audible from the corridor leading to the fireside. She hung her lamp and returned to her place.

Kaelan paced the fireside, at clear odds with Recca. "The child was helping Blind Grandmother!" she declared, unaware of her mate's return. "That alone shows she has at least some of her senses."

"My answer is no." Recca frowned at the questioner of her authority. The clan leader's word was gospel, all rebukes taken as a challenge for control. "I will not risk the safety of the entire community for one straggler."

"Straggler?" Kaelan threw up her arms. Recca's venomous glare did nothing to unnerve her. They'd been friends and battle comrades far too long. "We're talking about a girl the age of my Myrla. She's young enough to adapt. We should at least try."

"No!" Recca swung around the fire circle to stand toe to toe with Kaelan, a power move that more often than not quelled further argument. Kaelan grinned defiantly and set her toes on Recca's, grinding them into the soft dirt.

"She's a little girl."

Recca jerked her foot back and stomped it on Kaelan's. "She's big enough to cause damage. Unless you can prove she's in her right mind the answer is no."

Kaelan stepped back, her head cocked at a peculiar angle to mask the throbbing of her toes. "So, if I prove her lucidity she'll be welcomed?"

"Yes." The clan leader folded her arms across her chest.

"Then that's what I'll do."

"What?" Recca's arms fell limp by her sides.

"I'll teach her to read."

"How?" inquired Larkette, the youth instructor, from her place near the fire. "I'm sure she's never seen a scroll and hasn't any concept of reading. How are you going to teach Taelach language and morals without violating the contact laws?"

"It's simple." Jewel drew up on her knees to make herself more visible. "We teach her the same way we teach any other child—by primer scrolls, slate board and the morality fables."

Recca's stance began to soften. She was still unsure, but with Jewel's gentle persuasion, she listened. "You're going to teach her the signs and pronunciation of a language she's never heard?"

"We start with Aut letters and go from there." Jewel settled back as Kaelan rejoined her on their mat. "If she can speak Autlach, she can learn to read it and if she can read Autlach—"

"She can learn to phonetically speak our language and recognize our symbols." Recca nodded. "Kaelan, you wanted this, it's your project. Larkette will supply you with whatever you need. But this mustn't interfere with your daily duties. We need your pottery for winter stores. Educating a misplaced sister comes a distant second to the immediate needs of the clan, and as you said she appeared to be in a safe place—"

"Thank you, Recca."

Recca crossed the sands to bend close, her age-streaked life braid taking a parting swing between Kaelan and Jewel. "Be certain of this lost child's sanity before you adopt her. Don't bring a lunatic into my fold. And, next time, my friends," she said in a low, amused tone, "don't be so eager to step on my toes. Especially you, Kae. Those big feet of yours are too easy a target." She rewarded them with one of her seldom-seen smiles then turned back to the fire. "On to other business. A team has been dispatched to Zeilin Glen. Who's up for the next addition?" A young couple to Kaelan's left held their arms high. "Are you ready for the child?" One of the pair held up a near-finished swaddling blanket. "You ready for the flaming insults of a labored Autlach woman?" Their expressions became clouded.

"Who is?" Recca's gentlewoman, Ashklara, spoke up, her mothering tone calming the expectant raisers' frazzled nerves. "We all know what it's like. You have to tune the words out, because that is all they are, words." Ashklara spoke from experience. She had been the clan's lead birther until ill health had forced her to relinquish the title to Jewel. Her skilled hands had brought a good portion of those present into the world. "And don't let the mother convince you that you're robbing her of her child. The baby will be no more than a disposable burden, something to free herself of as soon as possible. Why most of them fight so hard, we'll never understand." Ashklara shifted in her skid chair and leaned a little toward the fire as her pale face searched for recognition. "We must endure the bad along with the good, mustn't we, Recca?"

"Most definitely." Recca placed a hand on Ashklara's thin shoulder, careful not to squeeze into her flesh the half-heart pin, which Recca wore the other half of as a cloak clasp. Ashklara had fallen victim to a long-term wasting disease that had destroyed her muscle and bone structure. She'd become a twisted form, slow and pained in movement but far wiser than her midnight blue eyes reflected. Recca looked after her as much as her duties permitted but always stayed close enough to phase away the agony at regular intervals.

"Ashklara speaks the truth as always," she said. "Birthings are never easy for any concerned. But as long as the child is healthy and the mother safely returned, it is well worth the effort." Recca pushed her mate's skid chair a little closer to the fire and tucked the blanket around her frail legs. "Jewel, who is your second tonight?"

"Wikkib, I believe." Jewel yawned. "On that note, I'm going to rest while I can. Wikkib?" She turned to her young assistant. "You'd best, too. If this mother is a first timer her labor could take days."

"A good thought for all those in skirts." Recca's slight bow meant dismissal. "There are broadback matters yet to discuss—"

"Like they won't know as soon as we crawl in the bed with them," sniped one of those remaining seated. "They tend to withhold themselves when we don't share the knowledge."

"Share and share alike." Ashklara's comment prompted a laughing chorus from the gentlewomen. "We have to even the odds some way or another."

Recca's expression grew exasperated. "When gentlewomen defend the clan they can be present for briefings. Until such a time"—she pointed to the main cavern's rocky entrance—"they should do as I request. They will, after all, hear what went on soon enough."

As Recca was not to be disobeyed, the gentlewomen retreated to their quarters, two of them pulling Ashklara's skid. When the last of their lanterns had faded Recca reached into a rolled mat and produced two bulging wine skins.

"Throw out the tea in your cups, my sisters. We have finer things to wash down our dinner." She passed the first skin to all who remained then Recca indulged in a second cupful. "To Serpent might!" She held the cup high in salute.

"To Serpent strength!" came the customary reply.

"Serpent strength? Serpent might?" mumbled Jewel as she peeked in on Myrla. "I suppose they believe we never hear their preposterous battle calls. If they only knew how Aut it made them sound." She flipped out the double sleeping roll and tossed the pillows to the open end. "But Klara's right, we'll know what they're discussing soon enough." She hung her skirts on a wall hook, draped her tunic over top, said her evening prayers, then slid into the coolness of the summer bedding before turning down the lantern. With the fold doors closed, the outside voices were muddled to the point she couldn't distinguish one from the other. The drone proved lulling and she slept, unaware of Kaelan's presence until she pulled close in bed.

"Jewel?" Kaelan tickled Jewel's nose with her life-braid. "Jewel?" Her second call drew out to a wine-tipsy extreme.

"Kaelan, you're lit!" Jewel brushed the braid from her face and sat up. "And you've been smoking pilta as well. That was the business tonight? Wine and smoke?"

"You betcha. Come back here." Kaelan jerked her back into the blankets and wrapped them tight so she couldn't escape again. "Broadbacks work hard." Her whisper brought goose bumps to Jewel's neck. "We deserve a bit of wine now and then. It's good for the soul."

"I'll remind you in the morning." Jewel struggled to free herself. "Let go, Kae. You're smothering me."

"Sorry, love." Kaelan hiccupped as she untwisted the bedding.

"Shhh." Jewel placed her hand over Kaelan's mouth, which now rolled into a grin. "You'll wake Myrla."

Hiccup. "Wouldn't want that now, would we?"

Jewel couldn't help but laugh. "What am I going to do with you?"

"Love me?" Another *hiccup*.

"I already do that. I meant your 'cups. You're bouncing across the floor. Much more and you'll be out in the corridor."

Kaelan let out a drunken chuckle and pulled Jewel on top of her, the phase she offered gentle though uneven because of the wine. *Perhaps you should weigh me down so I don't bounce away. Hiccup.*

Jewel kissed her mouth, sharing the wine that lingered on Kaelan's lips. *Tell me what you discussed before you even think of doing that.*

Kaelan jerked from another hiccup. "Please, Jewel. There's nothing to tell. The boundary line between the Tekkroon clan and us remains stable. The Autlach aren't an immediate threat. Things are good for the moment."

"You sure there's nothing more?" Jewel removed her headscarf and shook out the shoulder length waves Kaelan had long admired.

"Positive." Kaelan reached a hand to her lover's face. "The only thing on my mind right now is you." *Hiccup.* "Damn, I thought those were gone."

"Hold your breath." Jewel watched Kaelan draw a heavy breath

45

that puffed her cheeks. "You're not keeping something back, are you?" Her minuscule picking phase did little but share Kaelan's drunken sensation, spreading her hiccups. *Now look what you've done. I've got the infernal things, too.*

Serves you right. You know I wouldn't hold back. My hiccups are gone. Hold your air. That's it.

Jewel collapsed into Kaelan's arms as she exhaled. *I'm sorry. Picking wasn't called for. It's just that there are so many rumors of us moving to higher ground, further back in the hills. Leenzalia said she heard Recca was sending a crew to the secondary volcano bowl to survey for possible habitation.*

She's planning it. Kaelan lowered her to the tangled blankets and ran a fingertip path down her abdomen, enjoying Jewel's wriggling response. *It's a perfect spot, a natural fortress. Near the Tekkroon but not on their lands. Plans are to move next spring, if all goes well.* Her fingers found their way across the Jewel's curving chin and mouth, running inside the edge of her full lips. Jewel sighed and swatted the hand away.

Another migration? I thought we'd found a permanent home here. How could the volcano bowl provide any more protection than where we are now?

Recca says it does, lover. She says there's a small valley we can farm and build in, walled on each side by the slopes so we'll be separate from the Tekks and protected from the winter winds. It sounds perfect. Kaelan's heavy phase disclosed her intentions for the evening. *Tell me, Jewel of mine, tell me what you want.*

You, Kae. You and only you. Jewel wrapped her arms around Kaelan's back and let simple pleasure take over. They breathed heavily, the crests of their phase bathing them both in summer night sweat. Their minds blended in the depths of the coupling, heightened only when Kaelan added her gentle physical attention. She caressed Jewel's stiffened nipples expertly, kneading them between her fingers until her lover squirmed under her, delighting Kaelan into extending the touch down Jewel's belly and thighs until they both became lost in the pleasure of their phases. Afterward, Kaelan lingered on top, hands on each side of Jewel's head. She drew a work-leathered hand over Jewel's face and returned her fingers to the inner edge of her lover's mouth. Jewel flicked her tongue across their tips.

"See what happens when you tell me your business?"

"Yeah," Kaelan popped the wet digits across Jewel's slender nose. "You get hot."

"Hot and informed," Jewel whispered. "A rather enlightening experience for us both, don't you think?"

Kaelan shook with amusement. "Jewel, you can be quite the fire mind when you want. No wonder I stay so smitten with you." She pulled up on her hands then settled close beside Jewel, wrapping their legs together. "You ready for sleep?"

"That's what I was doing until you stumbled into the bed." Jewel nuzzled into the muscle at the crest of Kaelan's shoulder. She smelled of potting mud, fire and sweat, a not unpleasant smell and one Jewel had come to know as uniquely Kaelan. "What of the misplaced sister? What happens to her when we move?"

"She'll either be part of the clan or be left behind," Kaelan replied with a yawn. "I've a lot of work to do with her." She kissed the middle of Jewel's white on white head. "Sleep. The team will soon be back."

"Yes, Kae." Jewel had just drifted off when a light rap sounded on the folding door.

"Sister Jewel?" Wikkib's low drawl just penetrated the wooden slats.

"I'm up. The team back?"

"Yes, their cargo is awake and fighting her restraints something fierce. She's so young." Wikkib sounded nervous. The young ones were the hardest for her to handle. She found their hysterics pointless, often making her short with them. "She's younger than Myrla, and she's terrified. We'll have to phase her out again to induce her labor."

"All right, I'll be there in a moment." Wikkib's steps shuffled away, fading toward the main cavern entrance. "Kaelan dearest, the team's back."

"I heard. Do you need help calming her? My Aut's almost as good as yours."

"I'm sure it's nothing we can't handle." Jewel ran her fingers through her lover's short curls then rose from the bed, pulling on her clothes and retying her headscarf. "Tend to Myrla if I'm not back by first light?"

"Of course." Kaelan sounded almost insulted by the reminder. "She's going straight to the bathing pool after breakfast."

"You, too. There's glassing sand in your hair again. Be sure to shake out the furs when you get up." Jewel nabbed her slippers and parted the door. The cries of the Autlach mother pierced the thick night air.

"Another loud one. Must she wail?"

"She's scared," mumbled Kaelan. "Birthing hurts."

"She's not laboring. What we're hearing is nothing more than hysteria. If she's as young as Wikkib says, this could be a long one." She let a resigned sigh and slid the partition shut. "Kaelan?" Her tired alto slid under the door folds.

"Yeah?"

"Make Myrla recite her history to you before her exam."

"Sure. Love you."

"You, too." Jewel's light footfalls drifted away.

Kaelan pulled the blankets to her chin then rolled on her side. "History? It would have to be my weak spot." She lay in the stillness, listening for and hearing the soft sounds of her daughter's slumber. A younger girl birthing? That couldn't be a good thing. Why, the body wasn't mature yet, not to mention the mind. How was a half-grown girl supposed to handle a baby of her own? Kaelan's mind named the difficulties as she nodded in and out. Her head ached from the wine, ached until it made her sick. *Poor little girl, not yet grown, giving birth to a child she's not to have. Scared out of her wits and in the presence of strangers. Jewel knows what to do. She'll calm her, care for her. It's her nature as a birther. She knows best, she...* Kaelan began to snore, her alcohol torpor unaffected by the occasional cries of the young mother. One became accustomed to it. It was part of the Taelach existence.

Chapter Four

Learning requires emotion.

—Observer of a misplaced sister

Dawn had yet to reveal its face when the bell behind the smoker shed sounded. Rankil thought it part of some wishful dream until Granny Terry roused her with a poke of her cane. "Rankil, the bell. Dress and go see what they've left."

Still tying her waist lacings, Rankil scurried out the door and through the garden, the grass lapping cold at her toes. Yawning, she leaned against the shed's splintering outer wall and opened the box, crying with joy when she saw the contents. Kaelan had left three bulging sacks, each a wealth of Taelach information. Rankil hefted the sacks over one shoulder with an easy toss then turned toward where she believed the giver might hide. "Thank you!" she cried in Autlach, then hurried back to the house and Terry.

Once Kaelan was certain Rankil was inside, she made her way to the garden and began staking the hide markers that were to be Rankil's first lessons. "The girl is stout," she mumbled while setting the markers. "Grabbed up those bags like they were empty. She'll be a formidable opponent by the time she's through growing. Might be a proper beau for Myrla by that time, too." Tempted as she was to observe Rankil's excitement, Kaelan returned to her mount. Clan duty called. There were a number of store pots to be fired before summer's end and, after all, she had promised Recca.

Kathump! Granny Terry jumped when Rankil dropped the sacks onto the table. "Gracious! Did they leave an entire side of beast?"

"No, Granny Terry, three sacks for you. THREE!"

"You mean for you."

"For me?" Rankil picked at the complicated knot at the top of one. "And they're marked with some kind of odd symbols. I'm having trouble with the . . . okay, there it is." She spilled the contents across the table.

Terry placed the kettle to heat then drew her rocker close. "Tell me what you've found."

Rankil scrubbed the sleep from her eyes. "There's so much I don't know where to start."

"Try the beginning." Terry chuckled. "Pick up something and describe it to me."

"Yes, Granny Terry." Rankil untied the first cloth-wrapped bundle, revealing chalk sticks and a small slate, similar to the one Rankil had seen her father use for crop tallies. "A reusable scribe board, Granny."

"What an unusual gift. What else is there?"

Rankil gasped when the wrapping fell away from the second sizable bundle. "New clothes. Skirts with attached leggings." She passed both sets to Terry who smiled.

"I'm glad to see I wasn't the only one upset by your raggedness."

"Matching tunics, too." Rankil placed these in her lap as well, drawing the old woman's fingertips across the fronts. "Feel. They've piping at the collar and cuff."

"So they do." Terry nodded. "These new things mean we can use the green fabric for the finery it was meant for." She placed the garments on the bench. "Now, I know there is more than that in three sacks. What other treasures have your people left for you?"

Rankil remained silent as she unwrapped the next bundle. Not all the gifts were intended exclusively for her. "Something for you, Granny." She draped a fringed shawl over her grandmother's sloping shoulders. "However do they tat such patterns?"

"I wish I knew." Terry's face shone thanks for the unexpected kindness. She held the fringe to her face. "How does it look on me?"

"Pretty."

Terry blushed. "I always wanted a Taelach shawl." She settled back into her seat, rocking as she drew it across her shoulders. "But only the finest ladies can afford them. And the fact this one came by honest means makes it all the more special."

"You deserve it." Rankil turned back to the sack. The bottom contained a sleeping roll. The inside liner was of the softest fur and the top blankets protected by a water repellant hide coverlet.

"Why would they give me this?" Rankil placed the end in Terry's lap.

"They'd no idea what you did and didn't have so they've made certain all your needs are met." Terry stroked the liner's inner corner. "Letcher bear fur. And it's been cured free of stench. Just as well they gave this. I'd been wondering how we were going to handle the winter with the blankets we have." The kettle began to whistle. "Tell me what else you find as I cook." She shuffled to the fireside, pushed the kettle's rod from the flame and began heating the previous day's roast drippings for gravy.

"You need me to milk the nassie?" Rankil hoped the chore had already been done. There was so much here just for her, and she had just begun. She'd never dreamed of such luxury. Why, she was rich!

"The bucket's on the porch. There's enough in it for morn sup. You can finish up after we eat. I stopped when I heard the bell." Rankil brought in the bucket then dove into the second sack. Another blanket roll lay at the top.

"They sent a roll for you, too, Granny." Rankil left the bedding tied and reached back into the bag. "What the—" She pulled out a light wooden case with a beautifully carved top. The lid was hinged with brass and key locked, the bone key hanging from a string wedged into the top. The lid creaked as she folded it back. "Granny!"

The elderly woman spun on her heels to face Rankil. "Something wrong?"

"Arrows! A box full of arrows and a small bow!"

"A short bow unless I miss my guess." The meat pan sizzled as Terry poured milk over her roux. "I've treated enough Hunt riders to know the bow is the choice for most Taelachs when they fight. You'll have to practice at it to be as good as others your age, I'll wager. Knives and bows, that's what the Taelach use, even the wee ones. I suspect there'll be a knife for you in the sacks as well."

"A knife?" Rankil's forehead creased in confusion. "But we've plenty of knives. Why would we need more?"

"Not a kitchen blade." Terry placed several bread slices in the hearthside warmer. "All Taelachs carry blades, just as your father and other men do. Taelachs use them for most everything they do, even eating."

"Well, I don't see one. The rest of the sack is filled with wax-sealed spice pots and dried herbs. I can smell them without opening the bundles."

"So can I," said Terry. Once the gravy bubbled at the proper consistency, she placed it to the side and retrieved the nut-brown toast. "We'll sort through them later. Open the last sack so we can eat. I've lots to do, and you've snares to check, then hopefully meat to smoke this afternoon."

"Yes'm." Rankil's stomach growled as she opened the last sack. Granny laughed at the noise and layered another ladle of gravy onto Rankil's plate.

"Growing girl needs to eat. Now, tell me what's in the last sack before your food gets cold."

Rankil thrust her hand into the sack and pulled out a corked bark cylinder. She set it on the table and reached in again, pulling out another, then another. The majority of the sack contained the odd tubes.

"What are these?" Granny took the one she offered, fingers scraping across the bark until she found and popped the end cork. She placed a finger into the cylinder and pulled out a rolled piece of hide. It was painted with a large symbol and a corresponding picture. She held it out.

"What's on it?"

"A picture, marks of some sort, and a mark like the one on the bags. What are they?"

The old woman's face creased into what Rankil had come to know as frustration. "Seeing as you've never been to Rallings or beyond, I guess you wouldn't know. They're learning scrolls. I recognize them from when my sons went to the town scribe for lessons. Raskhallak forbid a *woman* should read and write." Terry's expression darkened. Her late husband, a Raskhallak devotee, had believed reading to be inappropriate and above the capabilities of a female. "Looks like they want you to read."

"Me?" exclaimed Rankil between bites of breakfast. "But I'm not smart enough for—" Rankil ceased when Terry's dark expression came to include her. "But those are just scribbles. How do I learn from that? Where do I start?"

"From what I've picked up, each symbol stands for a sound. Put the sounds together in figure shape form and they make words." Terry sipped her tea. "Is that all there is in the last sack, scrolls?"

Rankil choked down a half-chewed bite then shook the bag. "No, there's something in the bottom. Hear it?"

"I do." Granny took the sack and fished to the bottom. She clasped one of the final treasures and, trying hard to contain her amusement, pulled it from the bag. "And you doubted me." She drew the blade and held it up, the double-edge glistening in the morning sun. Long ties, beaded into an intricate pattern dangled from the leather sheath. "A boot knife." She replaced the knife in its sheath then held it out. "Try it on."

"But I don't have a boot to lash it to," replied Rankil in a disappointed voice.

Terry thrust her hand back into the sack. "Well, you do now," she said, and pulled out a pair of lightweight moccasin-style boots. "They feel like deer hide."

"They are." Rankil clasped them to her chest before trying them on.

"Do they fit?" asked Terry after a moment.

"They feel a bit snug, but maybe they'll stretch a little." Rankil loosened the lacings then stood, pushing her feet a little deeper into the boots. "Which side do I put the knife on?"

"Lash it so it rests on the outside leg of the hand you use most."

"That'd be the left." Rankil tied the blade like she'd seen her father do on many occasions, being careful to thread the ties through the boot's support loops.

"Left, huh?" Terry shook her head. "You've been very lucky."

"What do you mean?" Rankil paced the room with her new armament, stopping once to tighten the ties. The weight felt odd, almost distracting as it slapped against her calf. And the boots—they might be soft, but she knew blisters were inevitable.

Terry peered up at her with a sneer she'd seen on many others but never on her grandmother. It mimicked their attitude but proved so close to real that Rankil shuddered. "Bad enough you are a stinking white hair," Terry snarled. "But you're left-handed as well. Double bad luck makes you worthy of the fires."

"Burn witch, burn," mumbled Rankil. The words that used to frighten her now did nothing but infuriate. "I've heard it before. I guess that's why m'ma never let me slice things when Danston was around."

"It's pure grace your mother had the sense to save you from that fate." Terry began clearing the table. "Now, hurry up. The milker is bawling." Rankil resacked her treasures and placed them in the heavy trunk, filling the old case. She grabbed the bucket and made the straightest path to the little barn, through the garden.

There she saw it, a hide marker pinned to the post at the

garden's edge, an inked sketch with a group of figure shapes and another of the round markings she'd seen on the sacks. It was self-explanatory. The word was the picture—flowers and vegetables neat in rows. The picture was where she was, so was the word and the round symbol. Garden. "Garden!"

Rankil twirled around and around, stepping over rows and ridges as she repeated herself. "GARDEN!" She slowed to look at the marker again, careful to trace out all eight looping letters. She still couldn't say what they meant individually, but together they meant one thing. "GARDEN!"

Her mind whirling with the knowledge and its possibilities, Rankil picked up the bucket and headed again to the barn. She'd gone three steps when another hide caught her eye, then another. Suddenly, the garden was filled with pictography. It was all so easy to see—ground, dirt, white roots, fence. Kaelan had been thorough in placing Myrla's simple, but lifelike, interpretations in the most thought provoking spots. "Thank you!" She collapsed in the center of the garden, her arms and mind heaped with pictures and words. Rankil's education had begun.

Chapter Five

Emotions have taste: Fear is rancid, Hate is bitter, but love—love is strong, sweet and sour. Its flavor lingers, even when the acrid taste of fear overwhelms.

—Tekkroon saying

———————————

The week, then moon cycle, then the entire summer slid by, Rankil's knowledge growing with each of Kaelan's lessons. She never saw her mentor—Kaelan took great pains to remain unseen, but Rankil knew she watched, testing her knowledge whenever possible. Learning was fun. One morning a trail of hide markers led to the forest where trees, plants and several slower moving animals were labeled. Another sunrise found Rankil scarce awake, staring at the milk nassie. It was marked front to back, each piece of the baying animal's anatomy labeled with the descriptive word. Rankil considered leaving the tags but giddily removed them when she found that even the complaining animal's udder had been labeled. Things were perfect—as long the family stayed away. They made rare appearances that went well as long as Rankil appeared as she had been, ignorant, timid and obedient.

Then Tisph visited. He arrived late morning and lingered into the evening, unswayed by Terry's insistence Rankil was spending the day checking her snares and gathering greens. He poked through cabinets and boxes, searching for some sign Rankil had done less than what was required of her, but he found none. Terry had been certain all evidence of Taelach contact were hidden under the front porch boards.

Rankil returned at dusk, two fat hoppers and a sack of greens in her hand. She froze when she saw her uncle's thick-necked nassie grazing on the front lawn then turned, darting for the barn and her ragged clothes. But it was too late. She'd been spotted.

"There you are." Tisph stepped from the shadows, his worried voice masking the look of perverse infatuation on his face.

Terry came to the door, held it open, and beckoned Rankil in. "Hang your kill on the porch until we've eaten. Did you wash the greens?"

"Yes, ma'am." Rankil, trying hard not to shake, did as she was bid. She piled the greens into a bowl then carried it and a bottle of oil dressing to the table, Tisph watching through narrowed eyes the entire time.

"The girl's hands are dirty." He raised a thick brow at Rankil. "She and I should go down to the water hole and wash before we eat."

"No time," said Terry quickly and to Rankil's immense relief. "The food's growing cold. Use the basin. The water is clean enough for a quick wash." Tisph mumbled under his breath but followed her suggestion, pulling behind and pressing himself into Rankil as she bent over the basin. "Nice hair." He whispered in her ear. "Better than that tangle you used to own. Goes nice with those knee skirts. Tells me you know what you are." His wet hand found its way down her side to pull the blade from her boot. He placed the dagger on the shelf above the basin. "Women don't go armed." He shoved it to the rear of the shelf. "I'm surprised Terry allowed such a thing." His cold hand scratched up her thigh and abdomen, pausing on the soft flesh of her neck before it returned to the basin. "You will help me saddle up after sup, won't you? You know how I love to spend time with my favorite niece and with you being gone so long—"

"She doesn't have time." Terry's stomach soured as she became aware of her great-grandson's advances. "She has to clean the dishes, and then I have a stack of darning for her to do before bed. You're able to do it yourself, I'm sure."

"Then maybe I should just stay the night and head out in the morning." Rankil jerked away as Tisph dried his hands on the rear of her tunic. "Maybe Rankil could show me the snares she's been catching so much with."

"Soap bake is tomorrow." Terry handed Rankil a filled plate then turned her away from the table and toward the hassock. "Stick around, we could use an extra pair of hands to stir the ash pot and dip the stones."

"Figures," mumbled Tisph. "I'll just head back after sup. I'm needed at the farm anyway. What with Archell running off like he did."

"Archell's run off?" Terry poured Rankil a mug of tea and again pushed her away from the table. "When did this happen?"

"Five days back. He took off after I whipped him for those stupid songs he keeps singing. The nassies could care less if they get sung to or not. To top it all, the thief took three of my best string. I say good riddance. Never was as much a worker as he was an eater. He should be thinking of women at his age." Tisph turned to Rankil's direction at the mentioning, his eyes flashing their fantasies as he chewed. "Not just about his songs and nassies. It's not right."

"Did you look for him?" asked Terry, attempting to turn his attention back to her.

"No." He faced her again and took another helping of greens Rankil hoped he'd choke on. "I don't have time for a half-wit."

Terry stabbed her fork into a fish fillet, just missing the back of her great-grandson's still grimy hand. "You don't have time to look for your own son?"

"Not during harvest, I don't. I only got to come up here 'cause it's another day or two before the dark grain is ready to cut. Figured he might have headed this way looking for Rankil. He was always following her about." He leered at his niece. "Not that I blame him."

Terry rose from the table to refill her mug, catching his shin with her cane as she passed. "I'm sorry, Tisph." The apology was the sweetest sounding lie she could muster. "Hard to know where you are going when your eyes don't work. Poor Rankil by and large gets knocked in the leg. Guess today was your turn." Rankil smothered a laugh with her last bite of bread. She typically took heaping seconds but dared not in her uncle's presence. Granny had fed her well all summer, causing a growth spurt that failed to go unnoticed by Tisph's undressing gaze.

"The mountains suit Rankil." His eyes fixated on her from over the top of his mug, their depth of blackness adding to her fears. "You would think she'd been raised here by the look of her. Yes, she looks fit and firm." His eyes now focused on her chest. "She still doesn't talk much. Don't believe I've heard a word from her all evening. What's wrong, girl? Granny Terry got you afraid to speak? You run from her, too?"

"No sir." The reply echoed childhood fear and pain.

"Why would she run from me?" asked Terry. "I know how to treat a child, a skill that wasn't passed down given Archell has run for safer ground."

"Hold up, old woman." Tisph pounded the table. "Family or not, elder or not, no woman is going to speak to me in that manner as long as I'm alive."

"Really?" Terry drew the bread knife from its block and waved it his direction, her anger and disgust rising to a pitch as she spoke. "I can remedy that. The only reason you came here was for young Rankil, and we all know it. Leave her be. Go to Rallings and buy a whore if you're hurting for what Quyley doesn't want to give you.

Not that I blame her the way you stink of manure. Rankil isn't to be touched."

"Put down the knife." Tisph grabbed for the blade, but Terry countered with a wild swing that sliced the back of his hand. "Damn fool! You cut me!"

"Good!" She bellowed, backing away. "I'm telling you to leave. NOW!"

"Leave? You're throwing out your own kin 'cause of a Taelach?" Tisph wrapped a towel around his bleeding extremity, his blame for the situation now centering on his silver-headed niece. "White witch! You've cast one of your spells on her, haven't you?" He drew back from Rankil's blue-eyed gaze, sure she would inflict him with some similar effect. "That's fine, just fine. You care for the old bitch. You two deserve each other. Hateful and disrespectful, the both of you. I'll be damned if me or mine come back here again. I doubt Danston will either when I tell him what's going on." Tisph reached for his boot knife. "White witches are getting thick again. It may be time for another hunt. And, Terry, I'd hate to see you hurt, but you know how accidents happen."

Terror and protectiveness for her caregiver threw Rankil into a mental fury. She wanted Tisph to stop. She wanted him to leave and never return. The horror grew when he grasped his blade. *NO!* The call was internal and focused at her uncle. *You leave us be!*

"Witch! Get outta my head!" He aimed the knife at Terry. "Outta my head or I kill her."

"I'm out." Rankil found herself intuitively backing from something she wasn't sure how she achieved in the first place.

"Now, girl, it's high time we get to know each other better." Tisph jerked her close and forced his mouth over hers, "Ow!" then pushed her away as Terry sank the bread knife into his thigh. "Damn!" He shoved Terry to the floor and tossed the bloodied knife against a far wall. "I thought you were blind, old crone."

Terry felt for the cane he kicked from her reach. "I'm not so blind I can't see how sick you are, boy."

"She's Taelach, old woman. And if she were Autlach she'd be marrying age. That's old enough for me any day."

Rankil kicked and screamed as he forced his mouth to hers again, the cries a smothering high-pitched squeal Tisph's nassie echoed in its nervous nicker. She pushed against his embrace, trying to repeat the internal cry that had threatened him earlier. Tisph ignored her pleading and thrust a hand up her tunic, the other, still gripping his blade, tugged at her waist lacings.

"Tisph, NO!" Terry found her way to the fireside, grasped one of the iron pots and threw it at him. He deflected the heavy kettle and sent it skittering out the open door.

"Back off!" He took Rankil by the scruff of the neck and threw her toward Terry's bedroll. "Do as I say, or I'll be forced to hurt you, maybe Terry, too. Unroll the bed."

Rankil drew into a sobbing ball on top of the rolls. "No, please. Don't hurt Granny. She's been nothing but kind. Don't hurt her."

"Then do as I say." Tisph shoved Terry into the rocker and bound her wrists with kitchen rags. "Too bad you're blind. This is going to be good to watch." He turned back to Rankil, his face lit with a perversion so extreme she forced back the urge to vomit. Grinning, he sheathed the knife and removed his belt. "Let's play a game."

Rankil shrieked as the thin leather laid her skin open, jaw to high cheekbone, the gash continuing above her brow and into her hairline.

"That's for all the times you ran from me." Tisph swung again, this time the leather ripping across the arm protecting her face. "And that's for trying to mind phase me, you stupid whore." Rankil remained silent as he whipped her several more times, her urge to cry out, to fight suppressed by her fear for Granny Terry's safety. She fell limp, helpless with shock when he removed her bloodied tunic, unable to think or speak as he rolled her onto her stomach and jerked down her knee skirts. Rankil drove her head under a pillow and clutched it about her ears, wishing she understood what was happening. What had she done so wrong?

"Please, Tisph, no." Terry pulled against her restraints, jerking the rocker across the floor. "She's too young. A child. She's never harmed you. She can't help what she is. Please! NO!"

"She was born. That's enough." Tisph wrapped the belt around his niece's long neck and twitched her head from under the pillow, Rankil gurgling as the leather squeezed her windpipe.

"What's wrong?" Tisph tightened the belt. "You don't like this game? You wish Danston had killed you at birth? I tried to convince him, but Meelsa cried so hard for your life that he gave in to her." He tugged the leather until Rankil's eyes rolled back. "Beg me to quit, and I just might." He brought her just short of unconsciousness then tore the leather from her throat and bound her arms behind her back. Blood trickled across her face, into her mouth and nose, smearing with her tears. "Not much of a fighter, are you? I expected more than this."

Rankil could hear his sickening whistle as he unknotted then dropped his leggings—the same bouncing whistle that always landed Quyley in the birth bed some time later. Terry's pleas were reduced to a murmur.

"Rankil, child. Don't worry over me. Fight him. Run. Get away." Tisph rewarded the words with a slap that tipped the rocker back, knocking the breath from the old woman.

"I won't have you ruining my fun." He pulled Rankil's head back to see his, a face of deep evil, a possessed darkness that loved nothing or no one.

"Who's going to save you now? Where you going to run?" He rewarded her screams and kicks with a volley of fists to her head and back then forced her to her knees, face down on the blankets. "You're not pretty anymore, white witch. The ugliness is shining through. It makes killing you all the easier. Not like anyone misses a Taelach. You bitches don't have souls." His hands scraped her flesh, drawing her back.

It proved too much. Rankil wretched on the bed and passed out, oblivious to the worst, unaware of the booming call of her salvation.

"DAH, DON'T YOU DARE!"

༄

62

She dreamed of Archell. He sang to her in a baritone so pure he seemed right beside her.

"Rankil dankle, Rankil roo—Archell's come to help you through—To sing you all my little songs—And help you sort the right from wrong."

Rankil stirred, vaguely aware of the intense pain in her arms, her face, her groin. They felt tight and raw. Archell's song was too real, too close, too—

"Rankil dankle, please wake up."

He sat on the floor beside her, smoothing her silver head with his hand. He had grown and his lower jaw showed the beginnings of a beard. But it was Archell, Archell right down to a sliver of greens wedged between his teeth. He kissed her forehead, stroked her hair and continued his song.

"Skinny Rankil Rankil roo—Archell's come to help you through—To keep you safe from all that's bad—And stay here until you're good as new.

"Valiant Ranky, danky, roo—Archell's come to be with you— No more tears or cries of pain—'Cause Rankil's strong—she's Taelach fame."

He laid a hand to her shoulder now to show he knew, and she need not tell him.

"Don't be frightened, Rankil. Dah won't be back. Ever. Archell's seen to that."

Chapter Six

Death is the end of a journey—near-death just a bend in the road.

—Taelach wisdom

Despite Terry's diligent medical attention and Archell's constant companionship, Rankil became gravely ill, her deep cuts reddening with poison, her fever soaring until she lapsed out of consciousness. Terry could do little. She placed hot cloths on the wounds in hopes of pulling the infection to the surface, but it didn't help. The care proved exhausting, so much so Terry failed to notice it was time for their Taelach acquaintances to return.

At daybreak, Archell finally slept, curled at his cousin's side. He had eaten or spoken little since burying his father, and his eyes remained vacant. Archell's gentle nature prevented self-forgiveness for what he had done in Rankil's defense. Terry wondered if he would ever find the strength. She dared not wake him now, so she pulled a quilt over him and went about the morning chores.

Wearied to shaking, her forehead against the milk nassie's side as the bucket filled, she began to sing. Archell's tunes were contagious, easy to sing and pleasant to the ear. She supposed he'd create one in Rankil's memory.

Cheeks damp with tears, Terry finished her chores and turned back to the house. She felt useless. Rankil's body reacted differently than an Autlach's, making her healing wisdom trivial. She felt positive Rankil wouldn't survive the day unless she had some expert help, but where? How? The nearest physician was a day's ride away and if Rankil somehow managed to survive the trip, treatment would be denied her.

The rusted bell behind the shed clanged, rousing Terry from her grief. "I ask for an answer and it comes!" She dropped the bucket and shuffled toward the smoker shed, now hopeful for her grandchild's welfare.

"Wait!" she begged to the forest shadows. "If you can understand me, we need help. The Taelach you've been teaching, she's hurt. She's dying. Please, you have to help."

Kaelan stiffened and pulled deeper into the shadows. The girl had been injured? What could she do about it? Recca's laws prevented such contact. It was dangerous, a breech of her clan vows. A trap could mean her death.

"I'm begging you." Terry's arms stretched to where Kaelan hid. "Two wrongs don't make a right. Ignore her and she dies. Please, don't let this happen. She's a child."

"Our laws don't allow it," called Kaelan in Taelach drawn Autlach. "There is nothing I can do. Misplaced sisters are often better off dead."

"But she's not misplaced. You know of her. You thought enough of her to teach her your ways. She's studied hard and suffers now because of what she is. Should her own kind to turn their backs as well? You can't do this. You have to help."

Kaelan prodded Terry's mind for deception before she dared a step closer. "I make no promises, but I'll do what I can." Then against her better judgment and everything Recca expected, she followed Terry to the house. In the doorway, she froze, hand reaching for her boot knife. Archell had awakened, Rankil's head cradled in his lap. "A trap!" Kaelan stepped back. "You brought me here under the notion that only you and the girl were here. We have been nothing but kind to you. How dare you—"

"No, no." Terry worried her hands into her apron. "Archell won't hurt you. He's close to Rankil. They've suffered together."

"Rankil? That her name?" Kaelan nodded to Archell who drew back from his ailing cousin, permitting her full access.

"Rankil is the strangest name," he said in a singsong manner that drew Kaelan's attention. "It's not her fault. She's not to blame."

"Mother knows she isn't to blame for any of this." Kaelan touched Rankil's burning forehead and pulled back the blankets. "She's lucky to be named at all. Most sisters raised without a clan don't get names." She fell to her knees beside Archell and patted his shoulder. She needn't prod his mind. His thoughts were clear enough. He cared deeply for his cousin and would do anything to assist.

"I think I can help." Kaelan told him. "Would you draw some water from the creek?"

"Yes, Archell will. Archell will." He jumped to his feet and hurried out the door.

"What can I do?" Terry hovered nearby, leaning on her cane. Hope had momentarily replaced the exhaustion that lingered in her slow movements.

"Build a high fire so we can heat the water. I need enough free water to clean her wounds."

"Free water?" Terry pulled an armful of wood from the fireside box.

"Free water is boiled free of dirt, Blind Grandmother. It contains nothing to anger the child's body. I must have it to clean out the infection." Kaelan attentions were once again on Rankil and the coarse stitches in her face. The damage looked extensive, leaving her quite unsure where to begin. There were multiple scars on the youth's body but none issued with the hatred of the latest. They had been meant to kill. "Who did this?"

"Her uncle." Terry couldn't hide her contempt. "Archell made sure he'd never repeat it."

"That explains the fresh burial mound I crossed this morning," replied Kaelan. "So the boy killed for her."

"That and a lifetime of pent-up pain. Tisph was Archell's father. He beat the boy for his songs as much as he chased Rankil for being Taelach."

Kaelan's full mouth pinched with surprise then disgust. "Chased? You don't mean—"

"That's exactly what I mean," spat the old woman. "And he finally managed it." Terry coaxed the fire until it crackled high for Archell's return. "Rankil likes your songs, doesn't she my boy?"

"Rankil dankle is Archell's friend to the end." He filled the pot and swung it over the fire. "Rankil listens to Archell's songs. Never thought to call them wrong."

"Why would one call a poet's creations wrong?" Kaelan placed her knife in the bottom of the heating pot. "I need a needle and some of the thread you sewed her up with the first time. Some of the stitches have burst from the swelling. Archell, I need you to bring the water over here. You can help by wiping her down with a cool cloth."

Eager to assist, Archell settled on his knees beside Kaelan. "Does Archell need to keep dirty water from Rankil's wounds? Keep them clean so they'll heal up soon?"

"Yes, you do," answered Kaelan, astounded by his knowledge. "Did you hear me speak of the water when you were outside?"

He shook his head in that exaggerated way most mistook as a sign of idiocy. "Archell just knows. He learns things from the wind that blows." He sang a soothing verse while he cooled Rankil's fevered body. Gentle and kind, delicate beyond the capability of such large hands, he ragged her. Satisfied that Rankil was in good hands, Kaelan stepped back to warm by the fireside. Despite the warmth of the morning, she shivered. Be it fear or distress she wasn't sure.

"Amazing young man," she commented to Terry. "You say his family flogged him for his voice?"

"I'm afraid so. They say he's simpleminded. I say they're the ones without sense." Terry backed to the fire and held her hand over the pot. "It'll boil soon."

"So it will." Kaelan sat at the kitchen table to wait. "That boy is anything but dumb. He's what my people call a winnolla, a person so brilliant in one area it invades all his being. Besides menial tasks, he can do nothing but create and compose. It's the only way his mind will work. Has he put any of his songs in writing?"

"He can't read or write." Terry settled into the rocker that had proven such a prison three days ago, now wishing nothing more than to be rocking her snow-headed great-great-granddaughter in it. "He seems to keep the whole in his mind, hundreds upon hundreds of verses, one for every situation. Rankil told me of the one we're hearing now. She said he sings it when he's hurting. I don't know what he'll do if she dies. He can't stay here forever. They'll come looking for Tisph sooner or later. We did all we could to make it look like he'd been robbed, blood smeared his saddle, sent his nassie down the mountain." Terry turned toward the fire. "Pot's beginning to boil. I'll get the needle and thread you asked for."

Kaelan pulled the pot from the fire and fished her knife from the bottom. She wrapped the blade in a clean towel then ladled a fair amount of the water into shallow bowls to cool, setting the needle and a length of thread in the bottom of one before she returned to her chair. "You say Rankil has been studying hard?" She had noticed the absence of valued learning materials.

"Every evening. I've had to pry a scroll from her sleeping hands many times. She shares with me as much as she can. Lately she's been reading from the bundle of numbered scrolls you left a few visits back. It's a fascinating story."

"No story. Those are Autlach translations of history scrolls from my clan. My daughter helped make them."

"Daughter?" said Terry. "How old?"

"About Rankil's age. She was with me the first time I saw Rankil. Myrla has been a wealth of ideas. It's hard to judge progress when the only contact with your student is on a slate board. We're hoping Rankil becomes fluent enough in Autlach reading to begin teaching her Taelach in earnest this winter."

Terry leaned close. "Please tell me you're going to take her with you," she whispered in an almost begging tone. "She'll be killed, maybe worse, if she remains here. That or she and Archell will be forced to live like animals in the high ranges."

"We'll take her. The Serpent Clan can always use a strong member in its ranks." Then Kaelan smiled at the back of Archell's head. "And we have been known to take in a misunderstood Aut winnolla from time to time." She reached forward to touch test the knife handle. "Everything is ready. Blind Grandmother, I'll need your help as well as Archell's."

"Just tell us what to do." Under Kaelan's patient guidance, Terry took a place at Rankil's head, cradling it in her lap. Archell sat at her feet, his hands at her ankles should she awaken mid-stitch.

"Don't stop singing to her, Archell," said Kaelan. "Your songs remind her of your presence even when she can't respond." In the midst of his hum, she pushed a pain-relieving phase into Rankil's mind, prodding her for some sort of response. It could be difficult for the young to interpret a mental presence so she searched for any signal relief had been accepted.

Rankil stirred, brushing at her face.

Shhh, young one. Kaelan's words were slow, as she'd never phased in the Autlach language. *You're among friends. My name is Kaelan, and I'm here to help you. I'm relieving the pain while I tend your wounds.* She guided Rankil's hand back to her side, holding it there when Rankil squirmed. *No, don't fight. Your grandmother is here and so is Archell.* Kaelan stroked the unscathed side of her face.

Archie? Granny? Rankil settled when Terry and Archell added their reassurance.

See? They're close. Now let me help. You shouldn't feel any pain. If you do, tell me, and I'll take it away. Understand?

Yes. Rankil sank into unconsciousness as Kaelan opened and cleansed her wounds.

The infection proved deeper than Kaelan had anticipated. Jewel's knowledge and Taelach medicines were in order. She did what she could and was restitching the facial laceration when Rankil raised her first objection. *Hurts.*

Kaelan pushed another wave to mask the pain. *Better?*

Some.

I'm almost through. You've been brave. Kaelan dabbed at the drainage seeping from the loose stitches. *I'm going to put you into a deep sleep until I return.*

When? One word replies were common with youngster's phases.

Soon, and I'll bring back someone for you to meet. Kaelan began to push the phase.

Wait!

What's wrong?

Rankil forced her eyes open. Though the focus unsteady her swollen smile proved quick and her voice strained through her bruised throat. "So, I'm not alone after all." Put at peace by what she'd seen, she relaxed. *Ready.*

Goodnight, Rankil. I'll be here when you wake. Kaelan pushed the heaviest phase she dare, Rankil responding in deep even breaths. "You're not alone, Rankil." She peered up at Terry and Archell's pained faces. "I believe the Mother Maker has seen that you never were."

"Stay in the bed. We'll be back before light." Jewel kissed Myrla's cheek and tucked the blanket tight about her legs.

"I'll stay put, Jewel. I promise." Myrla hoped the guarantee would make her raisers' decision to leave her behind a little easier. "I'm old enough to be alone a while. Besides, the misplaced sister needs you more than I do right now. Go help her."

"From youngest mouth comes the profoundest wisdom." Kaelan winked at Myrla then pulled the divider curtain. "Come, Jewel, an hour's ride can take three in the dark."

"I'm ready." Jewel clasped Kaelan's assisting arm and rose. "Sleep tight, Myrla."

"Night." Myrla snuggled into her fur and pretended to fall fast asleep, knowing Jewel wouldn't leave until she was. Not fooled by her daughter's sudden slumber but confident of her safety, Jewel followed Kaelan through the clan's narrow escape tunnels and into the forest below the night watch's keen eyes.

"An Aut saddle?" Kaelan boosted Jewel up and pulled behind her.

"A loan from Archell so I wouldn't have to sneak a fresh mount from the corrals." She gave the nassie a small kick and guided it down the mountainside. "Thank you for agreeing to help. Rankil doesn't have a prayer without some tyroog root for those cuts. They're highly infected."

"So you said." Jewel pulled her skirts to a more comfortable arrangement. "I brought powders and salve from my birther's stores. An extensive infection needs treatment inside and out." She brushed Kaelan's swinging braid from her face and grumbled under her breath.

"Is the girl aware of what happened to her?"

"If you're asking if she still has her faculties after such a brutal attack, the answer is yes. She's able to speak a little when I phase away the pain." Kaelan thought of the suppressed anger she had sensed in Rankil. "But you must understand, Jewel, she's not much of a child. Her life has been a difficult one. She's bitter and mis-trustful, and so in need of parenting that—"

"Well, I would be to if I was . . . was . . . I'm glad the bastard who did it is dead."

"Don't be." Kaelan ducked to avoid a low branch crossing their

71

path. Despite the move, a twig scratched her cheek. She frowned, but said nothing. Such discomfort seemed trivial when another suffered so. "His death does more harm than good. The man's family will come looking sooner or later. And to make things worse, Archell is a runaway. He stole this nassie and two others when he fled home."

"Great Mother, what are we getting into?" Jewel tensed. "What if the family is there when we arrive?"

"We ride away. I'm not taking the risk. Sick as this child may be, your safety comes first."

"So should yours, Kaelan." Jewel steadied the sling in her lap and remained silent the rest of the short journey, preparing for the worst. Rankil might very well be dead when they arrived.

"Terry? Archell?" Kaelan inquired from the cabin's threshold.

"At the table. Please, join us." Terry beckoned them in. "Rankil's fever is rising again. Archell was about to draw some water to wipe her down."

Jewel hesitated when she saw Archell's hulking form. He was an intimidating sight until you saw his boyish smile. He gave Jewel one of his best, and her fear melted away. "Rankil dankle is so, so sick," he told her. "Please fix her up and do it quick. Archell fears for her."

"She'll do all she can." Kaelan led Jewel to Rankil's pallet, giving her lover a brief, phasing explanation of Archell's unusual talent as they went. "Archell, can you please get some water? We must wash before we tend her."

"Yes, Kaelan." He swept the water bucket into his arms and pushed out the door. Jewel made a summary view of Rankil's wounds and ran a hand across her forehead. Rankil's arms and face were an extreme red of fever and infection.

"Good thing you loosened the stitches." Jewel's accent wasn't as pronounced as her lover's. She shook out her skirts and unpacked her sling. "The drainage from her right arm is heavy. She may lose it yet. Blind Grandmother, has Rankil taken any liquids?"

"Not today." Terry shuffled from her rocker to her grandchild's side. "Nothing much has stayed down since the attack. Not even weak broth."

"Then we'll have to force them into her. The infection won't heal if she's dehydrated." Jewel turned back to her patient as Archell approached with the sloshing bucket. He set it on the table and collapsed on the hassock at Granny's feet.

"Archell's tired," he mumbled.

"So is Granny Terry." She patted his head. "Kaelan, do you need our help?"

"No, I think Jewel and I can manage." Kaelan rinsed her hands, sat cross-legged at the pallet's head and drew Rankil's upper body into her lap.

Rankil? Her prod received no response. *Rankil? It's Kaelan. I need you to wake up.* Rankil's eyelids fluttered. *Come on, Rankil, I brought someone to meet you just as I promised.* Kaelan nodded for Jewel to add her presence.

Rankil? Jewel's touch brimmed with maternal concern. She dried her hands then rubbed Rankil's leg. *Please, Rankil. I need you to wake up and drink some medicine for me.*

What? Rankil finally responded in a tired internal murmur.

Medicine, young one. You must take some.

Who're you?

I'm Jewel. Kaelan brought me here to treat you, which I can't do it until you wake. Jewel brushed a hand over Rankil's cheek before pushing a relieving phase. *There, the pain should be less. Open your eyes.*

Rankil rejoiced to find two Taelach faces smiling down on her. She was amazed to be seeing her own, astounded they actually cared. Why should they? They didn't know her.

"You thirsty?" Jewel seemed pleased by Rankil's nod. "Good, you can have something as soon as I salve down the cuts." She proceeded to smear a thick layer of foul-smelling gray oil around the stitches. Rankil lay in silence until Jewel reached her face then she winced, pushing Jewel's hand away.

"Hurts there, doesn't it?" Jewel looked at Kaelan. "Hold her firm. Any more of a phase will put her out again."

Kaelan's arm became tight around Rankil's head and shoulders. She held Rankil still no longer than necessary but not without considerable effort. Rankil was strong, powered by muscles formed by tedious lifting chores. *She's a tough one.*

What choice has she had? Jewel cleaned the worst of the drainage and doused the area with the antibiotic oil. "I'm through, Rankil. Please don't cry anymore."

But Rankil couldn't stop. She let wave after wave of terrified sobs, releasing what hadn't come of the assault. Kaelan and Jewel could do little more than comfort her as they did Myrla when she'd been scared or hurt, carefully rocking her. Terry and Archell were quick to add their input. Archell sang verse after verse of her favorite songs, each sillier than the last until all, Rankil included, laughed hysterically.

"Sorry," she mumbled when the trembling had eased and she'd downed the medicated water Jewel held to her mouth. "I acted like a little girl." Her facial muscles twitched angrily with her words, but Rankil knew it meant there was no nerve damage. Disfigurement was another issue. "Will my scars be bad?"

"There's no harm in tears," soothed Kaelan, pushing away the expected broadback resistance to emotional displays. "And, yes, you will have pronounced scars on your face and arms."

"But you won't be the first Taelach with them." Jewel pulled back her tunic collar, revealing a jagged circle on her shoulder. "I was run through during a Hunt when I was eight. One of my raiser's almost died protecting me."

"So, I won't be looked at strangely?"

"No," answered Jewel. "A scar is a mark of survival. If anything, it's viewed as honorable." She poured another measure of powders into the refilled mug. "Drink it all. You need the fluids and the medicine."

"Bitter. It's making me sick." Rankil's complaint became a gulp when Archell turned up the glass.

"Shush, Rankil," he said in his most serious, non-rhyming boom of a voice. "Do as you are told."

The room began to tilt and rotate as Jewel's medicines began to take effect. It was far different than the gentle numbing sensation of a phase, Rankil's eyes crossing as focusing became difficult. "Jewel?"

"Yes?"

"You wear skirts."

"I do."

"So you're a woman?"

"Yes."

Kaelan chuckled as she eased Rankil's head to the pillows. "Jewel is what we call a gentlewoman."

"Are you a woman, too, Kaelan?"

Kaelan stifled a full laugh when Jewel poked her in the ribs. "Yes, Rankil, but I'm not a gentlewoman."

"Then what are you?"

"The Taelach call my kind broadback. Auts have many terms for my kind, but none of them are flattering or correct. In essence, I care for my family and protect them from harm. You'll understand as you grow older."

Rankil puzzled over the explanation. "I'm growing tall and strong. Will I be like Kaelan?"

"All Taelachs grow tall and strong." Jewel pulled the covers to Rankil's chest and placed her arms across the top, happy to see that the angry red lines were beginning to recede. "Time will tell you where your heart lies. You're at a confusing time in your development. Not being raised by your own has made it more so."

"Will I ever be accepted?" Rankil allowed her burning eyes to close.

"Our plans are for you to be presented to our clan next spring." Kaelan smiled over to Jewel whose face could not hide her delight. "You're too young to be considered independent so you'll be presented as our child."

"Yours?" Rankil's eyes popped back open. "But you just met me. You don't know a thing about me."

"We know you need us." Jewel stroked away the moisture beading on Rankil's forehead. Her fever was breaking, a sign that made her leaving easier. "And Archell can join us if he wishes. All are welcome as long as they follow the clan laws. I believe Kae would back him." Kaelan put the medicines on the table and draped the empty sling over Jewel's shoulder.

"I would. It's time, my beloved. We must get back."

"I know. You need rest, sweet child. I'm putting you to sleep." She ignored Rankil's objections, forcing her into a deep healing sleep. *Goodnight, my precious babe.* Jewel kissed her cheek and stood, momentarily torn between the child she'd raised and the one who needed her now.

"Coat her wounds at dawn and dusk, Grandmother, and use a spoon measure of powders as needed for her pain. Sing to her, Archell. She needs your support."

"We will." Terry extended her hand in thanks only to find herself the recipient of Jewel's warm hug.

"Kaelan will return tomorrow. Rankil should be quite a bit better by then." Jewel then drew a surprised and pleased Archell into her embrace. "You're not above a little raising yourself, young man."

"I swear you'd have a swarm of children if it were permissible." Kaelan pulled Jewel to the door. "I'll be back soon." They slid through the late stillness to where their nassie was picketed behind the smoker shed. They were just inside the tree line when the rumble of hooves turned them back. Four sweat-slicked mounts drew to a halt outside the small cabin, four sword-wielding male riders sliding off and approaching the still open door.

"Dear Mother, what do we do now?" Jewel sat back against Kaelan. "They've no defense. The children will be killed!"

"Clan law says we ride away. There is nothing we can do."

"But we have to do something," pleaded Jewel. "We can't turn away. The sister child needs us. So does the boy, the old woman. We can't just—"

"We've no other choice." Kaelan urged their nassie up the mountainside.

"No!" Jewel jerked the reins so hard the mount almost flipped on its back. "I won't be able to live with myself."

"I won't risk your safety." Kaelan snapped the reins from her hands and veered the agitated animal back up the slope. "Maybe this is how it was meant to be."

"You're saying we were meant to disobey the Mother's will?"

"The Mother Maker doesn't have to live with Serpent law. We do. I know it seems harsh—" Her explanation stopped as a low-pitched wail rose from the cabin. It was Archell's voice, so pained it made one shiver.

"I can't stand it." Jewel hid her face in Kaelan's cloak. "They're torturing him! Mother's pity, Kae, we have to help."

"Yes, we must," muttered Kaelan as the noise rose. "We must." She turned the nassie back and retied it to the shed. "Stay here."

"I'll not." Jewel slid from her perch and drew her blade from her belt pouch. "I've seen my share of fights. Between our knives and phases we should be able to take all four."

Kaelan opened her mouth to object then stopped, knowing she would never convince Jewel otherwise. "Very well, but if I say run, you run and don't look back until you're safe with Myrla." Kaelan pulled their hoods up and took hold of Jewel's arm. "Stay beside me while we see what we're up against."

They crept to a low window and peered through a crack in the drawn shutters. Terry sat in her rocker, sword pointed to her throat while two burgeoning teens delivered blow after blow to Archell's midsection. The fourth, a chunky youth with Danston's high forehead, poked Rankil with the tip of his blade.

"She's out of it. Really out of it." Sallnox prodded his sister again then turned to his cousins. "Won't Archie speak up?"

"Stars, no. Even if he did the dummy would only sing." Eloc

ground his boot into Archell's stomach. "Where's Dah, Archie? Where're the nassies you took?"

"Leave him be!" Terry pushed the blade from her face and felt her way to Archell's side. She drew him into her arms and wiped his bloodied nose on her apron. "He has no nassies and Tisph was never here. Archell showed up a few nights ago cold and hungry. He's been helping me care for Rankil. Does that rate him a beating?"

"And just what happened to Rankil?" Sallnox pointed to his sister. "And what's that gunk on her face and arms?"

"She crossed paths with a letcher bear while tending her snares," said Terry. "The wounds are dressed with one of my herb remedies."

"Those aren't claw marks," stated one of Archell's brothers. "Those are from a strap like Dah's belt. We all know how his leather cuts."

"Yeah, we do." The smallest of the four, a boy no more than twelve, rubbed his shoulder. "Dah said he was riding up here. His nassie wandered back into the compound around dark. Where is he, Granny Terry?"

"All right." The old woman sighed. "He showed the other morning, took his pleasures with Rankil and left. You happy?"

"Dah finally caught up with Rank, eh?" Royce, the closest to Archell's age, gave his father's lewd grin. "She deserved what she got and more. Stupid witch, wish I'd been here to see it."

"Maybe we could finish the job." Eloc adjusted his belt line, hungering with the desires that had cost his father's life.

"We string the thief first." Sallnox grabbed Archell by the collar and pulled him toward the door. "Get your rope, Tilnor. Royce, tie him up and get him mounted."

"Oh, such big, strong, brave men!" wailed Terry when they ripped Archell from her arms. "Come here in the dead of night to hang your brother and murder your helpless cousin. And, Sallnox! You'd let them? I thought more of you."

"Shut up." Sallnox knotted Archell's bindings then shoved him to the others. "String him good. I'll watch Rankil until you get back."

"Sallnox, NO!" Terry threw herself over Rankil's body. "How could you possibly—"

He pulled her clear of Rankil once the others were occupied outside. "Not that. Think about it. If I don't end it quick for Rankil then Royce and Eloc will do what Uncle Tisph did, only worse. I won't hurt her. She'll just slip away." He settled with his knees on either side of his sibling's shoulders and pulled the pillow from underneath her head. "This is for the best." He pressed it into her face, her humiliation sliding away as he worked. Raskhallak was right—she was just Taelach. What his uncle and cousins saw in her he'd never know.

"Stop!" Terry pulled her great-great-grandson's black ponytail.

"Stars!" Sallnox knocked her hands loose, retook his position. "I'm only helping!" He pushed the pillow harder. "She won't hurt this way. It's for the best."

"For the best?" Jewel slid her headscarf noose-like around Sallnox's neck. "Maybe *your* dying is for the best." She jerked him backward, adding enough of a pain phase to emphasize her point. *Sorry little man. Have you learned everything wrong? It's love your family, not murder them.* Sallnox wheezed and collapsed at her feet. Jewel was strong for her slender build, her body tight from hard work. She shook him in disgust then released the scarf, her phase more than enough to keep him in control. *I should kill you, but I was taught better.* She shoved him to the door and turned his head so he could see his cousins bound to the hanging tree. Kaelan was removing the noose from Archell's neck.

"Rankil okay?" she called.

"Sleeping. Terry's with her." Jewel pushed Sallnox down the steps, dropping him at Kaelan's feet, where she released her mind hold. "Meet Sallnox, Rankil's brother. He was smothering her."

"Shall I finish him the same way?" Kaelan looped the noose around his neck and began to tighten.

79

"No, he's not worth the effort. We'll rearrange his memory like the others."

"What memory, white witch?" seethed Sallnox between rough jerks of the rope circling his neck. "How you planned your attack? How you stole Granny Terry and Archell for slaves?"

"Slaves?" Jewel laughed acrimoniously. "Attack? You stupid, shortsighted, snot-nosed brat! How dare you lie about the Taelach in our presence. We only want to be left in peace. We ask and take nothing other than our own. Taelachs defend. We never initiate an attack!"

"What about the ones you eat? You gonna hack us up for your fires?" His remark disturbed Kaelan so completely that she threw down the noose and walked into the house.

"Is that what they're saying about us now?" Jewel took up the rope and cut lengths for Sallnox's hands and feet. She passed the bindings to Archell. "Tie him tight, Archell, and we'll carry his useless hide inside."

"Archell will, lady Jewel." He followed her instructions and carried Sallnox into the house. "Sit." He tossed his cousin into the broom corner but remained by his side, looming, menacing, registering Sallnox's every breath. "You won't hurt my Rankil dankle again." Archell bore his teeth, gnashing them until Sallnox was certain of Taelach mind control. "Do and Archell might just eat you." Sallnox gulped and sat in silence.

"Now what?" Jewel joined the other adults at the low dining table.

"Terry and I were just discussing the options, or lack thereof." Kaelan took her gentlewoman's hand. "The children can't stay, that's a certainty. I guess they'll have to come with us back to the clan."

"What'll Recca say? She's thrown others out for less."

"It's a possibility, Jewel. A real one. If it happens, she may take Myrla from us."

"Not our baby. Not our girl."

"I know, Jewel of mine. There's only one other choice I can think of." Jewel grew anxious as Kaelan explained. "Terry has

80

agreed. Rankil and Archell will get what they need. It's the only option I can think of."

"But to live clanless?" replied Jewel. "By ourselves? Alone?"

"You'll have to be your own clan," said Terry. "There's enough strength in this room to handle most anything. Those children need a life. This is for them. Kaelan assures me there is a safe place you can build in, a bowl of some kind?"

"The volcano bowl?" Jewel cast her mate a puzzled look. "But the clan will be there next spring."

"If we leave the clan by choice it gives us time to teach the children Taelach ways. Then, when the Serpents arrive, we'll be prepared, and Recca'll have to accept the additions."

"And if we're thrown out there is no return," muttered Jewel. "I see the logic. We must retrieve Myrla and our things straightaway."

"I'm going in a moment." Kaelan then motioned to Archell, who was appreciating the newfound power he wielded over his cousin. "Archell, could you help Jewel and Granny Terry collect Rankil's things? Be sure to include all the lesson scrolls and slates. We can't have them in the wrong hands."

"Archell is a good packer," he replied. "Good packer and better stacker. We'll be ready by dawn."

"Good." Kaelan turned to Jewel. "A litter will leave too obvious a path so Rankil will have to be held. Think we should wake her for it?"

"It'll be easier for her if she remains asleep. You hurry back with Myrla." Jewel drifted to the door, anticipating a quick kiss before they separated. "Don't forget one of Myrla's dolls. She says she's too big for them, but a change this drastic may have her wishing for the security."

"I'll bring two. I'm sure Rankil has never had the privilege." Kaelan bent down, drawing Jewel into a passionate kiss. *Change can be good. It can heal old wounds and give new hope for the future.*

It can at that. You'd best go. The sooner you return the sooner we'll be making love in some exotic locale.

You fire mind you! Kaelan pushed back and smiled. "Convincing

81

argument. I'm off!" And Kaelan disappeared in the quick and silent manner Taelachs were known for.

"Well," Jewel turned back and stared somewhat perplexed at Sallnox, who was now convinced of his fate in the cook pot. She pitied the cowering boy as much as she detested him. Autlachs would never understand—the fear was too twisted with lore and religion. The Taelach would always be running, struggling for existence as long as the circle of lies remained unbroken. But, Jewel considered as she looked upon Rankil's swollen face, the task wasn't up for her to accomplish.

"Archell?" She reached for Sallnox. "It's time we take care of a few loose ends."

Chapter Seven

A Sister is never alone.

—*Taelach saying*

———————

"Kaelan, where in the Mother's name have you been? And where's Jewel?" Recca blocked the narrow escape tunnel as she toyed with her gold-handled blade. "I don't care one bit for this." Her seasoned brow rose. "Smells like conspiracy, and I know you wouldn't do that, my friend, so what gives? You switching your affiliation to the Tekkroons? I know they're more liberal than I choose to be, but I never figured you for this."

"No, Recca. It's nothing like that." Kaelan leaned against the wall, inappreciative of the delay. "Put that blade away, and I'll be happy to tell you what's going on."

"Good." Recca sheathed the blade, but continued to block the entrance, arms crossing her chest. "Does this have anything to do with the misplaced sister? Are you leaving the clan for her?"

"Her and another child, a winnolla with the gift of music. They need us."

Recca let a snorting laugh, shaking her age-streaked head against the foolishness she perceived. The stringent Serpent belief system had cost her people before, but she'd never lost anyone to living alone, much less an entire family. Normally, she wouldn't have allowed a child to be taken into peril, but Kaelan had been a long-time friend and could be trusted, even though Recca questioned the idea.

"You're going rogue? Wasting everything you've built here? Your station? And Jewel is willing to follow with so many single broadbacks willing to take her and Myrla in? You're a damned fool, Kaelan, an idiot extreme. I'm tempted to keep the child with us until you're sufficiently settled."

"We're doing what we feel is right." Kaelan eyed the way Recca's hand returned to her blade. On impulse, Kaelan's palm grasped her own knife handle, fingers tapping warning on the handle. "And I know my blade as well as you know yours, so don't threaten my family. Myrla will go with her raisers."

"No offense intended." Recca pulled her hand back. "I was only trying to figure your rationale. This is highly unusual. You of all people should know." Recca stepped aside but followed Kaelan through the interior corridors, dissatisfied by the manner in which she had retreated from another's challenge. But, dammit, this was Kaelan, a valued member of the community, and though Recca would never admit it, someone whose swordsmanship topped her own.

"At least tell me where you're headed."

"The volcano valley."

"Good choice. It's close to the Tekkroon, so it should prove safe enough. But you'll need winter stores, milk for the children. How, pray tell, were you planning to obtain these?"

Kaelan kicked a loose stone in her path. "However I can."

"Spoken like a truly desperate individual." Recca caught Kaelan hard by the elbow, turning her about. "My friend, I have a proposition you might just like."

"Whatever it is, make it quick." Kaelan turned toward her grotto. "Jewel and the children are waiting."

"It's simple." Recca released her hold, and they continued down yet another darkened passageway. "You need time to teach your new family. I need someone to map out the bowl's caverns. You willing to trade?"

"My services for what?"

"What do you suggest?"

"My clan affiliation."

"Still intact, provided the children know our language and customs when we arrive."

"They will." Kaelan's brisk pace slowed for a second, and she smile back at Recca, dissolving all tension between them.

"With you and Jewel guiding them they'll be quoting the Mother's parables." Recca laughed. "Go wake your daughter, Kae. Tell her of your expanded family while I have your supplies packed."

"I'm in a hurry."

"Aren't we always when we move?" Recca shoved Kaelan toward the living cavern. "Supplies will be waiting for you in half an hour. Go get your daughter."

Myrla proved an efficient packer when Kaelan woke her with the news. She chose her favorite two dolls, leaving the remaining three for the youngest clan members. "After all," she declared while rolling her bedding, "I'll be awfully busy with my friends."

"Got your winter cloak?" Kaelan placed their few pieces of jewelry and Autlach currency into her belt pouch.

"Yep, I'm ready." Myrla stood by the doorway. Late night or not, she was wide awake. "Never thought I'd live outside the clan. Isn't it dangerous?"

"Not where we're going." Kaelan folded the divider curtain and tucked it under her arm. The material had cost them several pieces of jewelry, and she had no intention of parting with it. "Let's go, daughter. Time is wasting."

Recca waited by the smoldering remains of the evening fire. She had three nassies packed for travel, two laden with food, the other with everything from cooking utensils to replacement arrows. A small, calf-heavy milker was at the end of the line, quite content to be chewing her cud. Archell's stolen nassie stood nearby, the Autlach saddle replaced by a Taelach riding pad.

"It's all here." Recca strapped a sword to Kaelan's back. "There's a second in the packs. Teach the lost sister how to defend herself. I expect to see you come spring with a stack of detailed maps. You'll receive prime quarters for your efforts."

"We'll be waiting." Kaelan lashed the last of their belongings on the packers, climbed onto her mount, and pulled Myrla up behind. "I'm expected back around dawn."

"Then get going!" Recca passed the lead line to Myrla and waved them away. "Keep safe, my sisters and good luck."

"Same to you." Kaelan whistled for the pack line to follow, ignoring the sleepy faces poking from the cavern opening. Recca would explain away their leaving, she was sure.

Progress proved slow with such a long lead line, but they arrived at the cabin just after sunrise, Myrla's excitement having faded enough for her to doze against Kaelan's back. At the sight of them, Jewel rushed out and pulled Myrla into her arms, startling her awake.

"No problems?" she asked between quick kisses on her daughter's forehead.

"What do you think?" Kaelan pointed to the snorting packers.

"I think Recca was either very generous or you stole the clan blind." Still clutching Myrla, she examined the supplies. "Everything we could want is here. What prompted the generosity?"

"I'm to map the volcano bowl's caverns. The supplies are part of my payment."

"See?" Jewel smiled. "This *was* part of the Mother's plan."

Archell trotted up the hillside as they spoke. He'd deposited his unconscious relatives in a small shrub knot down the road, roughing their appearance to match the planted memory of a vicious robbery by Autlach bandits.

"Nassies are packed and loaded tight. Let's get Rankil and ride until night."

"Jewel," a delighted Myrla said in broken Autlach, "he is winnolla! Will you teach me songs, Archell?"

"Will the pretty Taelach teach Archell to read?" He said with a mischievous smile.

"Love to." An instant bond was formed between the youths, a friendship blind to their differences. They chattered back and forth as the adults ushered them inside Terry's cabin, the merriment coming to a screeching halt when Myrla spied Rankil. "How will she ride?"

"With assistance." Jewel knelt to help Terry wrap Rankil in a new quilt.

"The patchwork was going to be her gift for the Pass End Feast." Terry lowered her grandchild onto the pillow. "But she needs it now." Terry's tense expression had settled into a reflective glow as her sightless eyes moved from Kaelan to Jewel. "She's yours. I'm too tired to provide what she needs. Give her the love she's been denied. Hold her through the coming nightmares. Listen to her fears and help her overcome them." Terry slid her grandchild's hand into Jewel's then reached for her grandson. "Archell, come lead your great-great-grandmother to her rocker and sit with her a while."

"Granny's heart is breaking?" He sat on the hassock before her. "Archell will stay."

"No, Archell," she whispered. "You go. I'm due a little rest." The rocker creaked, her eyes closed, and she hummed while her hand rested on his unkempt curls. "You've such a rare gift, my boy. Don't let anyone convince you otherwise. Use it. Let it grow into something grand." Her voice weakened as her breathing slowed.

"Granny?" Archell clutched her hand.

"It's all right." Jewel drew to her knees beside him. "It's all just been too much for her. I've made sure she's not hurting."

"Speak me a verse," whispered Terry. "Something about the hills in summer."

Wrapped in a comforting melody that helped link one ending to the next beginning, Archell's words went something like this:

"Mountains high with sunny slopes—Draped in carpet green—Flowers bloom in rainbow hues—Blessed is the view. We often wonder when we look—If this awaits us all—When this life is through, we are weary—And sweet reward is due."

Archell stopped singing as the chair fell still. He released Terry's hand and finished the words, choking back tears as he altered them to fit the moment.

"Mountains high with sunny slopes—She once again can see—Petals drop to pad her steps—In Forever she's renewed."

Part II
Angry

Chapter Eight

Your good, your bad—your children learn from them both.

—Jewel Kaelans

Fall winds found Kaelan's new family snug within the volcano dome's safe confines. They settled into a many-chambered cavern equipped with a natural smoke hole and shallow spring. Kaelan and Archell prepared for winter, stockpiling wood and dried nassie dung for the fires, while Jewel and Myrla swathed and bundled grasses for when the weather prevented the stock from grazing. Preferring to lone, Rankil hunted small game and gathered fall edibles, keeping the family from dipping into their vital stores. She had become sullen, a solitary figure, consumed by emotional scars far deeper than the physical ones jagging down her face and arms. She never focused it on others but appeared that way more and more often. Instead of the play and chitchat of the other children, she chose to refine her weapon skills, becoming a deadly shot with the bow and knife. Kaelan was beginning to teach her the more intricate points of swordplay when the first winter snow forced the family fully indoors.

"I had hoped Rankil would open to Myrla like she does Archell." Jewel replaced the lid on the heavy pot hanging over the evening fire. "Rankil seems disinterested in her, short at times. Do you think they'll ever find a common ground?"

"They will eventually." Kaelan looked to where the tallest of her foster children dozed in a remote corner. "Rankil is going through a myriad of changes. Her mind is giving her mixed messages. She feels a child at times, other times, she sees herself as adult. Broadbacks do that, my love. Adolescence is a confusing time for us, more so, I believe, than it is for gentlewomen. Myrla seems to be accepting who she is well enough."

"Yes, she does." Jewel settled on their ground mat. "But she craves Rankil's attention. I think therein lies the difficulty with their relationship. Rankil doesn't know how to accept or demonstrate affection. Her time with Terry wasn't enough."

"Jewel," chuckled Kaelan, coaxing the fire a little higher before feeding it. "You mean to tell me Myrla fancies Rankil? She just turned fourteen!"

"Don't you remember how I pursued you when you were Rankil's age?" Their daughter's happy laugh drifted from where she and Archell were engaged in a Taelach game. They were far too busy carving their moves into the dirt to notice their observers. "I remember you avoided me for over two passes."

"I hated you for the longest time," admitted Kaelan as she viewed Rankil's irritated reaction to the outburst. "Found you to be an annoying little pest. Then one day, close to winter like today, I saw you tending the smoker fires with Ashklara. You were a vision—hair a mess, face streaked with soot."

"Don't tell me that's the first time you found me attractive!" moaned Jewel.

"It was. It was also the first time I realized you felt the same about me. You became embarrassed when you caught me staring, then mad for making you blush. I couldn't take my eyes off you after that, took every chance I could to be near you, bothered your raisers until they gave me permission to court you."

"You were a bit on the wild side." Jewel pushed a strand of hair from her broadback's eyes. "Gaylord and Cirina hoped me to take up with someone already stabilized." She checked the cook pot and finding the contents thickened, swung it from the heat. "It's ready. If you'll get the mugs from the shelf, I'll warm the bread."

"Anything for you, my dear." Kaelan used the fire poker to flip the ends of Jewel's winter skirts. "Anything at all."

"Kae!" Jewel's reprimand turned to a laugh at sight of her lover's deep leer. "You're incorrigible!"

"And still a bit wild at times, in case you haven't noticed." Kaelan retrieved the mugs from one of the many shelves she'd mounted onto the cavern's walls and preceded to fill them with the aromatic stew. "I think I'll take Rankil mapping tomorrow."

"Please do." Jewel pulled crusty bread from the warming rock and placed two slices beside each mug on the serving tray. "It worries me when you go alone. Besides, Rankil could use a little, um, how should I say—"

"One-on-one attention from one who understands what is going through her mind at present?"

"Exactly." Jewel called the children to their meal, the start point for their evening lessons. Instruction consisted of conversations in Taelach. Rankil and Archell had only listened during the first evenings of cultural teaching but were beginning to comprehend enough to venture choppy questions and replies.

"There's half a mug left," said Jewel in her clearest Taelach. "Someone must empty the pot for me. It's shameful to waste what the Mother has provided us."

"This Mother you speak of," Rankil said, willingly receiving the scrapings. "Who is she?"

"She's the creator, the one who made us all." Kaelan stoked the fire against the icy breeze rising from the cavern entrance. "She watches us, guides us through life."

"So, she is like Raskhallak?" The adults were quick to reject Archell's comparison to the Autlach deity.

"No," replied Jewel. "She is not unforgiving and demanding like Raskhallak, nor does she have lower deities. The Great Mother simply asks we live our lives within certain guidelines and recognize the efforts she puts into her creations by doing what we can to preserve them."

Archell shook his head as he struggled to put Taelach beliefs into context with his raising. "But, Raskhallak says we are soulless unless we follow his commands. You are not soulless, Jewel, and neither are you, Kaelan. But, you don't believe in Raskhallak, do you?"

"No, we don't." Jewel said to him. She appreciated, how in serious matters, he attempted to refrain from rhyming verse. "But neither are we denying you the right to believe in him if you so choose. It's your choice."

"I never thought much of a god who said I was damned from birth." Rankil downed her remaining stew then cleaned the sides and bottom with her blade, catching the smallest of remainders. "Hard to believe in something that loathes your very existence."

"Most sisters would agree." Myrla rose and attempted to take Rankil's empty mug to the washtub with her own.

"I can do for myself!" Rankil snatched the earthenware away. "I'm not helpless."

"Never said you were!" Myrla masked her crushed sentiments with an indifferent sulk. "See if I ever do another helping deed for you!"

"Do them for Archell if you're so inclined." Rankil tossed the mug into the dishwater, lit a lantern, and made her way to the toilet dug in one of the cavern's rear alcoves. "I'll wash it as soon as I return."

"Don't bother. I'll catch it with the others." Jewel made a quick wash of the dishes while Archell, declaring it was his helping deed for the day, dried. He admitted he was still uncomfortable with the idea of a woman as the all-powerful creator but assured his foster raisers he embraced the idea of a kinder being watching over them.

"Rankil dankle is a moody girl," he mumbled in broken Taelach as his cousin retook her remote corner. "She is confused by herself."

"That she is." Jewel emptied the water pan by fanning the contents over the ground a distance away. "Let's see if your sweater sleeves are long enough. Kaelan swears they aren't."

"Kaelan is right," he grinned when the woven nassie fleece barely reached mid-forearm. "Archell is too big."

"No, dear." Jewel pulled the sweater over his head. "I just made the sleeves too short. It's nothing that can't be remedied." She returned to her mat and began to undo the right sleeve's bottom stitches.

"Told you." Kaelan began to pick the other sleeve. "Myrla, have you finished the head wrap I asked you to make?"

"I have." Myrla produced the handiwork. Jewel looked over the weave and passed it back to its maker.

"Well done. Tight stitches and sound knotting. Want to give it to Rankil tonight?"

"I made this for her?" The nassie fleece drooped in Myrla's slender hand. "Why would she wear something I made?"

"Because I expect her to." Kaelan's statement boomed across the stone walls in its most officious manner, rattling Rankil's defiant ears. "Come sit with the family, Rankil. It's warmer by the fire. We can't have you sick."

"I want to think." Rankil turned her back to the fire.

"That wasn't a request." Kaelan sternly replied. "Come to the fire with your thoughts. You can keep them and yourself warm at the same time."

Rankil took great pains in letting the others know how much she disliked the idea of joining them, thudding into the firelight and taking position as far away as possible, scooting closer only when Kaelan threatened discipline.

"Much better. You keep too much to yourself, daughter. Let

others in now and then." Kaelan nodded for Myrla to present her gift. "Myrla has been kind enough to make you a head wrap to ward off the winter winds."

"Thanks." Rankil grabbed for the wrap.

"No." Kaelan batted Rankil's hand away. "Serpent law bids the giver of a clothing gift get the privilege of trying it on the recipient. You will stand and let Myrla put it on you."

"Must I?" moaned Rankil.

"Yes!" Kaelan glowered. "You will not be rude to a gift giver."

Myrla had the momentary pleasure of demonstrating her affections to Rankil. She fussed over the fit, standing on tiptoe to straighten the headpiece around Rankil's flame red cheeks.

"It fits." Rankil scowled after one too many adjustments for her liking. "Thank you."

"I think you need mitts, too." Myrla stepped back. "Maybe some red ones." She thought of how they would match Rankil's blush. "Yes, definitely red."

"I don't need them, but thank you anyway." Rankil rolled the gift into a neat ball and returned to her seat, her shoulders slumped.

"We all need winter mitts." Myrla moved her mat closer, unsettling Rankil all the more. "And red is a good color for you. Snowberries will be ripe soon. You get the best color from them. I'll dye the yarn and knit you some in the next moon cycle or so."

Swayed by Kaelan's critical gaze, Rankil accepted Myrla's offer, her crimson blush fading as the conversation steered in other directions. Kaelan had let Rankil's ill moods go unchecked for too long, a situation she remedied the next day as they mapped.

"I know things are difficult for you right now." Kaelan held her voice to a gentle but firm tone. "But there's no reason for you to mistreat Myrla. She's only being kind."

"It's just that I'd rather be alone as of late." Rankil curled on a low boulder. Kaelan scribbled their position onto a heavy hide scroll, the torch's orange glow dancing high and back as she inked the small chamber's position.

"A need for solitude is one thing. Demanding it by way of hatred is quite another." Kaelan blew on the ink. "Manners are important throughout your life. My progenies will not be known for being lax in them."

"Yes, Kaelan." Rankil was quiet for a moment then tilted her head in a confused fashion. If anyone understood what was going on right now, she supposed it would be Kaelan. "Have you ever had so much going through your head you thought it might burst?"

"All the time. I've found it's preceeded by a period of no thought at all."

"That's what gets me." Rankil was relieved she wasn't alone. "It's all or nothing, empty or full. Why can't it be one thing at a time?"

"Anger, fear, joy, frustration and pain in one giant burst and then a blank. Hard to control, impossible to express so someone else might understand." Kaelan rolled the map and slid it into her sling. "Let's see what's down that right hand corridor." They proceeded in silence, Kaelan almost inaudible as she measured the paces to the next chamber.

"Kaelan?"

"Don't make me lose count." There remained silence until they reached their destination, and Kaelan had recorded the distance. "You were saying?"

"Never mind."

"You sure?"

"No, I'm not."

"Then tell me."

"Myrla."

"What about her?" Kaelan stopped estimating the chamber's size and turned to Rankil.

"I like her."

"I know that."

"She's always nice to me."

"That's because she likes you, too."

"But—" Rankil's face scrunched. "I think I'm scared of her."

"I know." Kaelan finished her estimation, dipped her stylus and noted her measurements.

"You do?"

"Perfectly normal at your age."

"It is?"

"Yes. So are the thoughts I'm sure you're having from time to time."

"You?"

Kaelan glanced up with a grin. "They cannot be outgrown."

"Don't think I want to." Rankil drew a lingering breath and tucked her chilled fingers into her underarms. Red mitts would be appreciated. "The thoughts are nice most of the time, almost sweet until I see"—she couldn't bear saying Tisph's name—"his face and then I get scared again but in a different way."

"Then angry?" suggested Kaelan.

"Furious!"

"Memories can hurt, daughter, and you have some bitter ones to work through." Kaelan picked up the torch and motioned Rankil to follow. "The nightmares will likely worsen before they get better, so will the anger. It's your mind's way of purging itself. It's all right to cry about it. It's all right to scream. But, it's never appropriate to take it out on others."

"Like I do Myrla?"

Kaelan's tools were now away, and her attention centered on Rankil. "To some extent you've done it to us all."

"I guess I'm jealous she had love and support when I didn't."

"You have it now."

"So I could cry, and you wouldn't be ashamed of me?"

"Not in the least." Kaelan could see the emotion welling in Rankil's eyes. "Here is probably the best place."

"Why?" Rankil gulped back the lump in her throat.

"Myrla isn't here to scare it back in you."

"Oh." First one, then a shrill line of angry wails escaped

Rankil's shuddering insides. Kaelan was there when her security was needed, wary but close when the fury threatened. The two sides of Rankil fought bitterly, her still dominant child clamoring for position against the adult presence that cried outrage, swearing revenge for what she had endured. It was good to scream, to bellow, curse and spit. She told Kaelan of the abuse, the ridicule. How she had been made to feel less than alive, left dirty until she knew no other way to be. She shed tears for the burns from the fire irons when she wasn't quick enough, and sputtered how she'd avoided the barn at all costs, Tisph's name unable to cross her lips. She would make them all pay. Somehow, some way, she would be vindicated.

Kaelan listened, asked a few critical questions but primarily listened, letting Rankil ramble and sob until she was spent. As one torch burned low, another was lit until only one remained in their sling. By then, Rankil sat in silence, her billions of thoughts expressed, her head empty once again.

"Did it help?" Kaelan's question echoed in the nothing.

"Kind of."

"Want to come mapping with me again?"

"Please." Rankil became aware Kaelan's arms surrounding her. She had supported her since childhood tears had won the struggle. Those arms had been there only when necessary, and Rankil knew they'd be there again. They had to be again. Her entire being required it. "Can I come tomorrow?"

"You're welcome whenever you feel the need."

Neither talked as they made their way back to the cavern mouth, the nothing in Rankil's head turning into a nauseating headache which forced her to bed the minute they returned.

Kaelan instructed the others to leave Rankil alone, assuring them she would be improved by morning. Only Myrla dared draw near, her eyes a brilliant blue of compassion as she offered a doll.

"She helps."

"She does?" Rankil's eyes fixed on Myrla and the faded, cheery-faced comfort in her hands.

"Yeah, she's the one I always hold when I'm scared." Myrla

tucked the doll into the crook of Rankil's arm. "Take her. I bet she'll work for you, too, if you'll let her."

"You think?" It no longer mattered if Myrla knew or not.

"I do care, Rankil."

"I care about you, too. Be my friend?"

"Promise you won't stay so mad at me?"

"I'll try. Promise not to expect miracles?"

"Can I hope?"

"Sure."

"We're friends then." Myrla drifted into slumber in the caress of Rankil's tousled hair, never stirring as Kaelan wrapped a blanket around the sleeping pair and tucked Myrla's other doll in her arms.

"First comes friendship," whispered Kaelan above Archell's snore.

"Then, what we have," Jewel said as she nuzzled a place in her partner's shoulder and slept.

Chapter Nine

No one steals food for the thrill of anything more than survival.

—Olitti Judalaes

Soon after the Pass End Feast, someone began stealing game from Rankil's snares. She followed the thief's tracks again and again but always came back empty handed, the prints so small they all but disappeared. Kaelan's attempts were no more fruitful. Whoever the culprit was, they took extreme measures to remain unseen.

"They're only taking what they need," said Kaelan between bites of leftover hopper leg. "There's always plenty for our eating. But I would like to know who's doing it."

"I find it unnerving," replied Jewel. "What if they're watching us?"

"If they were interested, they'd have contacted us," shrugged her broadback. "I say live and let live. They keep their distance, and we'll keep ours."

Jewel set down her mug. "But they could be the criminal element. Who else would live outside a compound or clan?"

"We are," replied Kaelan, waving the hopper bone her direction. "Are you guilty of some crime I should be aware of?"

Jewel placed one hand on her hip and laughed, "Like I'd tell you." She poured fresh tea and stoked the fire. "Did Myrla tell you the milker is going dry?"

"Archell did. The boy misses his morning cup." Kaelan sipped from her mug and patted the ground mat. "Bring me that last chunk of leg then rest your wearies next to mine."

"Gladly." Jewel took a generous bite of the dark meat and handed Kaelan the remainder. "I don't understand how the creature could be going dry. The evening milking is as much as ever, but the morning"—Jewel scratched under the edge of her head scarf—"there's none to be had. It's almost as if—"

"As if someone is beating us to it?" Kaelan glanced to where the livestock sheltered. "Could you brew me a strong pot before you go to bed?"

"I'll brew for both of us. You're not standing watch by yourself."

"Serpent gentlewomen don't stand watch."

"It's not safe for you to stand alone." Jewel rose to her knees. "I'm sitting up with you."

"This is not your call. I'll take Rankil."

"Oh, take a child over me why don't you?" Jewel filled the teapot with fresh water.

"It's either her or Archell, and he's not a fighter." Kaelan pointed to his snoring form. "He still has night terrors concerning his father. I'll not give him more."

"Rankil has them, too." Jewel added several measures of ground leaves to the pot before she set it on the fire rock.

"Not as often." Kaelan pulled her dagger to sharpen the blade.

"But they're much more violent." Jewel reminded her above the scraping. "Please, let them rest."

"No, Jewel."

"I'll be awake worrying over you anyway."

"*No!*"

"That's all right, Jewel. I'm awake." Rankil rolled to face the fire. "I can't seem to sleep tonight anyway." She reached for her boots. "Besides, I'm anxious to see who's been robbing my snares."

"You can't sleep again?" Jewel bent to roll Rankil's blanket furs. "If you don't begin sleeping, Mother help me, I'll pin you down and phase you out." She stomped past Kaelan and tossed the bedding in a corner. "Honestly, Kae, I'd think you'd have the sense to let the taller, stronger members of the family do the protecting."

"I am!" declared Kaelan. "That's Rankil and me."

"It's not." Jewel drew herself up proudly. "I'm the tallest next to you."

"Stand next to Rankil." Kaelan arranged them back to back then held her hands on the top of their heads. "Step away and see for yourself."

Jewel laughed when she stepped away. "Bless your soul, Rankil, at this rate you'll outgrow Kaelan. But"—she flexed a lean bicep—"it doesn't answer the question of brawn."

"Oh," replied Kaelan so Jewel might not take offense, "I believe it does. Show her what we've been doing with our mapping time, daughter."

"Can I?" Rankil's eyes lit with pride.

"She won't rest until you prove yourself." Kaelan chuckled as Rankil lifted Jewel and tossed her carry sack manner over her shoulder. "That says it all, doesn't it?"

"What have you been doing with this girl?" demanded Jewel when she'd regained her footing.

"We've been having stone rolling races." Rankil tied on her leg sheath and slid in her knife. "I won yesterday."

"You did?" Jewel cocked her head at Kaelan's humbled nod. "And I thought mapping was your sole occupation as of late."

"Glass blower, mapper, stone roller, I have many talents." Kaelan pulled on her cloak and set a head wrap about her ears. "Tonight, it's guard duty with another broadback. You finished with Rankil's cloak, my dear, or does she need a fur to fight the cold?"

"It's finished save for the bottom hem." Jewel drew the dark gray bundle from the sewing pile and draped it across Rankil's shoulders.

"It's hopper lined!" Rankil fingered the garment's supple insides. "So soft." She sniffed and turned away, ashamed of the happy tears stinging her eyes. "Thank you."

"Don't thank me. You've provided more than enough pelts to line all our cloaks." Jewel tossed Rankil her head wrap and red mitts. "You can keep yourself awake by hemming. Your stitches are always even." She held out the thread and bone needle. "I wish my sewing was as clean."

Rankil shoved the items into her pocket. "You become an expert when mistakes earn you lashes."

"You don't have to put in the hem if you don't want to," said Jewel quickly.

"I'll do it. It is my cloak." Rankil patted her pocket then turned to Kaelan. "I'm ready when you are."

"Then let's go." Kaelan led the way to the cavern entrance, pausing long enough to speak back to Jewel. "Finish brewing us a pot then get to bed, my pet."

"Don't worry your stubbly head about me," called Jewel. "I'm a big girl. Oh, and Rankil?"

"Yes?"

"Drop a stitch if it suits your fancy."

"I just might."

The nassies saw their nocturnal companions as a chance for attention and set about baying for a pat on the head. Kaelan gave each animal an affectionate scratch while Rankil mounded clean bedding straw. The milker's new colt tugged against his picket in hopes of a second scratch.

"Greedy," teased Rankil as she patted the creature between the eyes.

"They're gluttons for attention." Kaelan scratched the colt's coarse ear welts and set the torch into a bracket. "Don't make yourself too comfortable. We aren't here to sleep." She spread the hay wider before settling into it. "Want some help with that hem? I'm fair with a needle myself."

"I've only the one."

"Make that two." Kaelan pulled a tack needle from the stack of riding pads. "You'll never finish before the torch burns out. Let me help."

"If you insist." Rankil threaded her needle then passed the spool. "Where'd you learn to sew?"

"From Eeham, the gentlewoman who raised me." Kaelan wet the thread point and pushed it through the eye.

"You didn't have a broadback raiser?"

"Nope."

"That's acceptable?"

"Sure," said Kaelan, taking up the cloak's other side. "Single raisers aren't uncommon among the Taelach. Many times it is due to an untimely death, but occasionally, like with Eeham, one chooses to raise a daughter on her own. Lee, her life mate, died a few passes before I was born."

Rankil was silent for a moment as she stitched. "Did you miss having a broadback to talk to?"

"I always had someone to talk to. There were many who tried to get in Eeham's good graces through me." Kaelan pushed away a straw poking her side. "They came and went, but Recca was always there for me."

"The clan leader?"

"She hasn't always been clan leader." Kaelan chuckled. "When I was young, she was a metal smith. She still does it from time to time—beautiful work, fine detail and craftsmanship. She hoped I'd take a shine to it as well."

"You didn't?" Rankil pricked her finger and shoved it into her mouth to dull the sting.

"I prefer glass blowing and potting. The work is more delicate." Kaelan jerked the wet digit from Rankil's mouth, examined the finger, and shoved it back into her mouth. "Don't sew yourself to it, daughter. You won't appreciate the fur come summer."

"I might."

"Well, we won't be able to stand the stench."

"Thanks a lot."

Kaelan pointed to a break in Rankil's handiwork. "You missed a stitch."

"I know," Rankil replied.

"Your cloak. Your rules. Now move your rump before I follow the wrong line and sew up something important."

Rankil laughed, pulled the cloak free, then threaded a fresh length and began to stitch again. "Kaelan?"

"Yes?"

"When will I be allowed to wear leggings like you?"

"When you come of age."

"When's that?"

"Your eighteenth summer." She smiled at Rankil's irritated sigh. "Sounds like forever, doesn't it?"

"Just short of," Rankil mumbled. "Why eighteen? If I were Autlach I'd be old enough to marry now."

"Sixteen is not grown in Serpent terms." Kaelan put down her needle and motioned Rankil to do the same. "Let me put this into perspective for you." She rose and began to pace the straw-laden floor, arms crossed behind her back. "You've chosen your path, haven't you?"

"Broadback," replied Rankil. "I've known that for a while. My body won't let me forget it either."

"Not all sisters your age are so certain. Waiting until the age of eighteen ensures self-identity. The Serpent clan also expects you to have a trade skill by that age."

"Like potting and glass blowing?"

"Yes," said Kaelan. "But you already have two vital skills."

"I do?"

"You speak perfect Autlach, and you're an excellent hunter."

"Those are vital?"

"Most definitely," Kaelan placed her hand on Rankil's shoulder.

"We need fluent translators for trade and to soothe the hysterics of birthers."

"Birthers?"

"An Aut woman laboring with a Taelach child."

"Oh." Rankil shrugged. "Jewel told me all about that. I can see how my Autlach knowledge could be useful there, but hunting? I'm sure the clan has any number of able bodies."

"Not necessarily." Kaelan resumed her stitching. "You manage to find bounty in a season when most come back empty-handed. There's a knack to doing that. We've barely dipped into our winter supplies because of it. That's a thousand times more valuable than translation."

Rankil's stitches were growing close to Kaelan's as the torch began to burn low over the heads. "What about Archie and Myrla?"

"Melpra will teach him music. She's the clan's lead musician and records keeper. He'll learn to scribe and play the string box and time sticks." Kaelan tugged the cloak. "Look at your head wrap. Myrla is excellent at the loom and hand knitting. That and teaching will probably be her contributions."

"Suits her," replied Rankil. "Those are appropriate jobs for a gentlewoman."

"Don't underestimate her abilities or that of any gentlewoman sister," warned Kaelan. "She's a crack shot with a bow."

"Jewel?"

"Decent enough but lethal with a short blade."

Rankil was grateful the final stitches were almost in place. "Didn't she say something about tea before we came out here?"

"She did." Kaelan knotted her thread and bit it loose. She shoved the point into a broken harness strap then stood. "Think we could both use a strong mug about now. I'll be right back." She rounded the corner into the family chamber and tiptoed to the fireside. With a little prodding and several slow burning chips, she coaxed the smoldering fire back to life. One grew accustomed to the smell.

Jewel opened her eyes when Kaelan pulled the blankets to her chin.

Didn't mean to wake you, lover. Kaelan's mind touch was tender. *I was getting some tea for the night crew.*

How's Rankil faring? Jewel's question carried the equivalent of a kiss.

She's finished the hem. Kaelan extended another mental caress.

With a little help, I'm sure. Jewel shivered as Kaelan's phase intensity increased. *Rankil is waiting for you.*

I suppose she is. My thoughts will have to wait for a later time.

You've given me a pretty vivid image already. Jewel's corresponding thoughts were enough to make Kaelan shiver.

Jewel! Don't you dare say I'm the one with a dirty mind.

I learned from you.

You've had a good teacher then because that was quite inventive. Kaelan broke her phase. "To be continued?" she asked aloud.

"As soon as practical." Jewel closed her eyes. "Night, Kae."

"Pleasant dreams, Jewel of mine." Kaelan carried the pot and a pair of mugs back to the livestock cavern where Rankil paced and talked to the nassies.

"How long until dawn?" she asked when Kaelan's long shadow became visible.

"Three, four hours perhaps." Kaelan poured two steaming cups. "Find a seat. I'm going to douse the torch. Our culprit should show his or her face before daylight."

Rankil returned to the hay mound and took a long draw from her mug. "Think it may be another Taelach?"

"This far in the hills, it's possible." Kaelan smothered the light and felt a path to Rankil's side. "If it is, the sister is most likely clanless for a reason. Might be dangerous."

"Dangerous?"

"You have to commit a serious offense to lose your clan affiliation."

"Like murder?" Rankil could feel Kaelan's nearby warmth—a comfort in the cavern's darkness.

"No, proven murder or rape will earn you slow death in any clan. A clanless sister is probably a thief."

"I see." The warm drink only made Rankil sleepier. She yawned and stretched, trying to stay alert.

"I won't be disappointed if you rest your eyes."

"You won't be?" Rankil's head felt like a lead weight in danger of falling from her shoulders.

"Not a bit. I'll wake you if I need you."

"You won't tell Jewel?"

"I'll swear dead to rights you were wide-eyed the entire night." She pushed an ever so slight phase that soon had Rankil snoring. Kaelan maintained watch the remainder of the night, but her head also nodded as dawn approached. She was nearing full sleep when the nassies began to nicker. Someone was near.

Rankil, wake up. A moderate level of discomfort accompanied the prod.

RANKIL! NOW!

"Huh?"

Kaelan silenced the verbal reply with a phase pinch. *Shush! We have company.*

Ow! Milk thief?

Appears so.

What? Rankil could only broadcast confusion over what to do.

Keep still. Let them come to us. Kaelan received the sensation of a mental nod. She crept between the nassies and quieted them with a warming hand to their front flanks.

A slender shadow edged into the cavern and placed a bucket under the milker. Rankil could hear the liquid splash as the culprit worked.

"You going to drink that all by yourself?" Kaelan lunged forward and grabbed the form about the waist. The thief shrieked and kicked backward, planting a foot in Kaelan's groin. Kaelan cried out and her grip loosened just enough for the scrawny someone to bolt away.

"No you don't!" Rankil tackled the shadow at the knees, pulling it to the ground.

"Hold on!" Kaelan grabbed the torch from the wall, relit it and held it to the flailing figure's face. "Now let's see who had the gall to kick me there." The terror-filled brown eyes of a manure-faced Autlach girl no older than six stared up at them. She wailed at the sight of her captors and wet down the front of Rankil's new wrap.

"Don't eat me! M'ma says I'm rotten, too skinny to be much of a meal! I'll only make your belly hurt. Please! I want my m'ma!"

Chapter Ten

The stomach can speak louder than the mind.

—*Taelach wisdom*

"Don't lay her on the blankets. Her hair is infested." Jewel pointed to where she had spread a portion of the room divider from their Serpent grotto. "We don't all want the itch." She tended the unconscious child in her typical mothering fashion—stripping her clean of the urine soaked clothing, bathing her from a bucket of water and clearing her brown tangles of nits. "I know we can't spare the lamp fuel, but it's the most effective itch treatment I know."

"Use all you need." Kaelan scratched her head. "Maybe we all should wash with it just to be safe."

"Not a bad idea." Jewel slid one of her own tunics over the child's malnourished frame. "Did your phase turn up anything of use?"

"I just discussed the information with Archell." Kaelan shoved the girl's foul smelling, ragged clothes into the water and pushed the bucket away. "She's the eldest of three children. Her mother brought them here to escape an abusive home. They fared well over the summer but had to butcher their pack milker for food a few days ago. The mother is very pregnant." Kaelan blinked and shook her head. "And, Jewel, she knows it's a Taelach babe."

"How would she know?" Jewel stared at the dark-skinned child. "And the oldest? Why, she's just a baby herself. We have to help these people. They'll starve without assistance."

"But how do you convince a terrified child her mother's teachings are wrong?" Kaelan scratched her head again. "Do itch bugs fly?"

"No, but they do hop." Jewel thrust the oilskin at her. "Comb out your head before it spreads even more. Has Rankil finished changing? I want to soak her clothes before they stain."

"Last I saw, she was by the spring, sand scrubbing her cloak."

"Poor girl," replied Jewel, "I hope the smell comes out of the fur."

"You're not the only one." Kaelan wrinkled her nose.

Rankil returned as they spoke, shivering naked from the waist up, her soggy cloak and tunic draped across her arm. She sneered at the sleeping child, spread her things over the drying racks near the fire, and slid on a fresh tunic. Kaelan motioned her over and combed a thick coating of oil through her shoulder length layers.

"Bad enough I smell like piss," Rankil griped between Kaelan's tugs. "Thanks to her I get to smell like a lantern, too."

"Watch your mouth. It's not the child's fault we scared her so." Kaelan pushed her away. "Besides, the urine smell is gone."

"Good riddance!" Rankil shook out her hair as the other youths returned from their morning chores.

"I mucked the cavern for you, Rankil." Myrla grinned at Rankil's appreciative nod and sniffed the fuel-laden air. "The little girl has the itchies, don't she?" she asked in Autlach.

"Doesn't she," corrected Jewel with exact fluency before reverting to Taelach. "And, yes, she does, so keep your distance. We only have so much fuel." She resisted the urge to scratch. "Has Archell finished feeding?"

"All but," replied Myrla. "You know how he likes to sing them through breakfast."

"Sometimes at the cost of his own." Kaelan chuckled. "Ah, there he is." Archell lumbered into view. "Did the livestock enjoy their serenade?"

"Always do." Archell glanced at the tiny Autlach child. "Pretty little girl with pretty little curls—seems so very hungry. Are you going to leave her asleep?"

"We were waiting for you to convince her she's not dinner," said Jewel. "Think you could make her understand we want to help?"

"Archell can try." He settled beside the frail child and smoothed back her oil-laden hair. "Ooh, itchy bugs." His jovial face turned long. "An oiling for me as well?"

"For all of us," replied Kaelan as she shooed the others away. "Keep your distance and let Archell have a go. We don't have many spare clothes." She focused a rousing phase into the Autlach girl's open mind. "She's all yours, Archie. Do your worst."

"Worst?" He said with a sideways glance. "Archell always sings his best." A comforting tune rose from his chest as the girl began to stir. She squinted and shook off her daze, bringing her new surroundings into fuzzy focus. "Hello, pretty thing." He said between verses. "You're safe."

The girl gave him a curious look then turned her ear to the tune. "Nice," she muttered when he stopped. "Sing me some more?"

"Tell me your name and I will."

"Olitti. What's your name?"

"Archell." He sang her a silly upbeat melody. "Tell me about your brothers and mother."

"How'd you know 'bout them?" Olitti sat up. "Where am I?"

"Safe in my family's cavern." Archell couldn't keep from notic-

113

ing that one of the girl's eyes wandered. The brown iris of the left had faded, and the pupil was shrunken and opaque from disuse. "Are you hungry?"

"Yes!" Olliti's stomach gave an affirming growl. "You have food to share?"

"We have bread and milk. Archell will bring you some. Wait here."

Jewel passed him a laden tray when he returned to the fireside. "She can't see well, that's a plain fact." She whispered in his ear. "We'll introduce ourselves one at a time from a distance."

"Logical." Kaelan bent close as well. "Reduce the shock value. She'll talk to us before she can see us."

"Archell?" Olitti squinted toward him. "Who're you talking to?"

"Archell's family." He placed the tray by her side. "I have two sisters." He placed toasted bread in her outstretched hands. "Their names are Rankil and Myrla." Olitti mumbled her own siblings' names through bulging cheeks then reached for another slice. "When's the last time Olitti ate?"

"The other day when I robbed someone's snare." The little girl gulped down the second slice and followed it with a mouthful of milk. "A hopper ain't much eatin' when there are four of you, and that's all you got." Olitti flashed a gap-toothed grin then pointed to yet another piece. "Can I have some more?"

"Slow down, Olitti. You'll make yourself sick." Jewel made a small step forward.

Olitti whirled her direction. "Are you Archell's m'ma?"

"My name is Jewel." Jewel made certain her hair was secured under her headscarf before she stepped closer. "Your m'ma is having a baby, isn't she?"

"Yeah, how'd you know?" Olitti took a smaller sip of milk then wiped her cream-coated lip on her cuff. "M'ma is always havin' babies. Do you have a lot of babies?"

"Only Archell, Rankil and Myrla, and they're all but grown. I don't have any little ones left."

"You can have my youngest brother, Flynne. He's a pest. M'ma says he acts just like Dah."

"Where is your dah?" Jewel motioned Myrla to uncover her braids.

"He died in a fire." Olitti's puerile face darkened with memory. "M'ma rode off with us while the house burned. She said Dah was already dead. Said we had to leave before others came and took us away." She took a small bite of bread. "I don't really miss Dah much. He was always hitting on us." Then Olitti strained her eyes to the figures still out of her focus. "Does your dah hang around, Archell?"

He remained silent for a moment. "Archell's dah doesn't come around anymore." The expression he offered Jewel was tortured, agonized by mere mention of his greatest guilt.

"Then who takes care of you and Jewel?"

"I do." Kaelan stepped into the girl's range of sight. "It's nice to meet you Olitti."

"But you . . . the . . ." Olitti clambered into Archell's lap, climbing onto his chest where she held tight to his neck. "Help me, Archell! She'll eat me for sure!"

"Kaelan doesn't eat little girls." Archell wrapped his arms around her trembling shoulders. "She is kind to Archell. She'll be kind to you if you let her."

"But she's silver topped!" cried Olitti. "A Taewach!"

"It's pronounced Taelach, little one." Jewel took Kaelan by the hand and together they settled on their mat, a comfortable distance from the terrorized girl. "Kaelan wouldn't hurt you." She removed the scarf from her head. "And neither would I."

"But M'ma says—" Olitti's eyes were on the reflections the fire cast on Jewel's wavy hair.

"Your m'ma has been misled." Kaelan placed a loving arm across her gentlewoman's shoulders. "We want to help your m'ma."

"You do?" Olitti's curious one-eyed gaze had drifted back to her protector. "You like them, Archell?"

"They're part of Archell's family." He disentangled himself from her grasp and presented her with another slice of bread. "My sisters are Taelach, too."

"I sorta see them," she revealed between bites. "Can they come closer?"

"Sure." Myrla and Rankil were added to the circle. Olitti considered them as she ate, then, all but tripping over her tunic's hem, took a wary step toward Myrla so she could touch her hair.

"Pretty." She rolled a soft braid end between her fingers. "Blue eyes are pretty, too." She explored Myrla's face and, lifting her arms, touched her nose and cheeks. "Your clothes and milk skin are a little funny, but you aren't ugly like M'ma says."

"Thank you, Olitti." Myrla laughed as the little Autlach's fingers brushed her neck.

"You tickly, too?" Olitti wriggled her fingers against Myrla's collar. "M'ma says I'm too tickly."

"Didn't know you could be too tickly." Myrla took the girl's hands in her own and tickled the back of her small palms. "Can I be your friend?"

"You can." Olitti said, then turned to Rankil who, despite the need to seem sociable, remained sullen. "But your sister doesn't like me 'cause I wet her."

"Serves her right for scaring you." Myrla elbowed Rankil. "You're not mad, are you Rankil?"

Rankil drew up on her knees to frown above Olitti's head. "I'm not angry." She said in a low voice. "Just a little damp."

"Good!" Olitti jumped into Rankil's arms, throwing her back in a hard sit. "I like you. Paelu and Flynne will like you, too." Her hands drew across Rankil's head and face like she had Myrla's, pausing to trace the raised scar line. "Must have hurt."

"It did." Rankil brushed her hand away.

"How'd it happen?"

The question so distressed Rankil that she appealed to Jewel for a reply.

"An accident," said Jewel, rising to bring Olitti to Kaelan. "Rankil had an accident."

"Oh," Olitti stood before Kaelan, one hand in her mouth, the other twisting her makeshift dress. "You sure are big," she said, waving a wet finger. "Bigger than dah, and I thought he was huge!"

"I'm tall enough for what I am." Kaelan pulled two beads from her life braid and offered them to Olitti. "Does your m'ma have enough blankets for you and your brothers?"

"We got two," said Olitti, held the beads up to the firelight. "M'ma sleeps in her cloak. She says she's not cold but I see her shiver sometimes. We build fires but the wind comes in and blows them out. Mamma gets awfully mad when it happens."

"So would I." Jewel twisted a strand of Olitti's hair into a neat braid then added the beads. "We'd like to bring your brothers and mother here, Olitti. We've spare blankets and—"

"And food?" piped Olitti, dangling the braid between her fingers.

"Plenty of food." Kaelan rose to collect her cloak. "Can you take us to meet your mother?"

"I don't know if I should."

"We only wish to talk to her." Jewel wrapped Olitti's slight frame in a blanket and a double layer of Kaelan's heaviest footlings. "Will you show us?"

"Do Paelu and Flynne have to come, too?"

"Don't you think they're hungry?" Jewel clasped the cloak Kaelan placed over her shoulders. "It's not fair that you've eaten when they've not."

"I guess." Olitti twisted from Jewel's grasp. "Will Rankil carry me?"

"Me?" Rankil looked at Olitti then to Jewel who smiled.

"Rankil can go. Archell, too. We may need their Aut voices. Myrla, would you stay here and begin a stew?"

Myrla, though disappointed, started assembling a hearty meal. When she imagined the outside cold, the gray sky and stark winter surroundings, the cavern became less restricting. Her voice carried farther with the others gone so she sang while she worked, fracturing one of Archell's lighter songs with her out of key voice.

"I told you M'ma wouldn't like this." Olitti sat beside Rankil on a snow-cleared boulder, watching as her mother protected the younger children by brandishing the long stick she used as a fire poker.

"Witches! Demons!" Sharillia lunged at Jewel, who had no difficulty keeping out of the pregnant woman's way.

"Please, think of your children." Jewel indicated the rags covering their feet. "High winter is yet to come and—"

"We'll starve before serving Taelachs!" screamed Sharillia, waving the poker to halt Kaelan's slow advance. "We'll not fill your cook pots!"

"The only thing in our cook pot is hopper stew." Kaelan extended her hands to show her passivity. "You cannot permit the children to starve when food is available to you."

"You've already got one slave." Sharillia indicated Archell. "What else would you want with three children besides something tender to chew?"

"M'ma, behave!" Olitti wriggled free of her blanket and jumped from her perch, dodging Rankil's grab to bound to her mother's side. "They fed me, M'ma. They said we could stay with them. They have the most wonderful cave. It has water and a smoke hole so they don't choke up like we do."

"They have none of that. You've been crazed by them." Sharillia drew the girl against her great belly. "Stay with M'ma, baby. I'll keep you safe."

"But, M'ma, I'm tired of being cold and hungry." Olitti tugged on her mother's sleeve. "They want to help."

"Listen to her," called Archell from behind Kaelan. "Olitti speaks truth."

"Truth as it suits your mistresses." Sharillia's two youngest bawled and clung to her skirts.

"You're distressing your babies." Jewel searched Kaelan's face for what to do, but Kaelan showed no emotion, something Jewel knew meant her broadback was thinking.

"I'm protecting them from predators." Sharillia lunged again. Olitti jumped forward when she did, knocking the poker away. "Litti!" Sharillia pulled her beside her brothers.

"Shame on you, M'ma." Olitti spanked her mother's backside. "Jewel don't want to hurt us."

"Raskhallak help me!" Sharillia began backing into her cave shelter, pushing and pulling her children with her. "Don't follow me!" She cried. "I've a sword inside!"

"We've no intention of pursuing you." Kaelan turned away. "And if we'd wanted to slave or eat you then we'd have already done so. It's your decision. If you change your mind, Olitti knows where we are. Archell and Rankil, please go assist Myrla. Gather some fresh wood on your way. We'll be along shortly. It's a clear day so Jewel and I are going to enjoy the walk."

"Kaelan?" Jewel peered back at Sharillia's victorious expression. "Are we really going to leave them to the elements?"

"Course not." Kaelan whispered, urging her forward. "But, we can't make the mother feel she's being coerced."

"Then what do we do?"

"Let's get out of her sight, and I'll show you." Once behind a knot of high shrubs, Kaelan paused. He face twisted with devious intent, she turned to Jewel.

"Kae?"

"Shhh," Kaelan closed her eyes. "Listen."

"What?"

"Just listen."

Jewel turned her ear toward the Autlachs' inadequate quarters. A small child's whine rose from the cave. It was a pitiful cry, one for food that was beyond a mother's bearing. Kaelan popped open one eye and smiled. "Wanna help?"

"Why, Kaelan!" Jewel grinned. "You're decisively corrupt."

"No more than you, lover." A second, higher pitched whine rose, discordant with the first. Olitti's wail, which needed no encouragement, completed the trio.

119

"Now, this *is* something Raskhallak's witches would do," whispered Jewel as she overwhelmed young Flynne's mind with hunger pangs. "How long do we keep this up?"

"Not long." Kaelan was already tapering Paelu to a whimper. "The children's minds are fragile. We'll repeat it in a few hours if need be."

"If she is any kind of a mother another episode won't be necessary." Jewel backed her presence until only Olitti's cries were audible. And, after a moment, those ceased as well. "I'd so hoped it'd work."

"Fright can overwhelm judgment." Kaelan took her arm. "Our own children will be concerned if we don't return soon."

"Very well." Jewel walked beside her broadback. "Should we gather some wood on the way?"

"Wouldn't hurt." They were near their cavern, their arms laden with branches when Olitti's joyous cry pierced the crisp air.

"Jewel! Kaewan! Wait! M'ma's coming. She wants to talk to you."

Sharillia's children were a rambunctious lot, into everything and full of questions, their mother quite content to let them explore while she rested. On occasion, she helped with the easier meal preparations, discussing her life and lost Taelach children as she worked beside Jewel.

"Raskhallak says the pale-skinned babes are punishment for our sins." She shaped dough into loaves of quick bread.

"How could a helpless infant be a punishment?" Jewel lifted the loaves onto a long-handled paddle.

"A white hair is a scar, evidence of our disobedience of his requirements." Sharillia, ignoring Jewel's glare, began shaping another loaf. "I've yet to figure out what I've done to deserve three."

"What happened to the other babies?" Jewel almost dropped the paddle when she saw the Autlach's sunken expression. "You didn't?"

"Me? No!" Sharillia touched her stomach. "Taelach or not, I could never kill my own child."

120

"Then where are they?"

Sharillia pounded the dough, flattening a hole through the middle. "Longpass," she whispered. "He took them before I ever saw them. Punched me when he saw the first one, whipped me on the birth bed 'cause of the second. He would've killed me when he saw this one."

"How do you know you're bearing another Taelach?" Jewel drew the kneading board from Sharillia's trembling hands and began to reshape the loaf. "I've never heard of a woman bearing two Taelachs, much less three."

"Taelach babies are always moving. They never rest." Sharillia drew Jewel's flour-covered hands to her abdomen. "Or do I miss my guess?"

"No." Jewel smiled when the tiny body pushed against her hand. "She's Taelach. I sensed it on our first meeting." A second, stronger vibration responded to her mental touch. "What are you planning to do?"

Sharillia sniffed and arched her back against the baby's sudden roll. "She wouldn't have any kind of life with me. You want her?"

"You say that like you're disposing of garbage." Fearful her emotions would stress the fetus, Jewel removed her hand from the Autlach's stomach. She'd been hoping the offer would be made, but now felt Sharillia considered the child dispensable. "Of course we'll take the child. What other choice do we have?"

"About as much as I do about being here."

"You've the option to leave at any time."

"And go where?" Sharillia looked to where her children were clustered around Myrla, listening to a Taelach folk tale. "My children come first."

"Glad to hear we agree on something." An uneasy silence fell between them as they completed the baking. Then Jewel, after bidding Sharillia to return to bed, ventured to the livestock chamber. Kaelan was cleaning the nassies' triangular hooves, her pick scraping one of the packer's bars. She looked up at Jewel and smiled, happy to hear the ringing laughter drifting from the family cavern.

"The children are doing well."

"They're fine," Jewel sighed. "It's Sharillia that concerns me."

Kaelan dropped the hoof wedged between her knees. "What has she said now? Rankil stays so livid I'm surprised she hasn't asked to sleep out here."

"It's not what she's said, it's how she said it."

Kaelan tossed the pick into an empty bucket and drew Jewel into her arms. "What did she say to disturb you, love? Whatever it is, we'll fix it."

"She offered us the child."

"And this upsets you?" Kaelan stared at her mate. "I thought you wanted the babe."

"I do." Jewel pushed her head into the hollow of Kaelan's shoulder. "She offered like the baby was a burden, garbage. Why do Aut women think such a way? I'd give anything to bear a child." She shuddered as Kaelan pushed a comforting, calming phase.

I know you would, Jewel, and as much as I would adore seeing you in that fashion, it will simply never be. Jewel tightened her hold in response. *Does it matter how the child comes to us?*

No, it's just that—

You're a little jealous of biological differences you can't control?

More than a little. Jewel's grudging admission broke the phase. "Is Rankil still having problems with Sharillia?"

"I'm afraid so." Kaelan lingered in her embrace. "They can't agree on anything. Anything!"

"Sharillia provokes it."

"Rankil doesn't help matters by taking offense at everything she says." Kaelan brushed flour from Jewel's sleeve. "Though I do appreciate the way she stopped Sharillia from picking on Myrla."

"Archell had a hand in that as well. He reminded our guest her behavior could land her in the cold without her children."

"Congratulations, Archell." Kaelan laughed. "It's good to hear he's got backbone when required."

"And Rankil can have too much." Jewel grinned. "Did you see—?"

"Her take Myrla's hand at the evening fire?" Kaelan returned her lover's smile. "I suppose it's time I versed her on proper behavior."

"So you're opposed to it?" Jewel's pale face drew in mild surprise. "Remember how my raisers tried to keep our relationship supervised until I came of age?"

"And we sneaked around to do more than we should, didn't we?" Kaelan's face warmed with memory.

"Yes, but—"

"Want them to do the same?"

"No, but Rankil is younger than you were."

"Rankil is mentally older than I was at eighteen. It came to her out of necessity. She's no child, and she adores Myrla."

"But, Kae," sputtered Jewel. "Myrla is—"

"Like her mama—intelligent and highly aware for her age." Kaelan held up her hand. "And you must remember that Rankil was raised under Aut standards. You've had many birthers her age and younger. We have to give some allowances for such things." She caressed Jewel's face. "I'm not saying we allow them to do whatever they take the notion to. I say we give simple recognition to their emotions—holding hands, time together at the fireside, an occasional kiss without fear of retribution."

"A kiss?"

"Yes, my love, a kiss like this." Kaelan's lips brushed her cheek. "*Not* like this," then bent her back in an engulfing, body-feeling taste. "Notice the difference?"

"Just a little," Jewel pushed from Kaelan's eager embrace. "Behave. We must set a good example."

"So, we're back to sneaking around?" Kaelan retrieved her pick.

"Of course not. But we must demonstrate acceptable affection in front of the children. We're their only influence at present." Jewel glanced at the winter sun that crept into the cavern. "Rankil should be back soon, shouldn't she?"

"Hey now, steady on." Kaelan grasped the resistant nassie's hoof a little tighter. "Stubborn beast. I can't pull the pebble from that split without a little discomfort. Yes, she should be back any time. Game's becoming scarce for the best of hunters. She's had to expand her snares to keep up with the added demand." Kaelan flicked the intruding rock from the animal's foot and greased the hoof to prevent further splitting. "Can't have our packers going lame." The speckled-rump nassie gave an agreeing snort and nuzzled into Jewel's outstretched hand, lips reaching to nibble her tunic cuff.

"Watch your fingers. This one bites. Ask Archell."

"This one drew the knot on his back?" Jewel shied from the creature's wild gaze. "Not gelded, is he?"

"Nope. I'm hoping to breed him to the milker as soon she finishes weaning the colt."

"You're going to halter break it?" Jewel retreated to the gentler milker, stroking the grateful animal between the ears.

"No. Rankil is."

Jewel nodded. Serpent tradition bid the breaker of a nassie became its owner. "You're helping her build a base for Myrla's sake, aren't you?"

"We all need a helping hand at the start. Eeham provided me with two colts when I pursued you. Rankil deserves the same opportunity."

"I thought you won those colts in a foot race."

Kaelan blushed as she was caught in misinformation. "I was trying to impress you. Leonor had won three and had given you a gold bracelet. I was desperate."

"Leonor got the bracelet shoved up her fat nose when she got too fresh," said Jewel. "Acknowledging Rankil's affections will make some see Myrla as grown. Rankil may not be up to the competition when the others arrive."

"I don't know if I'd call it a romance." Kaelan hung the pick and joined Jewel by the milker. "Neither one of them are ready for that. I'd call their relationship a close friendship."

"The first sounded better to me." Rankil stepped into the cavern. Snow had driven deep into the folds of her head wrap. She held out two slim hoppers and a long, black-bellied tree snake known for its succulent meat. "Hunting's thin."

Jewel took the game. "We'll make do. And do you truly know what our recognition of your intentions means?"

"It means you know I want to be with Myrla when we both

come of age." Rankil shook the ice from her cloak. "I'll do whatever you want. Just let me be by her side until then."

"We're talking about two passes until Myrla comes of age," reminded Kaelan. "Two sounded like forever to you a while back. You have the patience?"

"An endless amount where she's concerned."

"But do you have enough self-control?" asked Jewel. "Announcing affections means you can't explore yourself with the older, single gentlewomen when you come of age. It's generally how a broadback perfects her pleasure phase." She peered hard at Kaelan, who looked away.

Rankil held her head high in conviction. A discussion of sex was not what she had wanted to stumble into. Her emotions, while they commonly lingered on intimate thoughts, went further than the physical and phase. She wanted to be Myrla's confidant and defender. "If she can wait, so can I."

"Can't argue with that." Kaelan clasped Rankil's hand. "You've got my permission." Her hand then landed on Rankil's shoulder, where she squeezed hard. "Within certain guidelines befitting your ages, the first being she agrees."

"I think I can vouch for her," said Jewel.

"Second," continued Kaelan, "your actions will stay polite and tasteful." Kaelan leaned close. "In other words, suitor Rankil, you misbehave, and I'll see to your personal misery."

Kaelan had succeeded in taming Rankil for she shifted her feet and smiled sheepishly. "Anything else?"

"I've a few questions." Myrla stepped around the corner laughing, and flew into Rankil's arms to kiss her cheek. "First, the bread is done. I pulled it from the heat. Second, does this mean I can wear a headscarf and, third, how long does a fifth birthing take? Sharillia's water just broke."

Chapter Eleven

Prematurity: that which reminds us how fragile life can be.

—Taelach Proverb

———————————

Hestralandra came into the world feet first, her scrunched, lanugo-covered face being the last to appear. She landed in the loving hands of her gentlewoman raiser, looked up at the world and wailed. Jewel cleaned fluids from the infant's passages, counted her fingers and toes, then swaddled the bare handful and passed her to Kaelan, who gave thanks for the precious gift and held the baby for all to see. Hestralandra lay quiet in Kaelan's steady strength until Jewel called for assistance, then was content to be passed to Myrla.

"The bleeding has slowed." Jewel stroked Sharillia's pale and sweat-streaked face. "She's weak. Help me move her closer to the fire."

Sharillia voiced discomfort as they transferred her to a warmer, cleaner spot. She fell into a deeper unconsciousness, never asking for her child. "The baby will fare better if you can convince her mother to nurse." Kaelan tucked a fur around Sharillia's feet.

"She'll have no part of it," replied Jewel. "We'll have to phase her out and put the child to her." She bundled the soiled birth bed and carried it to the cavern spring for soaking. "Did you find the colt's bottle feeders?"

"They're ready as are two nipples I modified. But the baby needs her mother's pre-milk, not thinned nassie."

"I know. Do you think her other children will notice if we keep her in a healing sleep for a few days? Mother knows she needs it."

"They'll be told she's recovering from a hard birth, which she is." Kaelan stooped by Jewel's side and helped dip the blood-caked linens into the spring's gentle flow. "You've done it before, Jewel. Hestralandra came early. She needs all the help she can get."

"She is small." Jewel motioned for Kaelan to glance over her shoulder at Rankil, who held the infant. "Looks like she's held one or two in her life."

"Undoubtedly," mused Kaelan. "She has younger siblings so I'd say she's held plenty." The topic closed as the newborn gave a little hunger-ridden screech. "Take her to her birth mother and see she gets her first meal."

"Join me?" Jewel brushed her wet hand across Kaelan's face then hurried to Sharillia. "The child needs to bond with you as well." Kaelan followed and helped roll Sharillia on her side. "Bring me the baby, Rankil. She needs to be fed."

"Sharillia's going to nurse? Didn't think she'd consider such a thing." Rankil, her brow raised, relinquished her bundle and retreated from the fireside, knowing this event was for the elders alone.

"She'll never know." Jewel eased Hestralandra's seeking mouth onto her mother's breast. "The Taelach do this with most premature births. There's no greater guard against disease." She lay behind Sharillia, her chest to the Autlach's back, her hand clasped in Kaelan's, who was on Sharillia's other side, supporting the baby.

Sharillia's features were covered by a light headscarf, forcing the infant's eyes on Jewel's hovering face. The association of nourishment went to Jewel and an instant maternal bond was formed. Kaelan burped the child while Jewel rolled Sharillia to the opposite side and the process concluded with a suckling Hestralandra drifting off in Kaelan's hands.

"Put her in the basket, Jewel, then come eat. Myrla made soup." Kaelan helped her make the infant comfortable then settled her on a ground mat with filled mug.

"I'm so tired, I'm half sick." Jewel pushed the food away and placed her head on the cold stone, hoping to soothe her splintered nerves. "I'd forgotten how exhausting a birthing could be. Let me sleep for a while. I'll eat when Hestra rises."

"You'll eat now." Kaelan shoved the mug back in her hands and held a bit of bread to her mouth. "Eat then we'll rest until Hestra wakes. I want to help again."

Jewel sat up, sipped from the mug and looked about the cavern. She hadn't realized the time. "Where are the little ones?"

"Archell and Myrla put them to bed. They were tired beyond thought, worrying for their m'ma." Kaelan pointed to three forms tangled in one bedroll.

"And where are my bigger little ones?"

"Sand scrubbing the bedding." Myrla supervised as Rankil and Archell twisted water from one of the blankets. "They didn't want to disturb the bonding."

"Thoughtful children." Jewel knifed the meat chunks clinging to her mug then cleansed the container with her final bite of bread. "We need to keep Sharillia phased, except for eating, for a cycle or more. Hestra needs the nourishment. She's far too skinny to be here yet. I'd say she was a good cycle, maybe a cycle and a half early."

"What problems should we expect?"

"There can't be any problems. Recca sent no shrouds or mourning sashes."

A small cough brought Hestra's raisers to her side. "She's all right," Jewel ran her finger over the infant's downy scalp. "Just a bitter bit of dinner." But she lingered near her daughter, watching her tiny chest rise and fall, her muscles twitch with a newborn's dream.

"You won't move from here, will you, love?" Kaelan pulled their bedroll close and placed Jewel in the furs, careful not to disturb the tiny hand wrapping her index finger. "Sleep."

"You coming?"

"As soon as I help with the bedding." Kaelan kissed the tops of two snow-white heads, stoked the fire, then assisted the teens in twisting out the last blanket. She assured them all was well then bid they do the morning chores and tend Sharillia's children as quietly as possible.

"Jewel and Sharillia need the quiet and loud noises will make the baby nervous." Promised a solid rest for mother and raiser, Kaelan sent the children to bed, settled beside Jewel, and welcomed a dreamless sleep.

Hestralandra woke twice during the night, each feeding two hours apart with the third discontented cry coming four hours later. Jewel nudged Kaelan at the baby's first whimper. "You wanted me to wake you."

"I know, I know." Kaelan drew the pillow over her head. "Me and my big mouth."

"It'll be you and your sore shin if you don't get up." Jewel lifted Hestra from her basket. "Come on, Kae, I'm too tired to phase Sharillia alone."

"Like I'll be much help. My head is pounding."

"She whines more than you do, my little Hestra." Jewel pulled the blankets back and left Kaelan shivering on the fur. "Come on, Kae, it's almost dawn."

Kaelan tightened her mouth in brief annoyance before smiling compliance at her mate. "You win. I'll be there as soon as I make a quick side stop." She tugged on her boots and dashed to the privy, returning to find Hestra still screaming in Jewel's arms. Rankil and Myrla were awake as well, stumbling about in search of something.

"What's wrong?" Kaelan followed Jewel's trembling finger to Sharillia's bed. The Autlach was gone. Her children's bed was just as vacant and the food stores were strewn about the cavern. Archell stumbled in from the livestock cavern. Blood drizzled from the back of his head, and his watering eyes showed the telltale signs of a mild concussion.

"The snow is high and howling in—Sweeping through the trees—Sharillia's fled into the dark—Woman with a blackened heart—She'll freeze her bitter soul." There was no rhyming of fact so his singsong stopped and his face scrunched. "I heard a sound in the livestock cavern, went to investigate, and she hit me from behind. When I came to she had taken all the mounts and every spare blanket we had stored. Four sacks of black grain are missing and so is our final side of beast. The colt's throat has been sliced and the milker is down with a knife in her side. Sharillia's left us to starve."

"Will she live?" Myrla stroked the milker's head as Kaelan stitched the gash in its side. Jewel had drawn some milk and now stood nearby while Hestra fumbled to suckle through the bottle.

"She'll survive. Sharillia managed to miss anything vital." Kaelan finished dressing the wound and patted the animal's side. "Wish she'd done the same with the colt. Such a good-looking animal. Straight legged and true backed. Shame we've been reduced to eating it. All right, Rankil, you and Archell help me get her up and walking." With shouts and earnest tugging, the milker regained her footing. She looked around the cavern, snorted, then dug her nose into the hay manger.

"Think she knows her babe is gone?" asked Myrla.

"Doubt she cares one way or another." Rankil brushed hay from the back of Myrla's knee skirts.

"Rankil, get your hands back!" Kaelan's stress level had peaked. "Go with Archell and start butchering that colt. Myrla, tend the fire and start breakfast. Some of us are hungry!"

"Yes, Kaelan." Rankil followed her cousin through the family chamber to the adjacent cavern where they had hung the colt to bleed. "I didn't mean a thing by it, Archie, honest," she stammered as they separated the sweetmeats. "She had hay on her skirts. I've done it before and no one got mad. What's wrong with it now?"

"Much." Archell bundled the meats as Rankil began to skin the carcass. "Rankil dankle must be careful."

"What changes hay on the skirts?"

"The hay doesn't change, Rankil roo, the touch does," he said, smiling in his wisest manner.

Rankil turned to face him. "You're not making sense. Was I out of line?"

"With the start of today, Sharillia's vicious display, yes." Archell began hacking manageable sections from the skinned areas. "Jewel knows you meant good, Myrla does, too." He paused in his slicing to speak. "Think, Rankil roo, you like Myrla. Myrla does you. Give it time. Get too rushed in Kaelan's mind," Archell grasped her wrist, "and things will never be good, never be fine."

Rankil took in the seriousness of his expression. "You think?"

"Don't touch your girl until the moment is right, ask Kaelan first so that you might." The Autlach chuckled at his cousin's hopeless sigh. "Poor Rankil dankle. She finds this so hard."

"Myrla makes me think of things I know I shouldn't." Rankil stretched the hide across a large rock and stood in thoughtful silence, a half-smile revealing her ideas. "Ever have those kind of thoughts?"

Archell raised his thick brows. "Sharillia was pretty to me until she showed how she could really be."

Rankil could see how he found the woman attractive. She wasn't much older than he was. "What changed your mind?"

"She insulted my kin." He butchered one of the colt's rear legs and laid it to the side. "My Rankil and Myrla again and again."

"She got back what she gave."

Archell's look turned long, and he scrunched his face. "Then she took her children into certain death and left us to starve." He said. "I believe I've lost interest."

"Cold and heartless is not your type, eh?" Rankil helped

remove the last of the usable meat. She broke the heavier bones into workable portions and piled the remaining carcass for disposal while Archell built a small, smokeless fire for drying the hide and another for drying meat. "I'll take the sweetmeats to Myrla."

"Sure I shouldn't?" he suggested, envisioning Kaelan's anger if they were found unsupervised.

"Nah, I hear Hestra bawling. Jewel is there." Rankil scooped up her soggy sling and returned to the family chamber.

"Nassie sweets are far from my favorite," commented Jewel when she relieved Rankil of her bundle. "But it's food." Then she smiled at the way Rankil glanced at Myrla. "The storm let up so Kaelan went to track Sharillia. You may sit with Myrla if you choose." Jewel winked. "Just don't brush off any hay."

Rankil blushed, rinsed her hands in the washbasin, and shook them dry as she approached Myrla. "I think I should apologize."

"For what?" Myrla set aside her handloom and motioned Rankil to share her mat. "Kaelan was upset, and you were a convenient outlet."

"Just the same," Rankil took up the loom to examine Myrla's delicate work. "What are you making?"

"A gown for Hestra. As small as she is, it shouldn't take long."

"You could almost fit her into a footling." Rankil smiled in such a contagious manner, Myrla returned the grin then giggled.

"Yours or Kaelan's perhaps." She ventured a look at Jewel's turned back then slid her hand into Rankil's. "Were you truthfully just brushing hay from my skirts?" she whispered.

"Of course!" Rankil caressed her slim palm. "I shouldn't think of you otherwise."

"No?" Myrla squeezed the slim hand wrapping her own. "I somehow doubt you could stick to that promise. I couldn't."

"Never said I couldn't, only that I shouldn't." Rankil grinned at Myrla's flustered stare. "Surely, I didn't shock you." Rankil pushed Myrla's gaping mouth shut, then slid her hand to her upper arm, where it lingered on her shoulder. "I wish we were older."

"This is becoming difficult for me as well," she replied. "But you have to understand Serpent customs. Kaelan and Jewel recognizing us as a couple is a major doing. I didn't have the nerve to ask permission for long skirts." She leaned into the touch, then shrugging and breaking her handhold, retook her weaving. "I must be content to have you near me. It's more than most our age get."

"I'm still accustomed to how I was raised," said Rankil. "It's hard for me to think in other terms." She fingered Myrla's collar, sniffed acceptance, then turned her attentions to Myrla's face. Her round features were slimming into the high cheeks and sharp chin common to the Taelach, her deep-set eyes framed by a curling set of lashes that, had they been Autlach black, would have appeared incredibly long. But as it was, and as Rankil preferred, the white lashes accentuated the mischievous twinkle Myrla was capable of. Those eyes turned to Rankil now, creasing to match the smile turning Myrla's lips.

"Still having thoughts you shouldn't?"

"Wouldn't admit to it if I was." Rankil moved closer, head lowered to line with Myrla's mouth. "May I kiss you?"

"Thought you'd never ask." Myrla turned her pink cheek upward. "Quick, before Jewel notices."

Rankil surprised Myrla with a kiss to the mouth, closed lipped, but full of longing, then pulled back with a ridiculous grin on her face. She chuckled at Myrla's tiny gasp and landed a second kiss on her cheek. "That's how it should be." Rankil's eyes brightened with enthusiasm. "Don't you think?"

"What we think doesn't matter if Kaelan finds you being fresh." Myrla scooted back a little, delighted though a little perplexed by Rankil's behavior. "And you are being fresh."

"Oh, good grief." Rankil stiffened with dismay. "I wasn't trying to be fresh."

Kaelan's voice rose from the livestock cavern.

"Rankil! Archell! Come lend me a hand!" Kaelan stumbled into the family chamber, Olitti draped over one shoulder. "Sharillia left a trail Blind Grandmother could've followed. The other children are in the hay, near froze like their sister." They placed Olitti near

Hestra's basket and drew a blanket over her. "Make some broth out of those bones, Myrla. The children need the warmth, and it will be a good stew base for tonight."

"But Sharillia took most of the fixings."

"I recovered some of them while I was tracking." Olitti was left to Jewel's loving attention, and Kaelan followed Rankil to the live-stock cavern. "I found the heartless bitch. She dropped things one by one as the way became difficult." Kaelan scooped up the larger of the toddler boys and smoothed back his snow-caked hair. "She left the children where they fell from their mounts."

"She what?" Rankil gasped when she touched the brittle child in her arms. He responded to her touch, shoving his thumb to his bluish lips and pulling to her shoulder.

"I'm cold."

"He's always partial to you," said Kaelan as they brought the boys to the fireside. "Let's go help Archell carry in the supplies." When Kaelan returned to the livestock cavern, she pulled the youths close, sharing her distressed expression. "To answer your question, Rankil. I followed Sharillia's tracks until they met up with four more sets. That's where I found the supplies."

"Four more sets?" cried Archell.

"Shhh." Kaelan pulled him closer. "I have no desire to frighten the gentlewomen any further. They have their hands full as is. Sharillia was near the supplies, dead, decapitated in some maniac display. Whoever did it wasn't out for robbery, they were out for revenge."

"How could you tell?" said Rankil, believing Sharillia deserving of the fate.

Kaelan's face drew with disgust. "Among other things, they cut out the woman's tongue."

"Her tongue?" Rankil set down the sack resting on her shoul-der. "That's Raskhallak's punishment for infidelity."

"Precisely," replied Kaelan. "And he hung her remains from a tree."

"How do you know it was a man?" queried Archell. "Taelach bandits could have hatched that plan."

"The damage was from a serrated Autlach blade," countered Kaelan. "And the executioner took the time to carve his name in her chest before leaving." She took a kindling twig and scratched the Autlach script into the cavern's dusty floor, the letters standing out against the stone, gray and damning to their survival. Kaelan traced them again and drew a line under them. "Need I say more?"

"You've said plenty." Rankil hefted one of the sacks onto her shoulder and headed to the family chamber, resisting her overwhelming urge to hover near Myrla.

"Grab a sack, Archie," Kaelan followed Rankil's lead. "And put on a comforting face. We have to make the children feel safe and wanted."

"Oh, Archell loves the babies." Archell gathered two bags. "He'd die protecting them." He stepped on the name carved into the dust, distorting the letters until they were beyond reading.

Chapter Twelve

Kindness warms more than any fire.

—Granny Terry

Tension and cramped quarters began to take its toll on Kaelan's family. No one slept enough. No one ate enough. Even tiny Hestra sensed the uneasiness, becoming restless at all hours. "I don't know how much more of this I can take," complained Jewel after a cycle of the infant's fussiness. "Every time one of us drifts off, there she goes. The fire chips are running low, too. How are we going to keep warm when they're gone?"

"Things will warm in a cycle or so." Kaelan refreshed her tea and pulled her cloak a little tighter. There was little they could do about the present situation, so why worry? "Spring is coming." Her eyes turned to the bickering children. "Then the clan will arrive and things will be back to normal."

"Normal?" Jewel dabbed spit from the baby's chin then placed her against her shoulder, prompting a shrill complaint. "They'll find us with not one but seven, *seven* children, four of them Autlach. You call that normal?"

Kaelan almost laughed out loud. Their lives were anything but typical and though she should have been miserable, vexed by the uncertainties, she was unreasonably, deliriously happy. She stretched now, wishing for a swig of wine to ease the stiffness and boredom that came with confinement. Then, with a smile to Jewel and a pat Hestra returned with a burp, she turned to the livestock cavern.

"Gotta give Archell a break, my dears. Try not to get into too much mischief while I'm away."

"Take some jerky with you. It'll keep you occupied." Jewel thrust the meat sack toward her. "We'll try not to run over each other."

"Set the little ones to clearing the stones they've scattered while playing. My toes are sore from stepping on them, and it should keep them occupied for a while."

"Until they begin chucking them at one another."

"Make a game of tossing them into a basket." Kaelan shoved a fistful of meat strips into her pocket. "Have Rankil rest until her shift. Her headaches have made her exceptionally ill-tempered as of late."

Jewel sighed and looked about, her tone the closest to a whine Kaelan could remember. "It's this confounded cave. It's getting to us all. I still don't understand your sudden notion to post watch. Is there something you're not telling me?"

"Nothing of the sort." Kaelan hoped Jewel wouldn't initiate a picking phase as the truth would finish unraveling her frazzled nerves. "I'm being cautious in case Sharillia tries to reclaim her children. She's no right to them."

"That's an understatement." But Jewel sensed there was more going on than Kaelan would admit. She was certain Rankil and Archell were involved as well but why involve them and not her?

Kaelan retreated to the livestock cavern, putting distance between herself and Jewel's probing mind.

Not fair. You did that on purpose!

Did what?

For shame. Jewel's phase dulled away.

"No shame," whispered Kaelan with a pat to the milker, "simply love for you."

"Hello, Kaelan." Archell yawned. "The time goes fast when you sing to yourself."

"Anything worth repeating?" Kaelan tossed him some jerky. "Jewel could use an upbeat melody to take her mind off the closing walls."

"Archell's sure to sing a song. Jewel still thinks you're doing wrong?"

"Yeah, I can't keep things from her forever." Then Kaelan realized the maturity Archell was beginning to possess. He wasn't the child Jewel still referred to him as. Archell was very much a man, young, but wise. Forced to grow quickly like Rankil, he was observant, able to sense his elders' unspoken exchanges as well as any Taelach youth. "I'm probably being overcautious, but I can't take the chance."

"I suppose we cannot." Archell's Autlach accent still slurred his Taelach speech. "Patience and forethought a certain peace makes—Soothes the soul when so much is at stake."

"Hope you've written it down." Kaelan turned him toward the family cavern. "If you haven't, do so before you lay down. That was quite insightful."

"Archell will before he retires." The hum of one of his infectious tunes lingered for Kaelan to continue. If nothing else, Archell's Taelach family offered the encouragement necessary to cultivate his rare talent.

"Recca will like his verse." Kaelan shivered in the morning chill then crept to the cavern entrance to observe the world outside. "Spring had best hurry, otherwise, we'll all be cavern-crazed when the clan arrives. Next break in the weather, threat or no threat, we'll have to emerge. Our sanity seems to hinge on it."

⨎

"Sun's out!" Rankil bounded around the corner into the family cavern. "Archie, Kaelan wants you and Myrla to help me gather fresh wood while it shines. And the little ones can play outside as long as they stay close to the cavern mouth."

"Gladly!" Myrla dumped Olitti from her lap.

"Gracious Mother, Myrla. Don't toss the children around like that." Jewel shushed the excited whoops of the boys then smiled, melancholy lessened by Hestra's continued peaceful sleep.

"Outside," she said, "the lot of you. Another moment of your woebegone little faces is one too many." Three little forms rushed past her. "Wraps and foot lacings before you set out. We've no wish for more frostbite, do we?" This stopped the youngsters long enough to put on protective gear, then they scrambled out the cavern, all but knocking Kaelan over in their haste.

"Here now, slow down. The snow will still be there, I am certain." She corrected their broken Taelach apologies and waved them outside. "There's your moment's peace, Jewel."

"Well, almost." Jewel turned to the older youths, who were wrapping themselves against the cold. "Myrla, would you mind taking Hestra with you? She's dry, fed and sleeping. The air should do her good. It is above freezing, isn't it, Kae?"

"It is."

"Good. Take her with you." Jewel strapped Hestra's sling across Myrla's shoulder and slid the sleeping child inside. "Here's a bottle. She shouldn't need it, but one never knows with an infant." Jewel turned back to the fire and began assembling the midday meal.

"Oh, no." Kaelan jerked the stir stick from her hand. "You need some sun, too."

"But . . . no . . . I . . . Kaelan!" She gasped as Kaelan carried her outside, and tossed her into a snow bank. "Mother but that's cold!" She laughed even louder as Kaelan collapsed beside her.

"It's invigorating." Kaelan rethought the comment when a snowball broke against her ear. "No fair, Myrla. I can't retaliate with you holding Hestra!"

"I know!" Myrla disappeared over a high drift behind Rankil

and Archell, singing as they volleyed more snowballs into the ground before them.

"Be mindful of Hestra and be back before dusk!" Kaelan pulled Jewel close. "Know why I dropped you in the drift?"

"In hopes of warming me again?" Eyes sparkling with mischief, Jewel shoved the tip of an icicle down the front of Kaelan's tunic, giggling at the contortions her lover went to shake it free.

"Know why I did that?"

Kaelan chuckled and tossed the remaining ice toward her. "So you can warm me up?"

"Nope, to see you dance!"

"Very funny."

"Indeed it was."

Kaelan sank to her knees to press a mitt full of snow against Jewel's lips. Her kiss dissolved the crystals.

"Good to see you brightening up." Kaelan's hands wrapped her slender shoulders. "I was beginning to worry over you."

"I haven't been myself." Jewel nodded to alert her of the Autlach children's observant eyes. "We're not alone."

"So?" Kaelan scattered the giggling threesome with snowballs, gave them a mental suggestion to concentrate on their play, then pulled Jewel just inside the cave mouth.

Kaelan! Jewel shuddered at the intensity of want expressed in her lover's phase.

Kaelan pressed her against the cavern wall. *Finally, a moment to ourselves.* She extended a leg around Jewel's knees to draw her hips closer. *I've missed your touch these last couple of moons.*

Has it been that long? Jewel's eyes opened to the renewed fascination with which Kaelan regarded her.

An infinitely, despairingly, desperate amount of time, Jewel of mine. Kaelan fumbled with her belt.

Your hands are ice. Take off your mitts.

Better? Kaelan raised both their tops, drawing skin against skin. *I'm sorry I've been so distant. Forgive me.* Then, against her better judgment and self-promises, she opened to Jewel, flooding their phase with her concern. *I've been positively awful, keeping clear of you like I have. It was unconscionable. There should be no secrets between us.*

Jewel gasped as renewed want dominated the angst, and the tension between them dissolved in the nuances of lovemaking. They freed their bodies of some of their winter layers, and Kaelan lifted her from the ground so Jewel's legs could circle her hips to brace against the wall behind. Now pressed together, the mental soon gave way to the physical, Kaelan's face buried in Jewel's hair, Jewel gasping against Kaelan's neck as they rocked and clutched for what they longed to give and feel.

When the distant laughs of children coaxed them from rapture, they were intertwined, steam rising from the stones they pressed against. Kaelan smiled and brushed straying hairs back under Jewel's scarf. "There's that fire mind I fell in love with so long ago. I've missed her."

"And she's missed your honesty." Jewel's soft fingers sifted through Kaelan's hair, pausing on her lips and chin. "What do we do now? What if Sharillia did share our whereabouts? Do you think Longpass will come after his children?"

"If he cared, he would have before now." Kaelan set Jewel down but continued to hold her about the waist. "The longer things go unchallenged, the better. The clan should be here soon enough. We'll move position and settle into a permanent home. Only a fool would attack then. The Tekkroon are so close."

"I just pray Recca will allow four Auts into the clan." Jewel watched the children roll down a nearby embankment. "We'd better bring them in before they get chilled."

"I suppose." Kaelan recovered Jewel's belt then smoothed her tunic down. "Promise we can finish this tonight?"

"Finish?" Jewel replied. "Kaelan, dearest, we've just begun."

"That so?"

"You'll find out tonight." Jewel burst from Kaelan's grip to herd her dark-skinned children into the safety of the family cavern, leaving a dreadfully distracted Kaelan to fantasize about coming events.

"Careful!" Rankil caught Myrla by the arm, preventing her from sliding back down an embankment. "Let me carry Hestra for a spell. It's slick going for some distance. I'd hate for you to fall."

"You don't mind?" Myrla moved easier without the baby's weight.

"Mind?" Rankil eased the sling over her shoulder, balancing it with the kindling bundle strapping her back. "I was toting younger siblings when I was five and that was while carrying heavier loads than this. It's old habit, isn't it Archie?"

"Sure is, Rankil dankle." Archell warmed himself in the radiant sunlight. He drew in a deep breath, "Fresh air feels good. Better than any wood." He squinted across the small piece of tableland they had climbed onto. "Where are we going?"

"Something I want to show you."

"Yeah?" Myrla knocked the snow from her boot tops then gave Rankil's upper arm a squeeze she returned. "Days are still short. We'd best hurry if we're to return before dark."

"Don't worry, My, we'll be back in plenty." Rankil's hand slid down her forearm, taking hold of her slim wrist. "We're almost there now." Hestra across her chest, Archell by her side, she trudged forward, supporting Myrla when the way became difficult with icy stones. She led them to small earth mound, climbed topside, and pulled the others up beside her.

"Though I know it is your wish." Archell pointed to the hold Rankil and Myrla had on each other. "Kaelan would not approve of this."

"You wouldn't tell, would you?" Rankil kept her arm around Myrla's waist. "Don't be a stickler, Arch. You know I mean no harm."

"But I promised Kaelan and—"

"What about how I feel?" Myrla slipped when she stamped her foot, and she clutched Rankil, struggling to stand as the snow began to shift beneath her. "What are we standing on? A boulder?"

She knelt, one hand grasping Rankil's leg for balance as she brushed an area free of debris. The surface below gleamed. "What is this?"

"I found it a while back." Rankil shifted Hestra's sling higher on her chest then stooped beside Myrla. "It's some type of metal. Nothing I've ever seen, but there's much I haven't. Is it Taelach?"

Myrla shook her head. "None I know. Any ideas, Archie?"

He shrugged, jumped from the rise, and began to circle it, pushing aside snow-coated vines to gain a better look. "Mound that rises from the dirt." He thumped the surface. "And hollow by sound. I don't know. Maybe Kaelan should be shown."

Rankil bounded from her perch to face her cousin. "Why does everything come down to Kaelan? Must she know everything I do? This is my discovery, my find. She doesn't have to, doesn't need to know about this." Rankil pulled a handful of vine to the side, revealing a corroded panel. A single red light blinked among the exposed wires and moss.

"Think she'd let us anywhere near this?" She reached in, touched the light and stepped back. With a hiss, a grind and a low swoosh of stale air the mound began to shake and a piece of the surface vanished into the interior. "Or this?"

Archell regarded the find with disbelief, and Myrla pulled tight against Rankil. "It's magic," she whispered into Rankil's tunic. "Magic."

"No, My." Rankil pulled up her head until their eyes met. "The Mother says there's no such thing besides the energy she has given all things, remember? This is something we don't yet understand. It's safe. I wouldn't have brought you here otherwise." She indicated the passageway before them. "Take a look, Archie. It seems bigger inside—a massive wagon, a transport of some kind?"

"Wagon?" Archell thumped the mound and stuck his head into the opening. The short corridor beyond burst into light and he jerked back, reluctant to go further. "Are you sure?"

"Positive!" With Myrla by the hand, Rankil pushed passed him and into the mound. "Don't be a child."

"Come on, Archie," said Myrla. "I trust her."

Archell raised his brows but followed Rankil's lead, at times very close to his companions. "Kaelan should be told," he mumbled more than once. "She should be told."

"Dammit, Archie." Rankil swore at him over her shoulder. "If I think she needs to know, I'll tell her. It's my call." She led them around a sharp corner to another portal, which opened in the same manner as the first. They stepped through, the lights cut on, and the hatch shut with a frightening screech which startled Hestra awake. Comforted by Rankil's familiar face and voice she soon quieted and gazed at her new surroundings, as did her caregivers. The room was dank with old decay.

Rankil led them to the center of the room and paused, hands resting on a high chair back. "This is what I wanted to show you." She turned the chair then stepped back, waiting for their reactions.

Before them sat the skeleton of a woman, long and lean, blond hair tumbling across the epaulets gracing her shoulders. She sat dignified, in an obvious position of authority, fingers still poised on the armrests. A terrible hole ripped across the front of her uniform, revealing bone where gut had been.

"Who was she?" Myrla asked, drawing back when the woman's hair broke at her touch. "How did she get here?"

Rankil depressed a key and pointed to the dust-covered screen before them. "I found this by accident, but this explains a little of it. It takes a few . . . all right, there it is." A pain-riddled face appeared before them, an ancient projection of their discovery speaking of long-ago events in a foreign but strangely familiar tongue.

"Captain Tara Conway reporting. This will be my final log." The woman held up her blood-saturated flight glove. "For obvious reasons, I'll not be making the rendezvous point. I'm sorry, Dr. Reccason. I've left you with a full plate. Take care of the others for me. See they adapt to the new environment. This species, the Autlach as they call themselves, seem a hearty breed, very like us

144

humans in their appearance. Keep detailed notes on your interactions with them." Her brown eyes brimmed with pain she would not allow in her voice.

"I launched the rescue buoys just before I abandoned the control station." She chuckled then shook her head. "Damn fools we were, tunneling into that sorry excuse for solid ground."

She sighed and a certain peace began to warm her expression. "Tell my children I love them. Joanna, too. We should have been married, Jo. I know you asked me a thousand times and I refused them all. Guess it was a game to me. You'd pursue. I'd evade. I never tired of it. Thought it'd last forever. Ah, but it's a little too late for that now, isn't it? Just don't let yourself get lonely. Find a pretty Autlach to snuggle up with. Rescue is at least six years away. That's a long time to sleep alone, and God knows no one else who knows you will want the job. And, Jo, one more thing." The woman collapsed back into her seat. "I think I would have said yes had you asked again." She drifted in and out of consciousness for several seconds, mumbled something unintelligible, then reached up and undid the loose plait running down her back.

"There, Joanna. Remember me like you met me—hair flying in my face as I barked orders." She closed her eyes. "And, yes, I have a final order. You didn't think I'd go quietly, did you? Don't worry, my friends, it's a simple one." Her voice sounded strange even to those who understood little of her command. "Don't count on what hasn't happened. Life is too brief. Conway out." The screen went dark.

"There was Taelach in her words." Archell looked respectfully at the seated form. "But some of them I've never heard."

"She must have been a great leader." Myrla settled into an empty chair. Their lifeless companion looked similar to the Taelach with her slim build and fair skin, but her eyes were almost as dark as Archell's. "I heard her speak of children and the Autlach, but she wasn't Taelach, was she?"

"I don't think so." Rankil reached again to the controls. "She's just the beginning. I've found much more. Watch." She brushed her fingertips across the controls, rotating a wall panel near Archell, causing him to startle.

"Rankil?"

"Sorry, Archie. Should have warned you." Rankil reached into the opening. "Take a look at this." She pulled out a weapon for them to see, a loaded handgun.

"What does it do?" inquired Myrla.

"Take Hestra and follow me." They made their way back to the main hatch. "The first time I handled it I accidentally set it off," explained Rankil as they stepped outside. "Was that ever a mistake."

"Why?" asked Archell.

"This is why." She aimed then squeezed the trigger, blasting into the snow fifty yards away. The others jumped at the bang, Hestra screaming her fear of the sound. "When it went off inside, it bounced around, almost hitting me before it stuck in the empty chair."

"But it was just a noise." Myrla placed Hestra in Archell's arms and took the weapon into her hands, observing the metal casing, the curve of the trigger guard.

"Don't point the hollow end toward anyone!" Rankil snatched the gun from her hands. "It's more than noise. Look at where the snow was disturbed."

Myrla dug into the snow around the impact site. "Is this what flew from it?" She held up the warm slug. "This little thing doesn't seem like much."

"But it moved so fast we couldn't see," Archell was beginning to understand Rankil's respect for the weapon. "Dug a hole where the hard ground should be."

"Point taken." Myrla extended her hand. "I'll be careful. Promise. I just want to hold it." She turned away and held the gun's butt end to her cheek, eyes focusing down the barrel. "Seems easy enough. Does it have an endless supply of those things it spits out?"

"No." Rankil eased the barrel down and slid open the firing chamber. "It holds six. There are more inside. More of these

146

weapons, too, in various sizes. They discharge different types of metal, but the effect is similar." She tossed a shell to Archell. "The metal is pressed inside these cases until it's used. I disassembled one of the whole ones. There's black powder inside. I think it's what pushed the pieces apart, but I don't know how."

"Now we know why she's been spending so much time hunting, don't we Archell?" Myrla relinquished her hold on the firearm. "What other discoveries did you make?"

"Let's go back inside, and I'll show you." Rankil held back the vines and motioned Archell through. With Hestra in the crook of his arm, he pushed back into the corridor. When Myrla followed, Rankil stopped her in the hatchway, drawing her in for a kiss. "Got to steal one when I can, pretty," she whispered into Myrla's ear. "Not much gets by Archell."

"Kaelan's faith in me is strong," he called from within. "Come along."

"Ah, Archie." Myrla grinned at her frustration.

"She's behaving horribly, Archell." Myrla stretched up to give Rankil a light peck on the cheek. "Simply awful." She darted into the corridor. "Come on."

"On my way." Rankil paused to touch her damp cheek, relishing the warmth rising from deep within her body. It was pure heat, an excitement difficult to ignore. She desired to touch Myrla again, to share her thoughts in the deepest way possible. When the emotions became overwhelming, threatening to spill from her mind, she shuddered and rushed to where the others waited.

"Rankil dankle?" Archell sat in the empty pilot's chair, Hestra perched on his knee, her blue eyes wide to the stimulus of his gentle bounce. As Rankil watched, she found herself longing to be Hestra's raiser, she and Myrla responsible for the little girl's upbringing. They could be a family to themselves, no one to say they were too young, no one to—

"Rankil?"

"Huh?"

Archell nodded toward the console.

"Um, yeah." She sat at the control panel. "Most of these things don't work. But the ones that do—" The view screen burst back to life, concluding her sentence.

"Why, it's the area outside the mound!" declared Myrla, staring at the screen. "How did you do that?"

Rankil guided her hand to the panel. "Like this."

"Good Mother!" The screen blurred then came back into focus when Myrla ceased moving her hand. "It's this side of the mountains we crossed coming into the bowl. Remember them, Archell?"

"I carried our Rankil across them. She looked much younger then, sleeping in my arms."

"I've grown." Rankil squared her shoulders. "Besides, you're not much older or any bigger than I am, Archie."

"Not anymore." His bounce reduced to a lazy rock and Hestra gurgled her approval. "Can that, that, picture guide show us more?"

"Like what?" Myrla sat ready at the controls.

"Our cavern?"

"I'll give it a try." The screen blurred again, the snowscape whirling by until familiar landmarks came into view. Then Myrla slowed, settling the screen onto the entrance of their underground home. "Everyone must be inside." She began to move the image back.

"Hold a minute, My. Turn back slow." Rankil squinted at the screen. "I thought I saw—Wait! Stop! There it is! Great Mother! Don't you see it? Look!" Rankil pointed to faint indentations in the snow. "Look! Nassie tracks! And they're wearing Aut booties! Kaelan and Jewel! We've got to get home!"

Rankil tucked two firearms and a box of shells into her tunic then led the way across the snowfield.

"Hurry!" cried Myrla as they began to slow their pace. "We've got to stop them!"

Rankil caught her hard by the arm, pulling her down on the drift they climbed. "They're already here."

"But, Jewel and Kaelan," Myrla said in a lower voice. "The little ones. We have to—"

"We can't rush in." Rankil reloaded the gun's empty chamber. "You and Archell stay out of sight while I see what we're up against." She dropped to her knees beside Myrla. "Do as I ask, My. Stay low."

"I will," whispered Myrla. "But if you don't return soon, I'm leaving Hestra with Archell and coming looking for you." She brushed the hair from Rankil's eyes.

Rankil looked toward the cavern then back to Myrla. There was so much she wanted to say, to express at that moment. A sense of desperation similar to the one she had felt in Tisph's grasp filled her heart, enveloping her until she had only one course of action. *You won't lose me that easily. I love you.*

Myrla shivered at the mental touch. Love—*me?* Only Jewel and Kaelan had ever linked to her and then it had been in a raiser's fashion, soothing panic, taking away physical hurt. This was different, almost threatening in its lack of control. *Rankil, I—I—*

Shhh. It's difficult for me, too. Kaelan swore she'd skin me if I tried this before we came of age.

Archell's watching.

I don't care. I had to let you know how I feel.

I need you, too, but this is hard. It makes me feel funny, almost sick.

Then we'll stop. Rankil pulled back. The entire exchange had taken no more than a second, but the effect lingered, leaving Myrla's head swimming. "I'll be back soon. Do you have your knife?"

"Always." Myrla drew her blade from her waist pack. "Just come back with good news."

"Knowing Kaelan's swordsmanship and Jewel's knife work, the battle will be over. And I bet Jewel is calming Olitti. You know how excitable she can be." Rankil looked up to Archell, who nodded his readiness.

"Keep safe." She stayed beside Myrla a second more, caressing her hair, then crept belly down toward the cavern, the winter white of her cloak fading her into the snowy backdrop.

The cavern was empty, pottery and foodstuffs scattered to ruin, the fire high with scrolls and linens. Kaelan's bow lay in pieces.

Rankil stamped out the least singed of the bedrolls and returned to the livestock chamber, her terror rising with every step. The milker was dead, finishing what Sharillia had started. How would they feed Hestra now?

As she slid out the entrance, she found herself repeating one of Archell's tunes, his running song, the words choking her throat as she glanced toward where the others hid. Nassie snorts cut into the crisp air, rising against a pair of excited Autlach baritones.

"Look what I've found!" A bearded Autlach held Myrla's knife-wielding hand. "You weren't going to cut me, were you, girl?" She kicked his shins as Hestra bawled in the sling across her chest.

"Too nice a blade for that." The Autlach squeezed her wrist until her grip loosened. He cut the sling free and held Hestra up by the strap. "Longpass was right. Sharillia was fat with another Taelach runt. This one looks just like his eldest."

"Get rid of it before he gets here," hissed the man binding Archell's wrists. "I don't like the way he fixes Sharillia's mistakes."

The first man stared at Hestra for a moment then held her at arm's length. "Not me. You do it. I can't kill a babe, even a white witch."

"Coward!" Archell's captor shoved him to the ground and grabbed Hestra's sling.

"No!" Archell lurched forward, wrapped his legs around the man holding Hestra, and jerked with all his might, sending the infant sliding down the far side of the drift. Her assailant fell behind her, tumbling head over heel, a target Rankil twice overshot before hitting. He fell prone and skidded into Hestra, knocking her further down the hill. The baby shrieked as her slide ended under a shrub, her cries more of cold and distress than any injury she'd received.

The noise brought the other Autlach to the top of the drift, his hands wrapped around Myrla's throat. "I don't know what you did, but put the noisemaker down before I break her neck."

When Rankil complied, he ventured a glance at Archell. "Taelach witchery can't be undone."

Archell took small steps forward. "The only lies are from Autlach tongues—Acid with deceit—The Taelach wish to live in peace—They have no quarrel, no wish to cheat."

"A singing idiot!" laughed the man, taking a backward step. "They've messed you up but good."

He glanced again to Rankil. "Come up here, broadback, hands over your head."

"I'll do as you say," she said in her fluent Autlach. "Do what you want with me but don't hurt her."

"Yours, is she?" The man loosened his grip enough for Myrla to gasp. "One of you is going to die for killing an Aut." He gave Rankil an appraising glance. "But you'll bring a higher price at the crystal mines, broadback, so I think I'll kill the girl." He pulled Myrla close to taste her neck. "But not quite yet."

As the color drained from Myrla's face, a rage like none other twisted in Rankil's soul. She knew what Myrla felt, the disgust, the terror, the very terror. And, suddenly, Rankil found herself not in the snow but at Granny Terry's. Tisph was pulling her head back with the belt, laughing at her helplessness. His hands became talons that scratched her back, his mouth burned her skin, his—

No! Her mental blast brought their attacker to his knees. He took Myrla with him as he fell, grabbing her by the braid when she tried to break free.

No! And Rankil was upon him, knocking him from Myrla with one hand as she placed her blade to his throat with the other. Tisph wouldn't chase her any more. He would never catch her again, never touch her again, never—

"No, Rankil dankle!" Archell grabbed her knife wielding arm with his bound hands. "He isn't worth the hurt."

Rankil pulled from his grasp, raised the blade to strike, then stopped, bewildered and quivering on top of the Autlach. How had she gotten here? Where had this Aut come from? Sensing her confusion, the man pushed from beneath her to slide backward down the slope. Rankil let him go, staring through him as he turned and ran.

151

"Rankil?" Myrla touched her shoulder.

"No," she replied in a whisper then she dropped the knife, rose to her feet, and stumbled down the hillside toward the cavern. It was winter and she was cold—nothing else made sense. Where were Jewel and Kaelan? Where was Archell? Myrla?

"Myrla!" She turned back to where she last remembered Myrla being only to find both she and Archell running toward her as Hestra screamed in Archell's arms.

"Run!" Myrla caught Rankil's hand in her own, pulling her forward. "For the Mother's sake, run!"

Rankil numbly joined their race, stumbling again and again as Myrla urged her along. A rumbling rose behind them. By the time they neared the family cavern the noise had become deafening, like the roar of rushing floodwaters, interspersed with the snorts and knickers nassies always made at a full run. Rankil slowed enough to look back then turned back to her run, all but passing Myrla and Archell as the apocalyptic sound of sixty nassie hooves closed in on them.

"It's him!" she cried when they reached the family cavern. "I saw him. We can't win!"

"Yes, we can." Myrla gathered the singed remains of Kaelan's map bag then grabbed a handful of torches, lighting one from the burning scrolls.

"Come on." Myrla took Rankil and Archell by the arms and led them deeper into the cavern. "We're following Kaelan and Jewel. We're going caving."

Chapter Thirteen

The Auts may outnumber us, but they can't outsmart us.

—Harlis Davies

———————————

"Hush her up." Blood roared in Rankil's ears. "Give her another bottle or something."

"She's teething," replied Myrla between pats to the baby's back. "That, and she's wet."

"Didn't you grab any wraps?" Rankil stepped to the edge of the torch light, hoping the dark would soothe the ache in her head. Kaelan had never taken her down this tunnel, choosing instead to map many of the surface caves. Rankil cursed the decision. Archell read her expression, took the map sling from her back, and draped it across his own.

"No use looking for what's not there, Rankil dankle. We'll push through. There's nothing else that we can do."

"But they're better supplied than we are," said Rankil. "We had the advantage of knowing where we were, until now." She turned to Myrla. "Shut her up!"

"I'm trying!" Myrla pointed to their surroundings. "She's as frightened as we are."

"Try harder," replied Rankil, clenching her hands to her head. "She'll lead them to us."

"What do you suggest I do?"

"You're a gentlewoman. Don't you know?"

Myrla stopped whispering to Hestra to glare. "And what's that supposed to mean?"

"Stop it!" Archell stepped between them. "Hestra needs changed. Rankil, take off your skirt."

"Pardon?"

"Your overskirts can be wraps so Hestra can nap."

"Oh." She tore the cloth free and handed a square to Myrla. "Give me the dirty wrap, and I'll hide it under a rock."

Myrla changed the child, and soon Hestra cooed thanks. "That's a baby." She slid her into the carry sling and passed the soiled bundle to Rankil. "All set. Which way are we going?"

"Pick a tunnel." Rankil waved at the passages as voices drifted their direction.

"Straight down the middle then." Myrla marched forward, head held high in defiance of the unknown. Archell remained by her side while Rankil stayed behind to hold off some of the trackers. Gun in hand, she shot at the first two men into the convergence then rushed down the darkened tunnel her companions had entered.

"Douse the light, Archie. They're getting close."

"No, Rankil roo." Archell grabbed her arm until she took up pace with his heated gait. "Myrla has a better idea."

"But we don't have time for—"

"Take her!" Myrla shoved the baby into Rankil's arms. She took the torch from Archell, lit the last one in Rankil's sling, and pushed

154

the new flame back at him. "Smell the grease?" She told Rankil. "It's the same stuff we use in our lanterns."

"The stuff Jewel smeared on our heads?" Rankil smelled the unmistakable odor of petroleum.

"It sometimes bubbles up in the deeper caves." Myrla pushed the others back and held her torch high over her head. "When I drop the torch, run."

"But—" Rankil flattened herself against the side of the tunnel and pulled her cloak around Hestra. "They'll be here any—"

Lights appeared around the nearest corner. "Great Mother! They're here!" She froze as the torch dropped from Myrla's fingers. Whether it was simple panic or the wrathful faces of those pursuing them that made her hesitate she couldn't say, but her next conscious thought was of Myrla taking her by the hand as they ran. That handhold became their mutual lifeline as they followed Archell's torch down tunnel after twisting tunnel. They weren't sure how long they ran or how far, but in time Archell called a halt and the spent trio collapsed to the ground. Myrla used her own saliva and one of the wraps to clean the worst of the soot from Hestra's eyes and mouth, then offered her the last bit of milk.

"They won't be following us anymore, will they?" Rankil gasped.

"No." Myrla locked apologetic eyes with her. "The slick could burn for days so unless they stumble across an intersecting tunnel, we're safe."

"Good to know." Only then did Rankil dare a look around. They were in nothing more than a wide spot in the tunnel. It was cramped but would have to suffice. "Any idea what time of day it is?"

"Late enough for Archell's stomach to be talking," he observed.

"That could be anytime." Rankil removed the torch from his hand. "Guess it doesn't matter. It's night in our world. The torch burned too quick when we ran with it. Maybe we should save what's left and call it a night."

"Might as well." Myrla yawned as she wiped the oily film from her lips. "Hestra's asleep." She placed the infant back in her carrier and bound it to her chest for warmth. "Good thing the deeper caverns stay a constant temperature."

"But it's still a bit damp. Maybe we'll be warmer together." She pulled Myrla into her lap, shielding them both from the cool humidity. "Think what you will of my excuse," she whispered.

Archell sighed but didn't say a word.

"Night, Archie."

"Night, Rankil dankle, Myrla and Hestra, too."

Rankil ground out the torch.

"Explain your presence!" Unknown hands slung Archell and Rankil into opposite sides of the tunnel as others pulled Myrla up a little more kindly, letting her shade her eyes from the glaring torchlight. "Do you have any idea of the damage you've caused?"

Myrla squinted toward the loudest voice. The accent was odd, perhaps one of the Autlach dialects she'd never heard. "We didn't mean any harm." She stuttered in her best Autlach. "We were being followed by bandits. The fire stopped them from getting to us. We are sorry."

A rumble rose from their captors and the voice eased to more of a parental tone. "Well, you shouldn't be caving so young. Especially with a baby." They brought Archell and Rankil to Myrla's side.

"Quite an accent you have," continued the voice. "Dark coloring, too. You must be from the southlands. Which one of these fellows is your husband?"

"I am!" Rankil dropped her voice as she wrapped her arms about Myrla and the baby. "Like my wife said, we were being pursued. The caves were our only hope. We dropped a torch when we were running and the next thing we knew fire was everywhere."

"Apology accepted," the voice replied. "We'll chalk it up to youthful stupidity." A well-fed Autlach with long gray hair and a bristling beard moved into the light. "Would you like a guide out of here?"

"We could use a hand." Rankil's protective grasp loosened. Someone removed the torches from their faces while someone else produced a water skin.

"Drink up."

Their rescuers took congenial, though removed, spots facing them. Except for the heavy Autlach, their faces remained cloaked and well out of the direct light.

"Tell us about these attackers," said a gruff tenor in the group. "Were any of them familiar?"

"Longpass." Archell took a second swig to quench his thirst. "Bad man."

"We know him," assured the voice. "Rapist, murderer, bandit, and every bit of it done in the name of Raskhallak. You were lucky to escape."

Myrla, remaining silent so her accent wouldn't again come into question, rinsed and refilled Hestra's bottle with water. Despite her efforts, a few drops spilled across her hand as she poured, leaving a smudge which caused the tenor voice to burst into laughter.

"A bottle when you should be nursing? And your complexion, young woman, it's streaking!" The tenor jerked up Myrla's cuff, revealing the ivory flesh of her forearm. "I think we can end the shadow games and make proper introductions." Before Rankil could become defensive, the tenor threw back her hood, revealing a rolling smile, razor short hair, loop upon loop of battle braid and ocean blue eyes which added to her good-humored face.

She cleared her voice. "Hello, my sister. My name is Jefflynn, supervisor of the gas well you destroyed today. You've managed to find a new way to pierce the Tekkroon border, something many have died attempting." Jefflynn cleared her throat again. "Stars, but it's hard to keep that voice up," she said to her companions as they lowered their hoods.

Several of the other Taelachs chuckled and Jefflynn's Autlach companion laughed heartedly. "There *are* a few things the Taelach

157

can't do well, sis, and copying a male Aut's voice happens one of them." He smiled jovially. "Now what about our three fire starters and their little one?"

"I don't like taking outsiders straight in like this," replied Jefflynn as she looked down the passageway. "And Medrabbi will probably have my hide for it, but, seeing as we can't just leave them here, I don't see any other way." She shrugged her shoulders and motioned for them to follow her.

"Come on, everyone. Let's show these people how the Tekkroon get things done."

Part III
Alert

Chapter Fourteen

Fear comes in many forms—fear of death, fear of pain, however, fear of change is by far the most prominent.

—Taelach wisdom

Astounding things happen when one is shoved into a culture technologically superior to one's raising. The brain accepts, denounces or refuses to acknowledge the existence of that which is different. Rankil, Myrla and Archell experienced all three mindsets to varying degrees during their first moon cycle with the Tekkroon, each discovering their own way of coping. Jefflynn, the Tekkroon's lead well master, and her gentlewoman Dawn temporarily took the trio into their grotto and then helped Rankil and Myrla settle Hestra into one of the smaller family dwellings carved into a nearby hill. Archell was quite content with his cubicle in the single's cavern. Serrick, Jefflynn's twin Autlach brother, maintained quarters just down the corridor and was happy to help Archell with whatever he needed.

No one questioned Rankil and Myrla's youthful appearance, nor did they pry their minds for answers. The Tekkroon respected privacy and publicly chastised unwarranted invasions. Rankil and Myrla maintained the social image of a happy family but privately they were unsure how to handle their new situation. Each turned away when the other dressed and, even though they shared a common bed, they never exchanged more than a hug or quick kiss on the cheek. They often lay back to back at night, discussing the day's events, their fear of losing control helping them maintain a comfortable distance.

Their greatest concern, however, remained Kaelan and Jewel. Myrla cried most every evening for them and insisted that a Gretchencliff portraitist draw Kaelan's and Jewel's likenesses so that she might share their images with the sisters who worked in the deeper caverns. The picture itself was a simple but realistic line drawing on stretched white hide, but Myrla painstakingly oversaw the portrait's creation, describing her raisers in such fine detail that their likenesses were uncanny.

For various reasons, most of which Medrabbi, the even-tempered, aging broadback mayor of the Gretchencliff Colony holdings explained in her slow, patient fashion, that little of the clan lands were open to them. They were restricted within the Gretchencliff borders, to the main square during the daylight hours, and to the food and household stores for necessities—practical places such as those. All other areas were forbidden without an approved escort. Medrabbi called it probation. Rankil renamed it boredom. They weren't allowed to carry anything heavier than children's eating blades and were denied the opportunity to do more than menial tasks. Myrla, once she had regained her composure enough to think outside of her search, was assigned to assist with the youngest community members in their housing area's crèche. Rankil and Archell spent long hours shoveling snow or cleaning ice from the external steam outlets of the Tekkroon's complicated radiant heating system. Like Myrla, they repeatedly inquired about Kaelan and Jewel's disappearance, but Medrabbi told them little could be done in the way of an above-ground search until the snow melted in the high passes. The avalanche risk was just too great.

Their lives continued in this monitored fashion until Medrabbi called them to attend a mandatory bonfire in the colony's main square. They were made to stand in full view of the community, all two thousand of the Gretchencliff, excluding those helping to maintain the Tekkroon's tight boundary lines, watching as they were given status and training assignments.

"All Tekkroons contribute to the clan's well-being." Medrabbi glared at the colony's youngest broadbacks, who grinned brashly back, and then to the wisest members of her elected council, who nodded agreement.

"You have all been observed during your probation, your qualities and natural talents taken into consideration when making your assignments." Medrabbi took Myrla by the hand.

"Lady Myrla, gentlewomen are the backbone of the Tekkroon, running many of the day-to-day affairs and providing an internal line of defense that has saved us on more than one occasion. I've been informed you have the gift of patience and understanding with the children. Those are qualities needed in a teacher, something we never seem to have enough of. You are to report to instructor Perrywinn, supervisor of Gretchencliff primary schooling, at the eighth bell tomorrow morning to begin your training. I am certain of your success."

Medrabbi then placed Myrla's hand in Rankil's. "Young Rankil, you, like your name, were difficult to decipher. There is an abundance of aggression hiding behind your scarred face, a power that must be forged into something positive lest it fester into hatred for those who have wronged you. We've seen you playing blade games with your cousin and know your skill level is significant, even with a child's utensil. Assuming this ability extends to the bow and sword, the master guard commander has suggested you join the ranks of the Powder Barrier, the elite of the Tekkroon forces. Upon completion of your training, special privileges will be provided to you and your young family, the least of which is larger housing." Medrabbi waved off Rankil's stuttering thanks and turned a speculative eye on Archell, who shuffled his boots across the saturated sands surrounding the fire circle.

"Ah, a winnolla is a precious addition to any clan. We have so few that the artistic-minded elders from every colony were scrambling to take you under their direction. But there was only one real choice for you." Medrabbi motioned to a tree of a gentlewoman seated on a folding stool which groaned under her weight. An obvious figure of respect, she dominated those around her, both in height and air of dignity.

"Maestro Lisajohn, the Bowriver colony's music master, has won the battle for your talents." Medrabbi was the only one who maintained steady contact with Lisajohn's penetrating gaze. "You are to move your belongings to her students' grotto. Music, verse and the presentation of such are to be your only concerns from this moment on."

"Archell will do his very best." The Autlach grinned in a manner Rankil had rarely seen. It was happiness, the purest of bliss. He had survived every impossibility to get to this point, the beatings and names now nothing more than an inconvenience on the road to this higher place.

"Very best?" Lisajohn was musical even in speech. "Young man, I expect NO less than excellence from you. You are winnolla, are you not? I have it on good authority that you are, but if you feel unworthy of the title and task—"

Archell's jaw tightened. There was but one true way to prove his worthiness to his new taskmistress so he breathed deep, held his head high, and let music flow from the depths of his gut. No sound rose above his pure, sweet melody, no noise would have dared pierce such perfection. Even fussing babes, including Hestra in Dawn's arms, quieted to the sound. Archell's voice rose from its depths to a falsetto within a single verse, the full range of his talent placed before the entire colony. The final note lingered in the silence, a tone so pure it resonated in every heart present. Archell returned Lisajohn's gaze when he was through, searching for some response on her unemotional face.

"Not bad." Lisajohn cocked the head topping the crisp folds of her collar. "Not good, but not bad. Your phrasing was atrocious, your tone too pure given the song's subject matter." She waved her hand to dismiss the faults as frivolous. "But those are common mistakes of the untrained. We shall discuss how to correct these errors in due time." A smile flashed across her complacent mouth. "We shall also begin placing your various tunes into a readable form. Mother knows a winnolla's tunes are the ones that seem to survive the ages." With a snort and a physical shift on her bowing seat, she motioned those around her to assist her to her feet, then, leaning on a crutch, gestured Archell to follow.

"Continue, Medrabbi. We shall be out of your hair very soon. Gather whatever you have accumulated on your short stay here, apprentice Archell, and we shall depart."

"You are welcome to stay," said Medrabbi with a bow. "There is no music scheduled this evening but I am sure our musicians—"

"I'll have to refuse the invitation." The gigantic maestro tucked her fold stool under her free arm. " 'Tis a twenty-minute cart ride to the Bowriver Square, and my escort is waiting. Good evening to you all and my apologies. I did not anticipate my presence would interrupt your business." And Lisajohn departed the square in a flourish of fabric, an anxious Archell close on her heels.

"Join us anytime, Lisajohn, you, too, Archell. Your interruptions are always welcomed. It was well worth it to hear that song." Medrabbi, like many in the community, had been noticeably moved by the Autlach's lyrics. "There is only one other order of business on my agenda, broadback elders' business. Unless there are other matters to discuss, we shall adjourn to the interior round for that undertaking." After several minor difficulties were brought to light and their solutions delegated to the proper authority, Medrabbi dismissed the crowd. Dawn, Hestra still cradled in her arms, her own two daughters trailing behind, ushered Myrla away from the square. Someone caught Rankil by the shoulders as she joined the flow toward the housing areas.

"Not so fast." Medrabbi's almond-shaped eyes forecaste the importance of the remaining evening. "There is more to becoming a Tekkroon for you. Much more."

"But Myrla," objected Rankil, attempting to turn back. "I should really see she—"

Jefflynn appeared at her elbow, grasping her arm and helping pull her toward an open door set into the hillside. "She's staying with Dawn tonight." Many more jovial faces and helping hands, all broadback, assisted Jefflynn and Medrabbi in shoving Rankil through the doorway and into the middle of a large cavern housing rows of tables and benches. A dozen or more heavy lanterns blazed inside.

"I think she's clueless to all of this, Medrabbi." Jefflynn took a seat on the edge of the mayor's cushioned bench.

"Quite possible, seeing her only exposure has been through the Serpents." Medrabbi bellowed for kegs and mugs to be brought from a side storeroom then called the round to order by pounding the table. Rankil stood before her. "Now youngster," she chuckled. "Do you know why we're here?"

"Just look at her," howled someone at a nearby table. "Babe, she is. You sure she's old enough for the Recognition? Looks to me she should still be tugging the bottle."

"The winnolla is old enough," said Medrabbi between draws from her mug. "He's past the Recognition. That's why I let Lisajohn take him tonight." She stared hard at Rankil until she dropped her gaze. "But Rankil still seems a might tender at times. She's still growing height-wise, but it's not uncommon for one of us to grow until she is nineteen or twenty." Her head tilted while she scrutinized one of the Gretchencliff's newest residents.

"Someone bring her a bench and a cup before she passes out from the stress." Then Medrabbi regarded her with a little more kindness in her tone. "You were obviously raised Aut, my girl. Your accent is far too defined for Taelach to have been your first tongue." Medrabbi reached forward and flipped up the edge of Rankil's tunic, revealing the marks dimpling her lower back and abdomen. "You're too young to have been flogged for a crime, and no clan I know of punishes on both the front and back. If maturity comes through hardship and survival, Rankil, I believe it's safe to state you're the eldest here. Besides, we've all seen you with that woman and baby of yours. You're very protective of them."

"I love them." Rankil's voice cracked just when she intended to sound the most mature. "Please don't take them from me. They're all I have left, all I've ever really had."

"We wouldn't dream of such cruelty," Medrabbi said swiftly as to dismiss the notion. "They should remain with you. But I demand honesty of you at this moment. How old are you?"

Rankil glanced at the Gretchencliff mayor and then to Jefflynn who nodded at her to provide the truth. "I'm sixteen, if you please." Then she stammered to add, "I'll be seventeen this next summer."

"Twelve or thirteen is grown for a woman in the Aut world." Jefflynn nudged Medrabbi in the ribs. "And as you said, she has had a difficult existence."

"I know. I know." Medrabbi tugged at her battlebraid and looked to the others, seeking their opinions. "Others know more of you than I so this is beyond me alone. We'll put it to a vote. Sixteen will require extra guidance on our parts, instruction as to what is expected"—Medrabbi pointed straight to Jefflynn— "insight as to what is required socially and otherwise."

"The other youths mustn't know of this exception to the rules," called out the broadback raiser of a youth Rankil's age. "Keeping one of the hormonal snots in line is hard enough without them all thinking they're grown."

"We all think we're grown at that age," laughed Medrabbi. "But I think it may be true in this case. Rankil's age will remain a closely guarded secret. Rise before me child Rankil, and we shall tally the vote. All in favor—" Medrabbi never got to the opposed as every occupant of the room rose to her feet. "Child Rankil is no more. Welcome to the Tekkroon and Gretchencliff, Broadback Rankil!"

Our world has changed. Archell had said earlier that day. He was right, thought Rankil as hoots of approval filled the room. It had changed for the better.

"The acceptance is noted in the clan records." Medrabbi thrust a filled mug in Rankil's hand and encouraged her to drink of the sweet ale common to the Tekkroon. "The Recognition is the oldest of Tekkroon ceremonies." The smell of burning pilta began to waft through the room. "A girl becomes a broadback woman with this ritual, capable of taking the responsibilities of battle, hard work and"—the Gretchencliff mayor peered at Rankil—"demon-strating love to the gentlewoman of her choice."

"Enough talk, Medrabbi." Jefflynn forced Rankil back to her bench. "Get on with it. Who has the shears?"

"I've got 'em!" declared a voice from the rear.

"Pass them over so Medrabbi will quit her speech making." Jefflynn grinned defiantly at her leader. "She's indirectly my responsibility so I should have a part in this, too. I am, after all, acting as her raiser in this regard."

Medrabbi latched onto the shears when they came near. "The shears will remain in the mayor's control," she said with a wry chuckle.

"Not tonight, good friends." An age-darkened head sporting a multi-looped braid pushed toward Medrabbi. "Tonight, I chal-lenge the claim."

"That challenge is recognized. Is the speaker who I believe?" Medrabbi strained to identify the voice then motioned the crowd to make way. "Ah, it is. Harlis, you grace the Gretchencliff with your presence. What brings you to us this eve?"

"New blood, Medrabbi, new blood." Harlis appeared in the round. She stood short for a broadback, her height further reduced by a spinal injury that caused her shoulders to be uneven. But she was also so thick in the upper arms that the openings in her royal blue tunic had been slit. "I had to meet the young people for myself. This one in particular interests me. I've been told she grew up clanless."

"Indeed she did, sister Harlis." Medrabbi clasped the clan leader on the back. "How long have you been lingering about?"

"Long enough to hear the winnolla's song, Lisajohn's usual criticism—and other matters." Harlis's gaze centered on Rankil.

"Your thoughts?" inquired Medrabbi.

"The Gretchencliff always do things differently than most." Harlis took an untouched cup and pulled a hard swallow from it, pale upon pale eyes never wavering from Rankil as she drank. Rankil dared to return the look, and their eyes locked for a moment. It was a brave though perhaps foolhardy move, one that many broadbacks took as a provocation but as Harlis was easy to humor, she took the stare for youthful mischief.

"I've spoken to several elder sisters regarding this matter and I believe—" Harlis dropped to the bench beside Rankil and lay her arm across her back. "I believe Rankil here is up to the demand." The clan leader's fingers grasped the top of Rankil's shoulder, squeezing hard enough to bring tears to most, a growl from Rankil. "I also believe"—the comment was intended for Rankil alone—"that the Serpent clan is too stringent in some regards, unbending to an obvious exception to the norm. You're a test subject for my council, the answer to the question does hardship make for maturity? Don't mess this one up, young woman. Medrabbi and Jefflynn have gone out on a limb for you. Screw up, and they'll both be your ruin. Understand?"

"Yes, clan leader Harlis."

"Harlis will do." Harlis flashed a grin. "Just remember where you've been and where you're going and you'll be fine. Now, someone hand me the shears. I'll take my right of first cut then I'll be off. An unattached gentlewoman in the Adner colony has requested my company this evening." Harlis winked at Rankil, released her grip then rose. "And I'd be a fool to refuse such a kind offer."

The clan leader snipped a small section of hair from the top of

Rankil's head then departed, the lock still wrapped in her fingers. "Farewell, young Rankil. We shall meet again—sooner than you think. Coach her, Jefflynn. Knock her on her ass if she warrants it. She's yours to mold."

"I will, Harlis." Jefflynn's expression became guarded as she turned to Rankil. The usual means of teaching a broadback her role, while tried and true, might throw astray some of Rankil's good beginnings with Myrla. But above all else, the Recognition must be true to its name. Rankil must feel the responsibility, the seriousness of her position, something that was often lost in the night's indulgence. No. Jefflynn stepped back as someone refilled the mug in Rankil's hand. No. Rankil should make her own decisions this night. Be they right or wrong, they were hers to make.

Someone poured a bucket of half-melted snow over Rankil's head. "Get used to cold baths!" Jefflynn joined the friendly mayhem as a second bucket rolled down Rankil's back. "They're the best alternative if your woman is not willing." Rankil voiced objection as she was lifted from the bench and placed face down on one of the tables.

"Quit your complaining. Tekkroons don't whine." Medrabbi began scraping the hair from the back of Rankil's head. "Don't move. I've already drank four mugs and will slice you if you so much as blink."

Rankil remained still, her eyes closed against the spinning sensation the ale created. First the back, then the sides of her hair disappeared, leaving a narrow mohawk strip on the very top when Medrabbi stopped to drain another mug. Now tipsy and quite insecure, Rankil kept her eyes closed to the laughs and whistles around her until the final section of hair was pulled straight for removal. Different hands finished the task, soft, gentle hands that rubbed her forehead and ears. A delicate, flowery scent accompanied the touch and Rankil looked up, straight into the plunging neckline of a well-endowed gentlewoman. Horrified, she tensed and jerked backward only to be pushed into the perfumed recess again.

"Never had one of you do that," laughed the owner of that generous pair of breasts. "Hold still now. Let me finish, and you can see everything." She removed the remaining tuft and someone jerked Rankil upright into a chair. The woman slid into Rankil's lap to run an exposed leg down hers, toes toying with her boot cuff. "Like what you see?"

All Rankil's attempts at communication failed.

"Hey, Jefflynn," shouted one of the onlookers. "What'd you say at your Recognition?"

"I don't rightly recall." Jefflynn replied as she observed Rankil's expression. "But I believe I managed an 'oh Mother yes' in there somewhere." She bent close, rotating Rankil's head so her nose pushed back into the center of the sweet-smelling woman. "Say something, Rankil, or Abbye will think you aren't enjoying her company." Then she hissed in a whisper only Rankil could hear: "Say it whether you are or not. It's expected of you."

"I . . . I am." Nothing further from the truth had ever come from Rankil's mouth. She was petrified, mesmerized and confused at the same time. Experience was pressing against her, nipping at her ears, gyrating in her lap. This older woman was beautiful, scantily clad, soft freckles running across her supple shoulders, everything a fantasy should be and willing to indulge—but Myrla! The objection threatened to fade as Abbye swirled her tongue into Rankil's mouth.

"I can't." Rankil pushed away to peer up at Jefflynn. "I can't."

Abbye sat back and glanced up in despair. "What gives, Jeff? Are my face paints crooked or something?"

"Nah, I believe it's more than that, Abbyegale. Rankil's the noble sort." Jefflynn sat down beside Rankil and began to explain the Tekkroon custom. Medrabbi turned away the few who had noticed the refusal, returning them to their gaming and drinks, pouring them a distracting round from her private keg.

"Abbye's a widow," explained Jefflynn. "She's not committed to a broadback. You're not violating anyone else's woman. Enjoy yourself as you'd like. Abbye will, believe me."

"No." Rankil swiped Abbye's saccharin flavor from her mouth. "It's not that. I just can't."

"Why not?" Abbye's touch was now more compassionate than seductive. "You embarrassed by your inexperience? That's what I'm here for. I'm to be your first pleasure phase."

"You can't be my first phase." Rankil drowned her sorrows in her drink. "I'm saving that for Myrla."

"We're not talking full physical relations. That's part of commitment. A pleasure phase isn't by most clan standards," explained Jefflynn in a low voice. "Mental pleasures have to be learned and practiced. Your job is to teach Myrla."

"It is?" Rankil looked again at Abbye. How could a pleasure phase possibly fulfill one enough that they could forget about involving the physical? "I thought Myrla and I would learn together."

"Sweet sentiment but not the way it normally happens." Abbye placed her arm around Rankil's slumped shoulders, took her mug, and drained the contents. "Most clans expect it to happen this way. But Medrabbi mentioned you'd been raised Aut, didn't she? That explains a lot. Tell you what. I'll stick around until the Recognition is finished. We'll play things up, put on a show that'll make everybody think you're ready and willing. Then," Abbye batted her lashes to remind Rankil of the delights she offered, "if you haven't decided otherwise, you can walk me back to my quarters and go back to your home. Deal?"

"You won't think worse of me?" Rankil glanced over to a young, single broadback who was being entertained by a widowed gentlewoman with wide hips and a shrill voice.

Jefflynn turned Rankil from the spectacle. "Don't compare your actions to those of one who is older and without an attachment of the heart. I told Medrabbi you might not enjoy this part of the Recognition. Abbye would've overwhelmed me at your age. I'm impressed you handled yourself so well. You're truly committed to Myrla."

Rankil took a moment to consider Abbye again before she

responded. Pleasure phases had to be practiced? Myrla should know this. "So it's all right? You don't mind, Abbye?"

"Nah." She kissed Rankil's shaved head, leaving a perfect, red mouth print Jefflynn removed with her cuff. "I would've done things differently if I'd known you were so serious about that pretty girl I've seen you with. Tekkroon broadbacks never take a woman at such an early age. They're far too content to play around with us widows and perfect their phases until sometime in their twenties." Abbye shook her head at the lewd nature of the other gentlewoman's dance. "Give it a rest, Webbic. There's still the marking to go. Save something for later."

"Ah, you're just jealous." Webbic snickered but stopped her dance, smoothing her skirts back to a less obscene height. "Somebody bring me some wine. I'm too parched to go on."

Jefflynn rolled her eyes as the other broadbacks stumbled over each other to obey the request. "She has it down to an art, doesn't she?"

Abbye was once again sitting in Rankil's lap, but much more primly than Webbic, who sprawled across two laps. Abbye's presence wasn't as intimidating now, thought Rankil as she listened to the tales of battlefield and bedroom victories circling the room. She was more of a sympathetic friend, she and Jefflynn the only ones who truly understood the dedication she felt toward Myrla.

Abbye made a good show of things, snuggling close and rubbing up in just the right way to keep suspicion at bay, but the touch was platonic the rest of the time. She matched Rankil cup for cup and both were quite relaxed when she was told to move from her seat. Someone stripped Rankil to her undershirt, exposing every scar dotting her arms.

Medrabbi reappeared at her side with an almost figureless thin gentlewoman on her arm. "This is Elreese, my woman of twenty-four passes and the Gretchencliff's second best skin marker." Medrabbi stumbled back a pace. "I'm the best, but seeing as I'm not fit to ink at the moment, I asked her to do the honor."

Elreese flicked her fingers for Medrabbi to sit down before she fell down and pulled a bench end close to Rankil. She laid hide-sealed pots of color, threading and thin curved needles across the wooden seat. "Someone bring a lantern close enough for me to work," she said brusquely, then turned to her partner. "Am I going to mark both sides?"

"Nope." Medrabbi garbled her reply. "Larza has volunteered to do the clan emblem."

"Not if she isn't sober." Elreese glared at Larza's ale-stained leggings. "How much you had?"

"Only two." Larza, a flare-jawed teen not far from the Recognition herself, straddled the bench on Rankil's right. She grasped Rankil by the arm and began to inspect the condition of her bicep. "I'll have to put the symbol a little lower than normal. That scar running off your shoulder will distort anything I ink onto it. How'd you get it?"

"I don't remember." Rankil ignored the shocked expression on Larza's face and took another swallow of numbing ale. "It's hard to recall what caused them all."

"I think I'll add the sign of a misplaced sister to your personal marker," said Elreese with a tad of reverence. "You deserve that recognition for just surviving." She dipped a long strand of thread-ing into the black color pot, wiped the excess on a cloth, then pulled the end through the eye of one of the needles. Someone pulled the surface of Rankil's upper arms tight. Elreese and Larza deftly slipped points under her skin and pulled out a few millime-ters down, the threads' knotted ends pinching into Rankil's flesh. It hurt, but in a purposeful way. They took stitch after stitch, never looking up from their work until the thread began to run short. Fine straight lines began to emerge on Rankil's arms, the right sep-arating into a star and stripe pattern very similar to the one on the downed spacecraft she had discovered. Just what was the relation? Should she tell her new people of the find, tell them about the small arsenal she had tucked between the tunics in her clothing box? Elreese, assuming Rankil's fixation on the emerging tattoo was pain related, paused to examine Larza's work then clipped the thread free of her needle.

"Rip time," she said to the closest spectators. "Grab her up."

They smashed Rankil into her seat a second later, holding her arms as the threads were removed in one hard pull. She tensed at the pain, but didn't pull away. She was Tekkroon. She was grown. Only children cried over such discomfort.

"Not a flinch!" declared Jefflynn in a proud parent's tone. "Medrabbi did right putting you in the Powder ranks."

"That she did," observed Elreese as she rethreaded. "Broadbacks normally howl and carry on like I'm killing them. Gentlewomen are much easier to work with."

"Yeah, they are," said Larza in mid-jerk of her first strand. "Medrabbi, did you finish her personal marker?"

"Reesie and I did earlier today." Medrabbi pulled a small scroll from her pocket and tossed it to Jefflynn who held it up for Larza. "A fair representation of her nature, don't you think?"

Jefflynn examined the scroll then looked at Rankil. "How much in the way Taelach symbols do you know?"

"Some. Myrla is still teaching me." Rankil blinked hard as a needle pierced her flesh again. The sites were becoming less sensitive though blood trickled down her arm.

"You know the symbol for battle?"

"Sure. It's the same as sword only with two handle marks."

"And the one for strength?"

Another gulp of ale dulled the sting. "A hand, isn't it?"

Jefflynn nodded. "A fist actually. And honor is indicated by circling the symbols." She lay the scroll next to the color pots and rolled up her own sleeve to reveal the faded red, blue and green band on her own arm. "Marks are your personal identity, your name written, your signature. The Tekkroon take great pride in their marks and try to live by their meaning. Individually, mine represent truth speaking, family and the oil pumps I work with. The banding means loyalty. All are important to me. Do strength, battle and becoming found represent you, Rankil?"

"I've had to fight for most everything."

"That confirms the strength and battle signs I included. The honor ring comes from the way in which you care for your young family." Medrabbi was far too drunk to stand. "What about the being found? Were you ever so lost that this mark has real meaning to you or do you wish to forget it all?"

"It's painful." Rankil could now acknowledge her past to the Tekkroon. There is no shame in survival by any means. "But I lived and want others to know I did. The marks are good. I'll wear them proudly."

"And so shall your woman." Elreese pulled back her neckline to show Medrabbi's marker of patience, stubbornness and fidelity on her shoulder. "A gentlewoman can wear her life mate's symbol if she chooses. It shows commitment and is more permanent than the custom of public blood marking. Some of the broadbacks have even taken to wearing their women's markers on their shoulders as well." She smiled at Medrabbi who rubbed her shoulder unconsciously.

"Speaking of blood marking," Jefflynn dabbed at the streaks trickling down Rankil's arm. "You need to do that if you want the other broadbacks to leave Myrla alone."

"How is blood marking done?" Rankil waved her mug in hopes someone would refill it. "Kaelan never mentioned that."

"It's a Tekkroon custom." Abbye offered to share her drink. "You stand in front of the clan and proclaim that pretty girl as yours. Challenges to your claim will be addressed, and then you mark her with your blood." Abbye drew close to run her fingers over Rankil's shoulder at the spot the mark would be placed. "It's a barbaric ceremony, a little degrading for the gentlewoman to be treated so much like property, but so romantic." Abbye's eyes reflected not-so-long-ago memories. "Talking about it makes me ache for Fince. She's been gone three passes now." Abbye retrieved her mug and downed the rest of the contents. "We never took a child. Thought we had plenty of time. Then came Longpass's initial assault on the border. Fince disappeared in the battle." Abbye sniffed, squared her shoulders then flashed Jefflynn a drunken grin. "But none of that matters now, does it?"

"Fince was a good friend, Abbyegale." Jefflynn refilled their empty cups, but held Abbye's back for a moment. "The drink won't make you forget."

"It numbs the pain." Abbye grabbed the cup, squeezed Rankil's knee and brushed her hand against her inner thigh. "As do other things." A wild whoop escaped her ruby lips, and she began to remove her stockings. "Finish those inkings so I can take this one home."

"You'll freeze on the way if you strip here." Elreese leaned back to view her handiwork. "All right. Turn her about so I can check Larza's doings."

Rankil was lifted and her position reversed. The rotation failed to cease when she was settled, and the voices and faces around her became blurred. She floated a few hand-widths off the floor. Someone held more drink to her lips and she gulped it, vaguely aware her stomach churned from the alcohol. Elreese examined the second mark and suddenly Rankil found herself out in the cold, Abbye supporting her weight on one side, Jefflynn on the other. Jefflynn helped her refuse Abbye's final tempting offer by reminding them both that they were too drunk to phase, and besides, Myrla was waiting. After a lingering kiss to Rankil's mouth and a mental caress that caused Rankil to reconsider her situation, Abbye stumbled into her room, and Jefflynn half-carried Rankil to her grotto, the pair singing a discordant version of a Taelach drinking song the entire way. Dawn greeted them at the door, shushing them for the children's sake while Myrla put Rankil to bed.

"I'm turning in as well." Myrla thanked Dawn for her hospitality and Jefflynn for bringing Rankil safely home, and shut the fold door to their room. Rankil was already snoring when Myrla slid out of her skirts and into the furs. She examined Rankil's new marks and affectionately rubbed her smooth head.

"Well, you said you wished we were grown." Myrla dimmed the lantern and laid her head to Rankil's chest. "That wish came true." Her hand caressed Rankil's abdomen, stopping just shy of her pubic area. Myrla knew broadbacks were no different physically than she was, but she had never seen, much less touched . . . Myrla jerked away and turned over, shaming herself for such behavior. The same hands now found their way across her own body, cupping her breasts and finger counting her ribs. How she wished the hands were other than her own. Rankil would kiss her neck, tickling her ears with whispers of what she wanted to do. It would be so right, so perfect—

"My, help me." Myrla lifted Rankil's head to the bucket she'd placed by the bed, holding it there until she finished purging her liquored stomach. "My damn head is exploding." Rankil swiped her mouth. "Drink can make you this sick?"

"Only if you drink too much." Myrla pushed the bucket away and held a cup to Rankil's lips.

She took several small sips then eased her head back on the pillow. "Thank you."

"You're welcome." Myrla pulled the blankets up and rolled back to her previous position. "Good night."

"Night." Rankil placed her hand on Myrla's shoulder, petting the ends of her unplaitted hair. "My?"

"Yes?"

"Would it be fresh of me to hold you tonight? It helps to have someone near when you're sick, doesn't it?"

"It helps." Myrla let herself be drawn into the embrace she had longed for. Rankil mumbled appreciation into the back of her head, then offered a fleeting mental touch that sent a wave of joy throughout Myrla's body, caressing her back and sides just as she had wanted even as it flooded her mind with the sordid details of the evening. *I love you, Myrla. It'll take a while, but we'll learn the ins and outs together. Can you be patient and let me learn from my mistakes?*

Always, Rankil. Myrla lay awake until late, wrestling with the knowledge that temptation had been faced and rejected for her sake. She wondered if it would be so simple for Rankil the next time, what with Abbye being such a figure of sexual desire and the promiscuous pleasure phases an acceptable part of young

Tekkroon behavior. Maybe resistance would be easier if she gave more of herself. Yes, that was the solution, decided Myrla as she drew deeper into Rankil's embrace. Archell was exploring his new world and didn't need their burden. She and Hestra had lost all else and were unprepared to live alone. Rankil was all they had left, and they couldn't lose her. Not now. Not ever.

Chapter Fifteen

If you insist.

—Rankil Danston

"Hold that piece at arm's length and steady!"

Rankil's arms locked in obedience of the command. She ached, her shoulder and back muscles screaming protest over the continued demand. A blazing hangover further deteriorated the situation, and the barn's animal smell topped her misery with nausea. Guard commander Stiles, a long-faced, turquoise-eyed broadback two decades or so older than Rankil, had been placed in charge of her indoctrination into the Powder Barrier and was taking great personal joy in making her newest charge's first day memorable. She barked orders close to Rankil's ear, giving her legs an occasional poke with the end of her finely carved staff. "They send a child to me? A little girl? What am I supposed to do with you? Nurse then burp you? This must be Medrabbi's idea of a joke."

"No, Commander," whispered Rankil around the strain of her stance. "I—"

"DID I GIVE YOU PERMISSION TO SPEAK?" Stiles's staff struck the ground just shy of Rankil's left boot. "You will speak only when spoken to!"

Three hours of continued badgering and physical torture began to twist the nausea into anger, the fatigue into intolerance. No title and prestige was worth this. And just who was Stiles to be treating her this way? She'd endured quite enough of it in her life and believed the Tekkroon above such behavior. Rankil snarled and held the heavy tube a little higher. Stiles wanted a response, a buckling of her will, a whining, something Rankil had learned to deny.

"So we think we're tough?" Stiles jerked the tube from her hands and replaced it with a single straw from one of the feed mangers. "Index fingers only."

It should have been easy after the weight of the pipe, so how could one straw be so heavy? Sweat beaded Rankil's face despite the morning cold. Her muscles cramped and burned. Her arms quivered. Then it became quite literally too much. She couldn't help but flex. The straw floated to the floor as the staff stung the ground beside her right boot.

"Don't do that again."

"What'd you say?" Stiles raised the staff again.

Rankil turned to face her tormentor. "You heard."

"What are you going to do?" Stiles returned Rankil's glare. "Bawl? Go running home to that sweet thing I've seen on your arm?" She circled the staff around Rankil's toes. "How'd you end up with such a good looking woman? Maybe I should show her what a real broadback can do for her. Mother knows she'll never learn from you."

"You leave her out of this." Rankil clenched her fists.

Stiles, upon discovering the sensitive spot, sniffed then planted the tip of her staff in top of Rankil's right boot, splitting the leather until the footling slid up into the crack. "Make me."

181

"If you insist." Rankil's upper lip began to curl.

Stiles immediately regretted her actions. "Listen, junior."

Rankil's fake right shadowed her left backhand, sending Stiles sprawling to the ground. "I won't be hit, and my woman is not up for discussion." She retrieved Stiles's staff and fractured it over her knee.

"Strength, endurance and a temper to boot. Pretty damn good shot, too." Stiles rubbed her jaw. "But, blast it! I'm getting too old for initiations. Too many of my teeth have been lost testing recruit dispositions." She looked up with a sigh. "And you, junior, just busted my new dental plate." She rose slowly, hands up to show her nonaggression. "Good moves. Where'd you learn the fake?"

"My brothers." Rankil looked at the broken staff in her hands. So this had been another test? Life had become full of tests.

"My brothers, what?" Stiles pointed to the faded patch on her left arm.

"My brothers, Commander." Rankil held out the staff. "I should apologize for my actions, Commander, but—"

"I insulted your lady." Stiles drew to a stand. "I was trying to get a rise out of you to test your temperament. Insults didn't work so I had to try something more drastic." She brushed the dirt from her tunic. "Just business, you understand. Nothing personal."

"Still, Commander Stiles," Rankil tried to explain away her reaction. The Barrier might well deny entry to a recruit who'd overpowered one of their experienced officers. "I *am* sorry about the staff. It was a beautiful piece of work."

"Should be. I carved half a pass on it." Stiles nudged the pieces with her toe. "I suppose I deserved that as well. I knew your history and shouldn't have provoked you like I did. But, we can't have pacifists in the Powder Barrier." She thrust her finger toward Rankil. "Nor can we have hotheads that fire off at every little thing."

"Commander," stammered Rankil. "I . . . I . . . ."

"I'm not finished." She retracted the finger but not her stern tone. "You happen to be neither of these things. Your temper is quick but not unjustified, exactly what my squadron needs. Take your piece, junior, and follow me. You'll need better attire if you're to be representing the Tekkroon."

"Yes, Commander." Rankil obeyed, her tube held in the vertical carrying position Stiles insisted she maintain. They crossed a grouping of small paddocks, Rankil jogging to keep up with her superior's agile gait. Stiles moved as if she floated just above the ground, her wide steps never crunching the crusted snow, much less making readable prints. Even her flapping cloak, a heavy, black, concealing garment, seemed mute among the Gretchencliff's daytime sounds. Others nodded respect for Stiles and smiled sympathetically at her panting charge. They offered words of encouragement and chin up signs so often Rankil began to wonder what she had gotten into.

They passed the singles and family housing and Rankil found herself out of breath and at the door of a small shop just north of the Gretchencliff's main stores. Stiles pounded on the door then swung it open without waiting for an answer. "Those uniforms ready?"

"Hello yourself, Stiles." Abbyegale looked up from her sewing machine to wink at Rankil. "I'm finishing the alterations on the last piece. The cobbler shop brought over four sizes of boots. You, as usual, didn't bother to give any measurements."

Stiles motioned Rankil to place her piece outside the door then pointed to the boots. "Close the door then find yourself something to replace those rags your feet currently reside in." She dumped the clutter from a chair, placed the seat near Abbye, and poured herself a mug from the teapot simmering on the room's radiant outlet.

"When you going to clean this place up, Abbye? You'll give my recruit the wrong idea about cleanliness."

"I'll clean up when I catch up," snipped Abbye, turning the fabric for another pass in the pedal-powered machine. "Your group keeps me overloaded with patches and replacements. I have little time for anything else." She clipped a stray thread from the garment's hemline and held it out. "Here, Rankil, try this on."

"You two know each other?" Stiles blew on her tea.

"Yeah," said Abbye, replacing the machine's needle with a heavier, leather-capable version. "You must have been on duty last night. We met at Rankil's Recognition. Didn't we, Rankil?"

"Yes, Abbye." Rankil overlooked Stiles's mistaken grin to search the room for a place to change. "How's your head?"

"Busting," she replied. "Same as yours. What're you looking for?"

"A place to change."

"Lose the modesty, junior." Stiles leaned back in her chair, raising the front legs as a sly smile formed on her face. "Abbye has obviously seen it, and I could personally care less."

Rankil bunched the soft tops of the new boots in her hand. "Commander, I—"

"I said strip! That's an order!"

"Yes, Commander." Rankil swallowed hard and removed her top and undershirt. Abbye made herself busy cutting a patch while Stiles occupied herself by gathering scattered pins on one of the worktables, saving Rankil further discomfort. The black knit undertunic Abbye passed her slid on easily once Rankil figured out the collar hooks, and a rough hide jerkin with side laces over that. They were identical to Stiles's except for the rank patch, and Rankil felt good in them, strong and somehow invincible. Such majestic clothing demanded respect.

"What you think, Abbye? Will they do?"

"Don't matter what she thinks," said Stiles before Abbye could respond. "I've final approval on what you do and don't wear from this day forward." She had Rankil turn then nodded her head. "A trifle large in the shoulder, but we'll remedy that. Are the leggings laying about, seamstress woman, or does my newest trooper go bottomless in the cold?"

"They were on top of the pile you moved." Abbye tossed Rankil the top pair and smiled at her, small-talking despite Stiles's preference she not with new recruits. "How is that lady of yours?"

"Fine," mumbled Stiles around her cup. "Just fine. Looking forward to spring as we all are."

"I didn't mean you." Abbye resumed sewing, the machine clanking and popping in time with the movement of her feet on the pedals. "I saw Annyalae this morning. She stopped by to pick up your new shirt. I was referring to Rankil's gentlewoman. Was she upset?"

"She made me fried bread and gravy before I left this morning." Rankil's stomach gurgled. Myrla had indeed roused her for an early breakfast, saying the meal was penance for drunkenness. But that wasn't what concerned Rankil. In fact, it had been expected. Myrla had been clear about her beliefs on alcohol. They were the same as Jewel's—the less the better. There was something more going on in the mind of that doe-eyed gentlewoman, something Rankil wasn't quite able to comprehend. She'd woke Rankil with a hungry kiss to her mouth, wrapping and drawing her bare, agile legs up and down Rankil's until Rankil fairly ached from the pleasure. Then Myrla had risen from the blankets to dress, pulling off her winter gown without turning away, revealing more than Rankil had envisioned seeing at this stage of their relationship. Familiarity sometimes bred casualness, but Rankil believed there was more than that. Maybe she should ask Abbye.

"Gravy on a sour stomach?" Abbye's grimace shook Rankil from her thoughts. "Well, at least you know where she stands." She watched Rankil struggle with the bottom lacings of her first pair of hide leggings. "How's the baby?"

"Baby?" Stiles peered inquisitively at her recruit. "I was told you wouldn't be assigned to the barracks after your training because you were committed but not that you had a family. How did you come to have a child at your age?"

"Right time, right place, Commander." Rankil buckled the top of her boots, slid her knife into place and straightened. Time would condition the leather, but for now it was stiff, though warm, with each piece lined with light cloth to keep the hide from chafing.

"I understand you've a knack for that." Stiles indicated Rankil should gather her new belongings and follow. "A family will not excuse you from basics isolation, night duty or from taking arms when the border is threatened."

"Yes, Commander." With quick assistance from Abbye, she bundled the uniforms, grabbed her piece and hastened to keep up with her superior. Midway across the main courtyard, she realized she had forgotten her cloak and begged for the chance to retrieve it. Stiles refused the request, stating, with a shake of the intimidating wrap on her shoulder, that the Powder Barrier wore a specific manner of cloak, one of which she would be provided as soon as she settled in the barracks. Her hopper cloak, Stiles added, could be picked up at a later time.

"I'll allow you tonight to say farewell to your family. There'll be no contact during the first cycle of training, so make it last."

"Yes, Commander." This time, they stopped outside the open walls of the Gretchencliff metal works, a freestanding stone structure whose interior heat was stifling even in winter. Twenty or more broadbacks, and to Rankil's immense surprise, three sweat-streaked gentlewomen and an Aut woman worked within, some hammering, others on complicated presses, each forging the items needed to maintain the Tekkroon existence.

Stiles spoke with one of them then vanished into the forge area's only fully enclosed room, returning with a sheathed rapier marked with the Powder Barrier's skull emblem. "Here, junior." She added the weapon to Rankil's load, wedging it between her arm and body.

"Run that stuff home then join me at the west stables." Stiles pointed the general direction the building lay. "We'll get you mounted and equipped. Ever done much riding?"

"No, Commander Stiles."

Stiles looked anything but pleased. "Tekks ride young, but you'll learn, girl. You'll learn quick. Now get home."

Rankil shuffled off, shifting her load to avoid dropping something into the slush and slop of the pathways. She managed to maintain the precarious balance until she reached the door of her little home then stood on the threshold, wondering how she was going to enter without assistance. The answer came soon enough as Myrla opened from the inside.

"You, too?" She took some of the load then held the door wide. "They've loaded me up as well."

"With what?" Rankil placed her piece against the wall, the rapier on their small eating table.

"Scrolls on teaching philosophy, slate boards to write assignments on—most everything." Myrla stepped back to admire Rankil's new attire. "You look incredible." She fingered the edge of the jerkin. "Is this your new uniform?"

"Yeah." Rankil smoothed the leather. "I love it." Her attention now settled on Myrla who had removed her headscarf and braids and pulled her hair back in the loosely banded style common to Tekkroon gentlewomen. She wore leggings, unheard of in the Serpent clan, and her long, belted tunic, again a style of the Tekkroon, was cut to show her upper cleavage. Rankil's gaze halted there, pondering the line. Serpent clan garments were never revealing, so she had never actually considered Myrla's endowments to any lingering extent. They came hurtling toward her now, as did the memory of the morning's bedroom disclosure, tensing muscles in new ways, teasing her nose with scent—Myrla's inviting own.

"You look beautiful." Rankil's gaze drew upward into her eyes and stayed there. "After tonight I have to stay in the barracks. It's only until I finish my initial training."

"I know." Myrla wrapped her arms about Rankil's waist. "Dawn told me last night. She said I could stay with them if I wished, but I think Hestra and I will remain here. They've too many responsibilities as it is. It's time I dealt with things myself."

"Your choice." Rankil gathered her tight, lifting her from the braided rug to deposit her on the table, the embrace continuing while Rankil slid into a chair and pulled Myrla into her lap. "I'll miss you and Hestra while I'm gone. Will you miss me?"

"Don't you know?" A kiss as sweet as the morning's crossed Rankil's lips. "You'll be missed and longed for. I've become rather used to sharing a bed with you."

"As have I," quipped Rankil, pulling back so she could view Myrla's face again. "There's a community fire tonight. Want to go?"

"Not tonight. I'd rather spend it here, just us."

"Let's go anyway, just for a bit." Rankil's eyes danced a hot blue flame. Myrla was hers by heart, and the time had come for it to be so in the clan's eyes as well. "The stories are always good, and we can slip away when Hestra becomes tired."

"All right, but just for a while." They clung together for a moment more, stroking one another's faces, their love expressed in the quick pace of their hearts. Then Myrla, overwhelmed by her requirement to return to her training, whisked away from Rankil's arms and pulled on her cloak.

"I'm sorry."

"I've gotta go, too." Rankil grabbed her weapons and bounded for the door. "Commander Stiles will rake me over if I'm not prompt."

"I'll collect Hestra from the crèche and have dinner waiting for you." Myrla blew a kiss over her shoulder and descended the stone stairway leading to the lower pathway. "See you tonight."

"The sooner the better," called Rankil, taking the path leading the opposite direction. She hoped a raking wasn't in order for either of them. Things were beginning to go as they should. The evening fire would only solidify it all.

"Good story!" Applause and laughter were amplified in the interior round. An evening snowfall had cancelled the bonfire and brought everyone indoors. They sat shoulder to shoulder, discussing the day's events. Even with the heat turned off and the ventilation slats open, the room was sweltering, everyone shedding their cloaks to combat the stuffiness. Rankil placed her small family at one of the benches near the round's center and bided her time. The overall mood was jovial, the stories humorous and tailored to the family air, a perfect evening to make it all permanent. When there was a lull in the conversation, she raised her arm for Medrabbi to recognize.

"And it's young Rankil with the next tale, I believe." Medrabbi waved her to the center of the room. "What yarn of wealth and glory do you offer us tonight? A harrowing one from your first day with the Barrier, perhaps?"

Rankil ignored the snickers of a group of broadbacks dressed similarly to herself, several of whom probably had stories of their own concerning her first day nassieback, complete with colorful descriptions of Rankil's multiple falls and rodeo throws courtesy of her unruly mount. "No stories, Medrabbi. I have something important to say." Rankil drew Myrla to her feet and gently pulled Hestra from her arms.

Elreese, who was sitting nearby, took the rosy-cheeked infant into her lap and held her upright so she could watch. "You may not remember this, young one," she whispered into Hestra's tiny ear. "But you can say you were here for it."

Rankil squared her shoulders and began to speak. "Most of you remember me from last night." Webbic, who was in yet another's lap, giggled loudly.

"And you all remember Myrla. We have been together since before entering the Tekkroon lands, and now I wish to seal our relationship by your clan standards." She glanced at Medrabbi in search of what to do next.

"A marking!" Medrabbi jumped to her feet. "What a perfect ending to the day." She pulled her boot knife and held it over her head until the room grew quiet. "Rankil wishes to proclaim Myrla as hers, unavailable to the courtings of other broadbacks. Are there any objections to this union?"

Myrla stood erect, unsure of what was happening but positive it was something wonderful.

"Silence means acceptance," said Medrabbi. "The union will

be." Medrabbi flicked the blade tip over her right index finger, drawing forth a tiny shimmer of blood. "Rankil, your right hand, please." Medrabbi used her index finger to smear an X on Rankil's palm.

"The stroke of my blade brings forth your soul, droplets of your inner being, your very life." Medrabbi drew her knife across the red streaks, opening the top layer of Rankil's flesh and, using the blade's flat side to spread the blood, thinly coating every crease of Rankil's hand. Then she drew behind Myrla and pulled her collar to one side, revealing Myrla's right shoulder. "Do you wish this woman yours?" Medrabbi asked Rankil.

"In every way."

"And does she desire you?" Medrabbi looked at Myrla.

"Yes," assured a breathless Myrla. "More than anything."

"Then it is done." She pressed Rankil's bloody palm onto Myrla's shoulder then placed another X of her own blood on the back of Rankil's hand. "Be it known only those who seal this relationship can unseal it."

"Remove the sealing cross before it dries! An objection has been declared!" Harlis stood in the round's doorway, holding it open for another to pass. A hooded woman pushed past her to the center of the round, her cloak sprinkled with snow, the gold handle of her boot knife glistening with cold moisture, her cloak held closed by two half-heart pins. Rankil didn't recognize the individual but Myrla did and she recoiled, crashing over Medrabbi's bench in her retreat. Her knees gave way, and she crumpled at Rankil's feet, sobbing in a distress she could only express in a single word.

"Recca."

Part IV
Adrift

Chapter Sixteen

To lose
Is to learn.

—Anonymous

Rankil Danston, the misplaced sister claimed by the Tekkroon clan, returned to what she once was—lost, longing for Myrla and Hestra, dejected by Archell's continued absence when she needed his wisdom and song. She eclipsed the sullen, withdrawn individual she'd been when Kaelan's family had taken her in, becoming a loner, an antagonist in any situation where her anger could be displayed. Her heart became hard and uncompromising. Love led to pain, to disgrace, deserting as soon as one grew accustomed to its feel. She wouldn't repeat the blunder.

"Get up, junior, and join the fun." Genevic, the gangly broadback who occupied the bunk over Rankil's told her as their squadron was enjoying an evening of gaming. "You've an excellent opportunity to show off. Odds say your aim will be wrong."

"Who'd bet on me?" Rankil sprawled belly-down across her bunk, face into her pillow to smother another throbbing headache.

"Those who desire to expand their purse," piped Genevic, jerking her leg. "Come prove them right."

"What'd you wager?" Rankil looked up, eyes squinted against the barrack's multiple lanterns.

"Most my Aut coinage, so don't miss." Genevic pulled on her again, agitating Rankil until she kicked back.

"Get your hands off me." She rolled to see her bunkmate's anxious face. "What are the odds?"

"Five to one against you."

"Give me sixty percent, and I compete."

"Sixty!" declared Genevic, slapping at Rankil's upraised hand. "You're insane. I was planning to spend my winnings on Isabella."

"Don't care." Rankil held her head in her hands as she sat upright. This headache had lingered, refusing to leave despite her efforts at relaxation. A Gretchencliff healer had given her powders to calm the ache, but they made Rankil woozy, something the Powder Ranks could ill-afford so she seldom took them. "Sixty still doubles your purse. Take it or leave it."

"But Isabella has her eye on a bracelet the traders brought back." Genevic pulled on her short braids. "I suppose she would settle on something less pricey, but the reward for me would be lessened." She grinned furtively. "And Bella's phase is worth any price."

"What a waste." But Rankil was pulling on her boots.

"Ah, Isabella is worth it."

"No woman is worth it."

"You don't know Isabella."

"And I don't want to." The light had become daggers to pierce Rankil's eyes. "You want my help or not?"

"Asking, aren't I?" Genevic followed Rankil to where the majority of the squadron had gathered, taking turns sinking their blades into a hay stuffed sack. Rankil examined the lay of the target then, stepping to the throw line, tossed her blade into the target's narrow center.

She extended her right hand to Genevic. "My fee?"

"No fair!" cried another squadron member. "We didn't know junior here had a profit in it. It changed the odds."

"You suggesting I cheated?" seethed Rankil, quick to retrieve her blade.

"Not directly," said the portly broadback who'd expressed the objection. "Your fee increased your concentration, heightening your senses. None of us thought Genevic would actually talk you into it what with your head splitting like it's been."

"Yours will be splitting, too, if you don't pay up." Rankil snatched her profits from the Autlach coins slapped into Genevic's outstretched palm then returned to her bunk, hurling herself across the top, oblivious to Commander Stiles's critical observation of the goings on.

"Dammit, Commander Stiles, my head is fine." Rankil's name had been withdrawn from the next morning's duty roster. Infuriated by the change, she'd stormed, without knocking, into the duty commanders' bunkroom.

"Cease the expletives in the same breath as my name, Junior." Stiles, still in her under leggings, looked up from the scrolls littering her worktable. "You will report to the infirmary as ordered."

"Couldn't it wait until tomorrow? Mounted maneuvers are this morning and—"

"And you can't imagine missing them?" Stiles pushed up her reading spectacles, gaining a clearer view of her youngest squad member. "The nassies won't miss your company nor you theirs. Your mutual dislike has become famous." Stiles's tone softened, as did her glare. "Besides, we cannot have our junior falling from her nassie, or worse yet, from a treetop post. The Powder Ranks must maintain their health." Though Stiles's mouth tightened with her next words, there was no concealing her concern. "You've been in four brawls in the past two cycles, the latest one earning your challenger a broken jaw. There's been a marked change in your temperament, junior. One I don't fancy. Any more fights or trainings missed because you can't see to aim your weapon, and you'll find yourself booted from my squad. You're useless if you're incapacitated by a splitting cranium."

Stiles stood before Rankil, placing one hand on the callow woman's lean shoulder. "I've no wish to lose you, Rankil. Go to the healers. Let them decipher the rattles in your skull then come back to me renewed." Stiles's warm smile diminished the officious voice she regained. "Go, junior, NOW! You try my patience."

"Yes, Commander." Rankil departed the Gretchencliff's Powder barracks, taking the wide, silent paces she'd been taught. Though the light hurt her inflamed eyes, she walked straight toward her destination, facing the rising sun, her head held high. Her station allowed for nothing less.

The Tekkroon medical facility rested deep inside the volcano, in one of the larger multi-colony hubs, which Rankil entered and exited the finely tiled medial before morning business began. The infirmary's elderly gentlewoman clerk greeted her and led the way to a small room furnished with nothing more than a tall lounger, shelves and a chair.

"Make yourself comfortable." The clerk lit the hanging lantern. "They'll be in shortly."

"They?" Rankil draped her cloak over the chair.

"Yes, they," replied the gentlewoman, pulling a pillow and blanket from the shelves. "Now take your boots off and lay back. You Barrier types are always short on sleep."

"What—" began Rankil, but the clerk pointed to her boots.

"Short on sleep *and* patience. Off with the boots." The clerk pulled the curtain. She had been correct. Rankil was tired and in pain. Her head only eased when she lay still with her eyes shut. She tried not to think, but the silence tempted her mind to wander and wander it did, thoughts on Myrla's well-being and how Hestra must have grown in the four moon cycles since the Serpent clan's refuge arrival at the Tekkroon border. Recca had insisted on Myrla's return and Harlis, for the sake of peace and trade, had reluctantly agreed. The reserved Serpents were small in number, but their combat abilities were legendary, an allegiance between the two clans necessary in light of Longpass's increasing attacks. Rankil fell asleep in mid-consideration of this and maintained an agitated slumber until the Gretchencliff senior healer woke her.

"Trooper Rankil?" Rankil grabbed the hand that touched her cheek.

The woman touched Rankil's other cheek with her cool, soft fingers. "Calm down and catch your breath. We've much to do this morning."

"Greetings, Healer Augustus." Rankil released her grip to peer at the healer and her golden, chin-length curls. "You brought company this time. I'm aware I can be a difficult patient but—"

Augustus's full, reddened mouth smiled at the observation. "I've patched you up enough to know you can be an aggravation but not about this. You have a serious condition which eludes me to the point I require assistance." She indicated her companion, who studied the scroll containing Rankil's medical history. "Healer Garrziko is more versed than I on concerns of the head. Shall we let her have a go?"

"Why not." Rankil found it hard not to return Augustus's jovial grin. "Anything of interest in my scrolls, Healer Garrziko?"

"You're young for such a lengthy file." The scroll curled in Garrziko's palm. "Evidence of gross malnutrition, extensive scarring, both indicative of the extensive physical and psychological abuse of a misplaced sister. How's your head today?"

"No worse than usual." Rankil attempted to sit upright, but Garrziko placed a hand to her shoulder, easing her back against the lounger.

"And what is usual?" Garrziko motioned for Augustus to bring the lantern close, raising the light level until Rankil winced. "Are we normally light sensitive?"

197

"I noted mild sensitivity during my last two examinations," said Augustus.

"So there's been progression." Garrziko felt Rankil's head, mapping the cranial features with her fingers.

"It used to come and go, but now it's become constant, sometimes to the point I get dizzy and nauseous." Rankil jerked from Garrziko's probing grasp. "Let go. Augustus has already done that and got nothing."

"You know how healers are." Garrziko said half-jokingly. "If it hurts we have to do it twice." She turned to Augustus and nodded, as if endorsing some previously discussed diagnosis.

"Healer Augustus will be leaving us now." Garrziko, with laggard movements, took the lantern and followed Augustus to the doorway where she spoke into her ear then closed the door and rehung the now dimmed lantern. "Well, Trooper Rankil, now there's just me and thee." Garrziko settled in the chair, lounging back, her legs crossed at the ankle. "Tell me about the recent occurrences in your life."

"As in?" Rankil rolled to her side to view the healer's inquisitive expression.

"What has happened since you became Tekkroon?"

"Too much." Rankil's aggrieved sigh prompted Garrziko to look critically at her.

"Expand on too much."

"I'm the junior in a Powder Barrier Squadron. Need I say more?"

"That'll keep you hopping, but there must be more. What else has changed in your life?"

"Shouldn't this be on my scroll?" Rankil shrugged then cleared her aching throat. She had vowed never to speak of what Garrziko asked. It made her think of love and that made her angry, causing her head to ache all the more.

"If it does not concern the biological it is not registered in Tekkroon medical scrolls. Social issues are addressed separately so you must enlighten me." She remained silent while Rankil stared ahead, refusing to address what troubled her mind.

"Silence says more than you know." There was no prodding in the statement, merely recognition.

"Don't toy with me. Everyone knows what happened." Rankil's hands drew into fists. "It was the talk of the Gretchencliff. Where were you?"

"I am not Gretchencliff," stated Garrziko. "I am McDougal." She flicked up the end of the bright tartan draping her shoulder. The tartan crossed her chest and wrapped her waist kilt-fashion. Rankil thought it looked childish on a broadback, but the dark streaks in the healer's short crop suggested anything but childishness. "Hence the plaid and the ignorance to an apparently very public display. Did this happen before the community?"

"Where else would it?"

"Did someone you care about reject your affections in a public fashion?"

"Might be easier if she had."

Garrziko raised her brows. "I suspect you don't mean that. Tell me what happened."

The healer being easy to talk to and their situation private, Rankil recounted what had occurred that evening in the round, speaking in accusing tones of Recca's sudden appearance, Harlis's senseless explanation and Medrabbi's heartfelt apology. Jefflynn had said the mate match just hadn't been in the cards (whatever that had meant). Myrla had sobbed. Hestra had screamed. Rankil, restrained after she had rushed, knife drawn, toward Recca, had watched her family escorted from the round and the Tekkroon clan. Recca wanted no part of a misplaced sister who thought herself worthy a family at the age of sixteen. If the Tekkroon wanted her they could have her. The Serpents would not recognize the union. Garrziko remained silent while Rankil spoke, focusing on her body language, the tightness in her jaw, the tension in her shoulders and her fisted hands.

"Look at yourself." She finally interrupted from her reclined position, "View the manner in which you're laying. You're balled, curled in on yourself with every muscle braced against an anticipated blow. No wonder your head hurts. You've spent so much of your life on the defensive that relaxation is unfeasible."

"No, my first Taelach raisers had me speak on my upbringing. They believed it would help sort my emotions. Lot of good it did." Rankil brought her legs around to sit upright, shrugging out the knots in her shoulders. "I still have night terrors, days on end I can't sleep. And if that wasn't enough, they take my Myrla! Damn the Serpents! And damn the Tekkroon for not stopping it!"

"You're mad at far more than the clans," said Garrziko. "And, yes, your adoptive raisers did well in keeping you talking. It has aided on a certain level. You've been able to function normally thus far."

"You call double vision normal?" Rankil glared at the healer.

"Comparatively speaking, yes." Garrziko strummed the chair's curving arm. "I think it might do well to see what could occur without such guidance. It's not something I typically show my patients, but you might benefit." She rose in a manner that suggested she loathed anything besides utter repose. "Are you ready?"

"To leave here? Need you ask?" Rankil bounded into her boots.

"Leave your cloak," said Garrziko with a lazy wave to the outer passage. "We can reach our destination through the inner tunnels. We'll return for your wrap later. And leave your blade behind as well." Garrziko seemed insistent. "It could bring trouble where we're going." She led the way through a maze of narrow passageways, suggesting Rankil memorize the course as key tunnels led to the cavern squares of all the Tekkroon colonies. When they were deep indeed inside the volcano's belly, they paused at the barred, guarded entrance to a small cavern.

"You must understand," Garrziko waited while the sentry unlocked the heavy gate. "I am not the same type of healer as Augustus. I am an emotional healer. I deal with diseases of the mind."

"Diseases of the mind?" Rankil took a quick step back. "Are you saying I'm—"

"No, no. Quite the contrary, I intend to show you just how much in your right mind you actually are." The guard swung the door back and Garrziko stepped through, looking back to insure it was secured behind them. "Dee?" she called. "You about?"

"Be with you shortly."

"That's fine." Garrziko turned up a dimmed lantern by the entrance. "Did we beat everyone up?"

"Nearly," called Dee, this time in a voice closer to their location. "Brighten things up for me, will you?"

"We will." Garrziko pointed to a dim glow in the room's center. "Help me turn up the lights and raise the wheel, Rankil. This place is dismal in the dark."

Rankil did as asked, remaining silent, apprehensive and somewhat nervous that Garrziko might leave her in this barred, clean-smelling hole. But, when the flames brightened, and the lanterns were raised, the cavern became pleasant—the stone walls painted with vibrant outdoor scenes, the space attractively arranged with lounging sofas, chairs and tables, the stone underneath covered by rich rugs. It was a luxurious space, very unlike the simple furnishings in the majority of Tekkroon housing.

"Impressive, isn't it?" Dee stepped from one of several carved side chambers. She was an almost Autlach-short, older broadback with a stomach that declared her love of food and thin hair that could not hide the massive spider-web scar on the back of her head. "Ziko said you'd be visiting today. Have you breakfasted?"

"No." Rankil still focused on the odd space she occupied. "Where are we? It has an infirmary's smell." She turned to Garrziko. "I don't think I like it here. You're not going to leave me, are you?"

"Only for the day." Garrziko draped over one of loungers. "I'll retrieve you when I return from my rounds."

A sudden, cursing wail from one of the side chambers made Rankil grab for her absent knife.

"Don't be alarmed, Rankil, is it?" Dee placed a laden tray on a side table. "That's just Easton's way of saying good morning."

"Wha . . . what's wrong with Easton?" The veins in Rankil's temples throbbed in time with her quick pulse.

"The same as everyone else who inhabits this cavern." Garrziko sipped from the mug Dee had given her. "Relax, I wouldn't be dining if we were in peril."

"How many live here?" Rankil's eyes darted about the ornate chamber.

"Forty-three." Garrziko blew the steam from her mug. "Twenty-nine broadbacks. Fourteen gentlewomen. Only twelve are allowed free roam of the common cavern. You'll meet them soon enough. They'll be rising as it suits them."

"And you best eat before they do," added Dee as she distributed rolls onto small plates. "Everyone here eats like it's to be their last meal." She grinned and patted her midsection. "Me included."

"I'm not hungry." Rankil swirled the contents of the mug warming her hands.

"Nonsense." Dee laid a plate of rolls by Rankil's elbow and took a seat in an opposite chair. "Everyone must eat."

"But what about the others?" Rankil fingered a roll then licked away the sugar it had left on her hand. "Aren't they allowed in the common area?"

"Only with an attendant," stated Garrziko around a bite of her own breakfast. "You won't have much to do with them. Easton is the one I really want you to meet. You and she have quite a bit in common."

Dee turned to give Rankil a long, respectful look. "If you've been through half what Easton has you have my sympathies, as well as congratulations for persevering." She glanced to Garrziko. "Survivor or not, Easton might well hurt her. Should I use the restraints?"

"Would be prudent," said Garrziko. A shuffling sound turned the healer's head, and she smiled, rising to greet the sound's creator. A slim gentlewoman with frizzing hair stood in the doorway to her room. She approached the breakfast table, withdrawing when Garrziko extended a greeting hand toward her.

"Good morning, Shaedra. Meet Rankil." Shaedra peered at Rankil with an expression somewhere between terror and fury. She took the plate and cup Dee offered her and settled at a table a safe distance away.

"Excellent, Shaedra," praised the healer. "You're becoming efficient at controlling your flight instinct."

"This one is damaged goods, too," Shaedra muttered in mid-attack of her meal. "She here to stay?"

"No, just visiting." Dee placed a cloth napkin by Shaedra's elbow. "And you're not damaged goods, Shae."

"All right then, I'm an overly cooked bit of meat." Shaedra jerked back her robe to reveal the scars where her breasts had been. "They said burn witch burn, and that's exactly what I did. Clear to the bone in a couple of spots. You ever been burned, girl?" She asked Rankil.

"A few times." Rankil could see that three fingers on Shaedra's left hand had been reduced to discolored nubs.

"Like this?" She held out the charred extremity.

"Rankil has other scars." Garrziko placed her steady hand on Rankil's arm. "She was raised Autlach."

"Another Easton?" Shaedra took up her breakfast and scurried toward her room.

"There goes Shae, running like the scared hopper she is." A towering broadback swept in from another room. "Ignore Shaedra's foul manners, my young friend. We've all been burned in one way or another. Easton included. Shaedra merely forgets such things in her panic." The tall woman plopped down on the foot of Rankil's lounger and proceeded to pull on her boots, which, Rankil noted, were Powder Barrier standard issue.

"Rankil, meet Beverlic." Dee passed Beverlic a plate and mug. "And she's right about Shaedra. Her experiences won't allow her to associate with others, including those who now care for her."

"Severe incapacitating paranoia." Garrziko pulled from her

203

lounger, stretched, then shook out her kilt. "I have patients to see. Rankil, Dee will be your guide the rest of the day. Simply do as she says, especially around Easton. Bev, you are looking well this morning. How about enlightening our visitor with your reason for residing here."

"I like the atmosphere." Beverlic shrugged. "Beats the barracks, eh, junior." She tugged Rankil's rank patch.

"Your actual reason, Beverlic." Garrziko drifted toward a barred passage. "Until evening," she called back, and the bars slammed shut behind her.

"Lonely sound, isn't it?" Beverlic traced the glaze on her roll. "Junior, I'm here because, well"—she cast Dee an exasperated look—"it's the Mother's injustice and my bane. I'm here because my mind can't seem to stay where my body is."

"It's defined as flashbacks." Dee rose to refill their mugs then redeposited herself in a nearby chair. "Beverlic sometimes can't separate past events from the present. She relives them in graphic detail."

"And they're all gruesome battle memories." Beverlic sighed. "I was a good officer in my day. But now I never know what might bring the memories on or how I'll react to them. Lost my post and my family to it." Beverlic ducked her head in embarrassment. "Any more, I can go for days that way."

"Like a waking nightmare?" queried Rankil, alarmed by the realization her own traumatized mind occasionally cast similar flashes.

"Waking nightmare is a good description." Dee rose as several more women emerged from their rooms. They were introduced, some acknowledging Rankil's presence, others ignoring her entirely. Only one, a hollow-eyed gentlewoman terrorized by Rankil's Autlach accent, became aggressive, and Dee and Beverlic removed her to a smaller common area deeper in the stone.

"Just until she calms." Dee assured Rankil. "And it won't be the first time she's been removed for such behavior."

Rankil began to understand why Garrziko had brought her to

this disturbing place. She saw herself in many of the occupants. Shaedra's distrust, Beverlic's flashbacks, both were part of her own makeup. The conversation around her was light, even cheery, with everyone making light of their own maladies, but Rankil could not participate nor did she want to. The weight of her aching head threatened to pull it from her shoulders. Dee was there when the pain became blinding, placing a cold cloth on the back of Rankil's neck while Beverlic shooed the others to the opposite end of the cavern.

"Rankil?" Dee held a cup to her acidy mouth, encouraging her to drink. "Garrziko thought you might need this." The liquid had a bitter medicinal taste, but Rankil downed it, soon finding the pressure in her chest and head easing, so much so she momentarily dozed, awakening to Beverlic's appraisal of her relaxed state.

"She's better, Dee. Come have a see." She leaned over Rankil, removing the cloth from her neck.

"I'm fine." Rankil shook her head. It must have been her head, for it was attached, though numb and distant, to her shoulders.

"Yes, your color isn't near as washed." Dee held another cup to her mouth, just strong tea this time, and insisted she drink. "Get up and walk about while you do. It'll clear your head."

"Don't believe my head has ever been so clear," replied Rankil, but she stood up anyway and was pulled about by Beverlic.

"Ziko would be pleased by your reaction." Beverlic propped her against the wall where Rankil leaned, panting, her head against the cool painted stone.

"Pleased?" Rankil peered at Beverlic from the corner of her eye.

"Yes, pleased." Dee dabbed a cloth across Rankil's temples. "A non-reaction would have indicated you were beyond help."

"But the others?" Rankil turned until she faced the pudgy broadback. "Am I to sink to their—"

"Level of insanity, depth of withdrawal?" suggested Dee. "It appears not. Garrziko brought you here to shock your system, to force you into realizing you must take control."

"Control?" The tea calmed Rankil's turbulent stomach.

"Of yourself, dear girl." Garrziko, who had been listening from a hallway, crossed the cavern to stand by Rankil's side. "Your past is encroaching on your present, so much so your mind will eventually lose the ability to differentiate between the two."

"Is that what causes my headaches?"

"That and simple stress." Garrziko led Rankil to a lounger. "You have put a tremendous burden on yourself. You try to block out your tragic beginnings, but they keep coming back to leave you feeling unloved even when rejection is not the intention."

"Love brings pain, and I'll have no more of it." The rehearsed words came from Rankil's mouth, but now they had no meaning. "I'll have—"

"One cannot live without love." Garrziko sat sideways in an overstuffed chair, her legs thrown across one arm. "Didn't you love Myrla?"

"Yes, and now she's gone. And so is Kaelan and Jewel and baby Hestra." Rankil's chin rested heavy on her chest. "I couldn't stop what happened to Kaelan and Jewel, but I still had Myrla and Hestra. My headaches all but stopped when we were together so it must have been right."

"You held onto them because they were tangible," said Dee. "They were a physical something to show your worth, that you were loved. When they were taken you felt rejected again."

"But we were a family!" wailed Rankil, letting out a gut-deep sob. "A real family. I wasn't the convenient slave, the pitied misplaced sister in need of basic teachings so she'd be acceptable to her own people. I was Rankil! Strong, steady Rankil! I found game when others returned empty-handed. I worked hard to make things right. And everything was falling into place. I was worth something. I was important! I was needed! And then . . . and then . . ." Rankil's tired face began taking on a new, educated expression. "I held on too tight. Something had to give and no amount of work was going to stop it. I've always worked for something outside my reach, worked to keep away the beatings that came anyway, worked

206

to keep away hunger that was always there, worked because I was trying to be an adult, and adults are supposed to work."

"And now you're still working." Garrziko motioned behind Rankil's back for Dee to ready a room. "You're working to overcome the obstacles set before you since your arrival in this world."

"There're so many." Rankil could not resist when she was led to the space made for her. "What'd you put in that tea?"

"Nothing that hasn't already lost effect." Garrziko eased her onto a bed stacked with generous pillows. Dee removed her boots. Beverlic was somewhere in the background, urging Rankil to, for once, listen to her inner needs. She needed rest, uninterrupted, dreamless slumber of the type she had experienced her first night with Granny Terry.

"What about Easton?" She heard herself mumble as they pulled a blanket to her shoulders.

"She'll be here when you wake." Garrziko watched as her patient returned to her curled position.

"But my post. The Barrier. I thought I would be allowed to leave."

"You're not a prisoner." All but Garrziko had departed, and the healer again lounged, almost wilting into the chair at Rankil's bedside. "And your post will be there when you return. You're not the first nor will you be the last Powder Barrier trooper to inhabit this room on a temporary basis."

"Oh. How many of them have been misplaced?"

"Just you." Garrziko pulled a pilta from her robe, lit the leaf and inhaled before continuing. "Easton was never in the Barrier. She barely learned the Taelach tongue before she completely snapped."

"Snapped? As in broke?"

"Her past overcame her present. And snapped is a cruel term, unprofessional of me really. She couldn't help it, just as you cannot."

"Am I to—snap?"

"Certainly not. Your illness has manifested as unceasing

207

headaches, your mind's cry for help. Easton had no noticeable symptoms. She was a diligent student, learning Taelach, even had a gentlewoman who fancied her."

"What happened?"

"The young woman had a change of heart. Easton felt rejected, and it boiled inside her until it steamed over. She abducted the gentlewoman and demonstrated her distress in the only way she knew how. She killed the girl."

"But I know better," whispered Rankil.

"Do you? How many fights have you been in as of late? And I understand the last one was quite brutal, that it took three to pull you off your challenger. Easton thought she was in control, too. Then her early torment came back to complete the damage. It frequently does with misplaced sisters."

"So how do I prevent it from returning to me?" Rankil was desperate to finish the conversation before sleep overtook her.

"We examine your past and recognize how it's affecting your now."

"I don't like the sound of that."

"It isn't pleasant, but it is healing." Garrziko flicked her pilta ashes into her hand then, with a comforting pat to Rankil's arm, drew to her feet and loped to the door, calling back over her shoulder before she exited. "Sleep. If anyone deserves a respite, it's you."

In complete agreement, Rankil fell asleep before the door shut.

Chapter Seventeen

When experience is compared to experience, there is much to learn.

—*Sarah Garrziko*

Easton Outbrook had a brilliant mind, one that rationalized murder as acceptable reciprocation, but a brilliant one nonetheless. The thick, amber glass blinder covering her eyes was locked about her head, preventing her phase from hurting those who tended her needs. The blinder, along with wrist and ankle tethers, kept her restrained during her first meeting with Rankil.

"Garrziko says you grew up like I did." Easton blew at a strand of hair that lay across her binder. "Fun, wasn't it?"

"Fun?" Rankil glanced up at Dee who stood behind Easton's chair.

"Yeah, fun. Unpredictable, exciting." Easton tilted her head back and forth, timed by some unheard beat. "Savage."

"I'd hardly call my beginnings exciting."

"Where's this girl's sense of adventure, Dee?" Easton ducked her head enough to brush the pestering hair from her face. "She's too serious. Let me loose so I can make her laugh."

"I doubt she'd enjoy your sense of humor," responded Dee. "Besides, I still remember last cycle's little incident."

"Your fault." Easton carefully crafted her words to remove any sense of blame. "You saw my chinstrap was loose and chose to ignore it."

"I didn't ignore it. You bit through the leather before I could get a replacement over your head." Dee maintained a pleasant tone. "And we're not here to discuss your escapades. We're here—"

"I'm no idiot, Dee Dee," shouted Easton, cracking her head against the chair back. "She's here because she knows the game. She, like I, has played and won. We're both victors. Comrades in disfigurement."

"I'm not your comrade in any regard." Rankil rose from her seat. "There is no point in this. Dee, can I go?"

"Anytime you wish." Dee unlocked the room's metal reinforced door.

"Come back." Easton bore her teeth in frustration. "Ah, damn you both for making me conform. All right, I'll cease being obtuse if you'll just stay a while." Easton's face became falsely complacent. "Come back, please. I get bored by myself."

Rankil looked about Easton's stark quarters then retook her seat as the door clicked locked behind her. "I suppose it would get lonely in here."

"It's called the Pit for a reason." Easton relaxed in her restraints. "Your family big?" She asked in Autlach.

"Not overly." Rankil responded in kind. "Three brothers, one sister. My uncle had the big family. Eight, no, nine. Quyley was carrying another when I left."

"Auts breed like hoppers." Easton shook the same annoying strand from her face. "How many you take out before you left?"

"Take out?"

"You know, exterminate, cut down, pick off. How many did you kill?"

"Why, none." Rankil took Easton's knitted brows for disappointment. "My father sent me to care for one of my elders. She was blind and—"

"And you killed her for sport." Joy returned to Easton's face.

"No, she was good to me."

"Then what did you do to get revenge?" Easton pointed to herself. "I poisoned the well with nassie shit and dead hoppers. You should have seen it. They crawled about for days, clutching their bellies and moaning, begging me to help them when they couldn't walk. I helped them all right." Easton grinned in a malicious, twisted manner. "I gave them fresh, cool well water, as much as they could hold. Then I watched them die." She glanced up at Dee. "A deal is a deal. Garrziko said—"

"Finish the tale," said Dee in perfect Autlach.

"I believe I've heard enough—" began Rankil, but Dee cut her off as well.

"Easton will finish."

"Easton doesn't want to, you web-headed moron. Screw the both of you. Go away if it suits you. We could care less." Easton bent her head to her chest and began speaking to herself.

"Then I'll finish for you."

"This ought to be interesting," mumbled Easton, immediately back to her self-conversation.

"Easton buried them in the Aut manner," Dee said in a mocking tone. "Then she came to the high hills and the Tekkroon. End of story."

"Methodical, boring and so fucking wrong it hurts," panted Easton. "I didn't bury a damned one of them. I sat them around the table like I did every evening, cooked a meal, and then I sat at the table with them and ate."

The strange confession rang true. Rankil had often envisioned herself equal to her siblings, eating alongside them. Easton was no different. She had just made it happen in her own manner, her own deranged, morbid manner.

"I never ate with my family," said Rankil when Easton began fidgeting.

"Well, I did, and that's not the half of it." The chinstrap could not limit Easton's grin. "I tried on everyone's finest clothes, used all their combs, rolled in their beds and then," Easton held her breath in anticipation, "then I did everything to them they had done to me, by whip, pole, chain and whatever else I could find I gave them lash for lash what they'd given me."

Rankil remained silent, staring at her boots. Her constant headache, rested by a day and a half's sleep, was reduced to a wishy-washy sensation between her ears. "I always wanted to do those things," she said in Aut, then abruptly switched her speech to Taelach. "But I never thought of killing them."

"Never?" queried Dee, still in Autlach, very close to her ear. "You never once considered it?"

Easton drew her mouth in annoyance. "She's scared to admit it."

"I'm scared of nothing!" Rankil drew up in her chair, locking eyes with Easton in a brief test of wills.

"Yes, you are!" Easton bounced against her ties. "You're still scared shitless of your fucking Aut family. They're days from here, but they still have a hold on you."

"Shut up!" Rankil flew from her chair, her hands flexed for Easton's ivory throat. Dee pulled her back into her chair.

"She's right." Dee grasped Rankil's fist in mid-air, sending it smashing against the chair arm. "I'm not the enemy. Your fear is. Admit to it, and it'll be easier to handle."

"I'm not scared! I could outfight any of one of them!" Rankil's right hand remained clenched.

"But all of them?" Dee whispered in her ear. "All at once? You knew what would have happened if you'd lashed out, and fear of that situation is what kept you from doing so."

Rankil stared ahead. "Most of them I could have fought one at a time, all my brothers together. My father Danston would have been tough, but never . . . I never could . . ."

"Never could what?" Dee pinned Rankil's arms to the chair. "Never could what?"

"I couldn't fight off my uncle!" Rankil fell limp in her seat. All her strength was gone, and she was once again in need of rescue. The scars on her face and arm throbbed. "He had me facedown on a bedroll, whipped me until I couldn't move and then . . . then . . ." The realization of what had happened came hurtling back. She'd longed to die, wished to die, but she'd been spared. Spared by Archell!

"Archell saved me. He killed Tisph. Killed his father for me."

"For love of you." Dee released her grip. "And you say you have no one to love you. Sounds to me that Archell has given you the ultimate in love. Where is he now?"

"Yeah." A seldom seen lucidity flared in Easton's eyes. "Not half-bad for a damned Aut."

"He's winnolla under Lisajohn, Bowriver's music maestro." Rankil sniffed. "I need to speak to him. I have to thank him."

"And you will." Dee fished for her keys. "Good job, Easton. Your reward will come tomorrow."

"It will or I'll pinch your little head off," hissed Easton in full return to her typical status. Then her expression switched again, and she looked at Rankil. "Kid, you think you had it so rough, don't you? Well, I had three uncles, and I didn't have an Archell."

"I suppose I was lucky."

"Damn right you were," Easton mumbled then she began to shake. First, she appeared near tears, but then a laugh rose from her, a bitter, hollow laugh that soon became uncontrollable.

"Look at me!" she shrieked. "Telling someone they should thank an Aut, a fucking man at that!" She let loose a scream of lost control then pulled a dangling lock, tearing it from her head. "Nice or not, girl, don't ever turn your back on him or any other Aut." Easton's vacant gaze followed the lock to the floor, where it lingered, fixed on the blood droplets which clung to the roots. "'Cause you'll bleed if you do."

213

Part V
Anew

Chapter Eighteen

Quit searching. You'll find what you need when you really need it.

—Rankil Danston

———————————

Rankil's nineteenth summer found her again in the hills with Archell, the duo filling their bellies with fresh berries. Mountain berries were tarter than those they'd grown up eating, but that was all right. Berries were berries, and they were far from the only available food source. Not knowing her actual birth date, Rankil had proclaimed the breezy summer day her claiming anniversary and was taking advantage of the off day. Archell had requested the holiday as well and was picking over a laden bush, searching for the ripest fruits.

"Berry time, Archell?" Rankil lobbed a sunburst berry at his tunic.

"Yes, Rankil dankle, berry time." He returned the throw, splatting a rotten berry against her elbow.

"Did it have to be a sour berry?" she moaned, flicking the seeds from her sleeve. "I'll never get the stain out."

"Save yourself pain, have Abbyegale wash the stain." He popped a handful of berries into his mouth.

"Abbyegale is my friend, Archell, a friend who won't do my laundry under any circumstances. Believe me, I've tried."

"And Clarrina and Quinnway?"

"Friends, too, though Quinnway longs for more."

"Quinnway's looking for in ways?" Archell teased his snow-headed cousin. Rankil always dodged the approaches of eligible gentlewomen. She remained polite but resistant to them all, saying her heart and mind weren't ready for it.

"Quinnway volunteered to scrub the battle sweat from my back. That tell you anything?"

"Yes," he laughed, pummeling her with another berry. "Quinnway is still single, which makes Archell want to mingle."

"You go right ahead but count me out. My life is complicated enough without a relationship," Rankil swiped at her tunic as she looked down the slope at the closest guard tower. "You through gorging or are we going to waste the entire afternoon in this patch?"

"I'm through." The Autlach drew his hand across his mouth then, pointing at the tower, came to stand beside her. "So many towers, the scene it sours."

"There are eighty-seven last I heard, plus another forty or so portable stands that rotate about. Even the fields are guarded when they're being tended." Rankil shook her head. "It's a sorry day when the fields are no longer safe." She peered up the slopes. "You know what I really want to do today?"

"Dine on the cake Abbye said she'd make?"

"No, that'd be you. Let me show you what I'm wanting." They trekked to the top of the slope and there, Rankil pulled her cousin down on the grass. Archell knew her requirement and soon they were laying head to head, each resting on the other's shoulder, watching the cumulus clouds float by.

"Rankil dankle?" He patted her head. "Did you hear them say that Taelachs come from far away?"

"That we come from the stars? Yes. And considering my discovery winter before last, it's possible." Rankil returned his pat, feeling the tight braid he now kept his hair in.

"Did Harlis like what you dared share?"

"I'd say. Never heard so many hallelujahs before," she replied, chuckling. "Such finds seem to be a cause for celebration and work. They dug around the thing until they could move it. It took forty, count them, Archie, forty nassie teams to pull it from the ground."

"That is a lot, Rankil dankle. Have you seen it since?" Archell rolled a grass stem between his fingertips.

"Yes, the technicians," Rankil still stumbled through the lesser-used Taelach words in her vocabulary, "they had me show them everything I knew. Then they shoved me out the main hatch and haven't let me near since."

"And the weapons to which you were drawn?" he prompted, drawing the grass between his thumbs. He held the wedged stem to his mouth and blew out, vibrating the blade until it whistled.

"The weapons smiths are trying to duplicate them." Rankil's attempt at copying his whistle left her hand wet and the grass sticking to her upper lip. "Darn it." She pulled the stem from her mouth. "Why can't I do that?"

"You're no musician." He whistled again, proving his point. "Plus you spit when you should hum."

Rankil tried again with a fresh blade, and again, she coated it in saliva. "Ah, well," she laughed, slapping the soggy grass from her palm. "I've no musician's delicacy, and you've no mind for war. I guess that makes us even."

"I think I've the better," he said with a stretch. "You've seen too much fighting in too much bad weather. It can't be good for my Rankil dankle."

"On the contrary," Rankil sat up. "Battle practice has proven most therapeutic. Lets me play out my aggressions in a constructive manner."

"And does battle for real still hold its appeal?" He pointed to her bandaged forearm.

"Garrziko taught me to separate my battlefield actions and my childhood from all else in my life, review them in my meditations, considering each action, its outcome and my emotions when it was occurring."

"Garrziko has taught you much, but she failed to teach you to duck." He again indicated her arm.

"A lucky shot from a man who didn't know he was dead." She flexed and twisted the arm to show him there was no actual damage. "I heal quick these days. Meditations seem to help that, too."

"They are kind to the mind. But how long is your healing time?"

"Tired of me already?" Rankil teased her cousin. "I get another three or four days. Maybe five if the infirmary is backed up again."

"Then?" asked the Autlach, raising his brows at her shrug.

"Then I go where all good soldiers go, wherever I'm needed."

"That simply?"

"That easily."

"No questions?"

"A Powder Barrier trooper does not question her post."

"Oh." Archell scratched his head. "You are right, Rankil dankle. I have no mind for such grind."

"And I'm glad of it." Rankil began descending the slope. "Come on, Archell. Abbye did say something about a sweet cake, didn't she?"

Archell trotted to her side. "A massive sweet cake is yours for the take."

"With a home-cooked meal to match?"

"Food and friends until the day ends."

Rankil picked up her strides. "Can't be late for that. Race?"

Archell buzzed past her. "At your pace you'll have to chase!"

"Cheat!" But Rankil held back, letting him win this one. The competition wasn't important, the companionship was something her heart, her forlorn heart needed.

❧

Morning muster found Rankil quite refreshed, having spent a relaxing afternoon and evening in the celebratory company of friends, the night in restful sleep, the dawn in meditation. She heard her assignment, then, musket in hand, rapier at her hip, crossbow and quiver strapped to her back, she set out for one of the lower pastures. Tower duty in the fields was easy, reserved for those recovering from minor injuries. Her stand was already in place so she shimmied up and was in position when the harvesters emerged from the trees surrounding the field.

The harvesters, mostly gentlewomen, a few with infants strapping their backs, came from several different clans which relied on Tekkroon support. They all greeted Rankil with waves. Tekkroon guards, with their expertise, always made one feel safe and Powder Barrier troopers, with their loud, metal throwing weapons, doubled the sense of security. Rankil maintained the reassuring presence expected of her, hovering over the workers' heads, their only protection should Longpass's ranks break the borders.

Genevic, who'd also suffered a mild injury, relieved her at noon. They exchanged brief pleasantries at the tower's base then Rankil made her way back to the Gretchencliff Colony for the midday meal and an infirmary appointment. Healer Augustus proclaimed her wound almost healed and scheduled her stitches to be removed two days later. This suited Rankil and, after she returned to the barracks, she was lounging on her bunk, taunting the newest junior when Genevic returned from her post.

"Seems you have another admirer." She threw a folded scrap of writing hide onto Rankil's chest. "Pretty girl, but very shy, almost as if she was scared to talk to me."

Rankil glanced down at the scrap. "Another one? That's the third in as many days."

"They love us Barrier types." Genevic draped her cloak over the bedstead then hopped onto the top rack, shaking Rankil's bed with her landing thud. "We're irresistible in uniform."

"You maybe. I just wish they'd leave me alone."

Genevic's skinny face popped into her view, its grin upside

down. "You're an odd sort, Rankil, but I like you anyway." She retreated then reappeared, Genevic's braids catching on her great nose as she spoke. "Say, what do you single types do on quiet evenings like this? Isabella has been assigned to do health education and vaccinations in the refugee clans so I'm alone the next few nights."

"You two ever going to make a home?"

"When we're ready. Probably by summer's end." Genevic, stifling the sneeze her braids had tickled out, reached down, all but sliding from her bunk as she grabbed the folded scrap from Rankil's chest. "Isabella wants you to her room for dinner, with a date. How about this girl?"

"Give me that." Rankil snatched the note from her bunkmate's palm. "It's for me."

"Then read it already!"

Rankil did so, then, with a quiet smile, shoved the note under her pillow.

"Well?" queried Genevic, her upside down face grinning.

"Well, nothing." But Rankil's contented expression suggested otherwise.

"You're not going to tell me?"

"No."

"Does she at least spark your interest?"

"Possibly."

"I hate it when you're cryptic."

"I know." Rankil crossed her arms behind her head and closed her eyes. Genevic, knowing she'd never coax the information from her quiet comrade, dropped to her feet, grabbed her cloak and left.

"Odd sort, likeable, but odd." She called back as the door creaked shut. "Odd and quiet."

As soon as she was gone, Rankil reached under her pillow, pulled out the note, and read it again, tracing the words as she read.

"Myrla," she whispered, filled by the temptation to crow the proud news. "She's turning eighteen!"

Rankil received permission to skip morning muster, and after some quick trading with the duty commander, was able to duplicate her previous day's post, reaching the field just after dawn. She had taken a scrubbing bath the night before, and, though Genevic was no barber, her bunkmate had trimmed her hair. She was the picture of broadback availability, her leathers cleaned, her cloak pressed smooth between her bedroll and bunk platform. Breakfast had been out of the question—her stomach had been too knotted.

The harvesters straggled to the field in groups of three to five behind the small cart that would carry their endeavors back to their clans. Having no fields of their own, they brought in crops on contract, every basket of white root they took paid for with two for the Tekkroon's huge stores. Rankil acted as the Tekkroon representative in this regard, counting the baskets placed in the carts under her stand, assuring everyone did as agreed.

Three basket-wielding gentlewomen caught Rankil's attention early on. None wore the smaller clans' customary headscarves of paired gentlewomen, and they were all about Myrla's build but when none of these proved to be Rankil's true beloved, she became frustrated and disappointed as noon drew near. She was scanning the tree line as her duty required when a pair of gentlewomen donning the scarves came to their cart to sharpen their hoes. The first scraped her hoe to a gleaming point then passed off the hone and returned to work. The second worked slower, cleaning her hoe before honing it, humming off-key as she worked. It wasn't the discord that caught Rankil's attention, it was the tune. It was one of Archell's!

"My?" Rankil glanced down between the slats in her stand.

"Rankil!" Myrla wanted nothing more than to close the distance between them, but she dared not. "I thought I saw you yesterday, but I couldn't be sure. Your replacement said she knew you and promised to give you a message. I'm glad you received it."

"You're wearing a headscarf."

"I'm promised."

Rankil's heart sank. "Then why approach me?"

"I'm being forced to take a partner."

"Can't you talk to whoever took over your raising?"

"Recca is my raiser."

The name still angered Rankil. She paused, separating the emotion from her now before she continued. "Baby Hestra?"

"Well. Given to a family that had lost a baby to influenza."

"Oh." Rankil glanced about. No one had noticed their conversation. "Who is she?"

"Huh?" Myrla had stopped honing.

"Who're you promised to?"

"Leonor."

"Jewel's old beau?"

"Leonor requested me shortly after Recca brought me back. Her way of finally defeating Kaelan, I suppose. She lost her gentlewoman during the crossing and wants me as a replacement. I've run twice, but Leonor caught me both times. Now Recca promises to kill you if I do, and Leonor keeps such a close eye on me when we're together—"

"So there's no love between you two?"

"Possessiveness on Leonor's part but no love. I'm only wearing the scarf because Recca keeps me cavern-bound if I don't. I could never love anyone but you." Myrla peered up between the stand's slats to see Rankil's sparkling blue eyes peer back.

"And I you. Does Recca have a fire scheduled tonight?"

"Every evening, weather permitting." Myrla looked away as they were no longer alone. The elder broadback who approached held up three stacked baskets, placing one in her clan's cart and two in the Tekkroon wagon. Rankil nodded confirmation and the broadback shuffled off again with three empty baskets on her shoulder.

"I'll be there," whispered Rankil as soon as it was safe.

"At the fire? You're an outsider. You won't be allowed."

"I am Powder Barrier," boasted Rankil while twirling her musket. "I have unlimited access to all Tekkroon holdings, and the Serpents are technically on Tekkroon lands."

"You won't be safe." Myrla pretended to retie her sandal lacings. "Recca won't allow your name to be spoken. She calls you a misplaced abomination."

"How else am I to challenge Leonor for your hand?"

"Don't. Leonor is a seasoned warrior."

"As am I."

"As you are what?" Genevic appeared under the stand. "Hello, again." She smiled at Myrla. "I promised you I'd deliver the message."

Rankil jumped from her perch, landing beside Myrla. "Genevic, meet Myrla."

"*The* Myrla?" exclaimed Genevic in delighted surprise. "You're right, Rankil, she is a beauty." Then she frowned. "But promised by the headscarf she wears today. Illicit liaisons are not advisable, my friends, especially one involving a Serpent's woman. They kill for such things."

"And I'll kill to keep her," said Rankil in a low, determined voice.

"I've no doubt you would." Genevic accepted Rankil's boost up the stand. "But you should have a second for a challenge."

"That's not a rule." Rankil began counting baskets, a continued reason for her presence.

"It's my rule." Genevic frowned down between the slats. "Only an ignorant sister throws a challenge in a foreign clan without backup, and seeing as you're not ignorant—"

Rankil felt fortunate to have such a steadfast friend. Myrla did, too, and smiled up at the skinny broadback. "Genevic, would you come with Rankil?"

"Thought you'd never ask." And all was in place for Myrla's liberation.

"Will you wait up? I'm on light duty because of my knee, remember?" Genevic trotted to keep up with Rankil's hurried gait. They were just outside the Serpent encampment, faint shadows against a moonless night. "Rankil." Genevic cursed the Autlach who'd caused the ache in her leg. "We have to check in with the watch."

"Why should we?" protested Rankil over her shoulder. "We're Powder Barrier."

"The Powder Barrier is not above manners." Genevic pulled up the hood of Rankil's cloak. "If you're going to do this, then do it right. Give them no reason to doubt your sincerity."

"I've never been so serious about anything in my life." But Rankil turned toward where the watch stood, leaning on their spears. "Good evening." The watch stiffened and glanced about.

Genevic stepped up, pushing Rankil behind her. "We humbly request audience at your fire."

"For what reason?" queried the tallest of the pair, eyeing their uniforms as she spat pilta juice.

"None of your—" began Rankil, but Genevic elbowed her hard.

"It is a delicate matter intended for the clan leader's ears." Genevic bowed slightly, honoring Recca's mention.

"Recca says there's to be no outsiders." The second guard, squat and somewhat bent at the midspine, frowned. "But the Tekks say that isn't supposed to apply to you Barrier types. Let me check." She wheeled about and jogged toward the background glow.

"We'll wait." Genevic nodded at the remaining guard who scowled, turning the glower on Rankil who grinned brazenly back.

"You Powder heads all think you're something special." Pilta spit splattered against Rankil's boot leather. "I say you're nothing without your muskets. All noise, no skill. So much hype for so little ability."

Rankil kept silent, grinning beneath her hood until her teeth stood out, knowing it infuriated the guard. Genevic nudged Rankil again, urging her to be chivalrous. The momentary standoff ended as the second guard returned.

"Recca says to make it short. She's indulging you because you're Powder heads."

"As long as she permits it," said Genevic, again forcing Rankil behind her.

"Hey!" Rankil whispered as they walked. "What's with taking over? This is my problem."

"Have you ever seen a mate challenge?"

"No."

"Then shut up and follow my lead."

Unable to argue with such logic, Rankil straightened and stared ahead.

The Serpents, downed to a mere thirty-six in number during their escape to the volcano bowl, surrounded a sand ring where a small bonfire lit their tired faces. Rankil scanned the group for Myrla, not finding her where Recca's mats were located but instead sitting, her knees to her chest, beside an older, sullen broadback with close-set eyes. One of her arms circled Myrla's slim waist. Myrla pulled against the hold, creating a gap the broadback would close by jerking Myrla close again. Myrla would mumble something, the broadback would reply in a venomous tone then the process would repeat, Myrla pushing away again. Rankil kept her instincts in check while Genevic addressed Recca.

"The Tekkroon send their greetings, Serpent leader Recca, and their wishes for continued—"

"What is it the Tekks want?" said Recca in an acid tone. "And why can it not wait until morning?"

"We are sorry for the hour," started Genevic, but Recca's eyes hardened with distrust.

"Out with it, then be gone. The Tekkroon have most of my warriors, half my nassie stock. What do they require now, my gentlewomen for their beds?"

Of all the times for Recca to say such a thing, thought Rankil, observing the emancipated manner in which Myrla was regarding her. She expected this night to end in Rankil's arms, and Rankil would settle for nothing less.

"We come concerning a sensitive matter," Genevic was saying. "One that is best discussed in private."

"There are too few of us left for anything to be personal." Recca folded her arms across her chest. "Speak before us as a whole."

"As you wish." Genevic bowed. "The young are determined creatures, their hearts becoming so wrapped in the doings of love that they seldom think of the consequences. They—"

"You're challenging a Serpent?" bellowed Recca before Genevic could continue. "You're challenging outside your own clan?"

"Humbly, clan leader Recca, it is not I who challenges. It is my companion." Genevic indicated Rankil, who remained deep in her hood. "Her heart cries for Myrla."

"Myrla is mine!" Leonor leapt from her mat. "Recca's promised her to me. Who dares challenge such an arrangement?"

"I do." Rankil stepped forward, pulling back her hood to glare at Leonor in a possessed manner. "Myrla and I were together long before Recca offered her to you. I have right of first claim."

"You!" Recca's hand clenched her blade. "You had a child's fascination and an unhealthy one at that. No abomination will claim a Serpent. I'll not have it."

"I've no wish to engage you, Recca." Rankil stepped back. "But forced committal is outdated, slavery for the woman it is pushed upon. It makes us no better than Auts."

"You speak of Tekkroon liberties." Recca sheathed her blade but kept her hand close. "Myrla is a Serpent by birth, and now she is promised to a Serpent warrior. Leonor has nassies, gold and status. What do you offer, girl, besides inexperience and the terrored beginnings of a misplaced sister?"

"I bring friendship, love, knowledge of Myrla's hopes and dreams." Rankil watched Leonor crouch in a fighting posture. "I bring a heated home in a Gretchencliff family community she already knows. What more could you want for her?"

"You've said nothing of wealth, girl." Recca's condescending tone revealed her intentions never to release Myrla, not to a Tekkroon, not to one so young, never to someone with the reputation of a misplaced sister. "Have you monetary security?"

"I have over a pass of unspent credits in my account."

"Worthless outside Tekkroon borders," spat Leonor, flashing the numerous gold bracelets circling her arms. "Enough questions, Recca. Let me kill her so we can return to our discussion."

"No, no fighting yet. I'm still trying to determine her right to challenge at all. What else do you offer, girl?"

"She doesn't have to prove herself worthy to challenge." Genevic stepped to Rankil's side. "You know she's inexperienced in the ways of the challenge, and you are using it to question her ability, which is to your advantage. The only criterion is a willingness to fight for what she desires. Rankil has that. The challenge should take place. Now!"

"Perhaps it should at that." Recca's mouth twisted into a grin. "Clear the sands." And they were as Rankil was of her cloak and knife, Leonor of her hatchet and dagger.

"The rules of the challenge are but one," Genevic told Rankil as she took her cloak. "There's to be no outside assistance." She laid her hand on Rankil's shoulder. "Leonor's aging. Losing this challenge will cost her social standing and what may be her last chance for a family. She's fighting for her life."

"And I'm fighting for Myrla's," replied Rankil in a low, thoughtful tone. Her eyes were open, but she was meditating, preparing her mind and body for what might happen. She could not lose control.

Recca called the competitors to the sand, placing them a dozen paces apart. Myrla stood an equal distance between them. "You have two claims for your affections." Recca told her. "One is a valued member of your clan." She indicated Leonor. "She is wise, strong and will provide for you. The other," she waved at Rankil, "is a lowly foot soldier of an outside clan. You can resolve this conflict without bloodshed by following your clan leader's and raiser's wishes. Choose Leonor, and there will be no bloodshed."

"You won't put the blame on my head." Myrla pulled off her headscarf and moved to Rankil's arms. "My emotions were clear, but you still promised me to Leonor, a decision that would have landed your best warrior dead by my hand before I slept in her bed. You forced this fight. Any injury is your doing."

"And your loss," replied Recca in a foreboding tone. "Separate from your choice, Myrla. She must defend your foolish heart."

Myrla did so after she and Rankil exchanged quick whispers and kisses. Wikkib motioned to Myrla, and she joined Wikkib on her mat, glad to be in the company of another anxious someone. Wikkib, orphaned just before her eighteenth pass and too old to be assigned another raiser, had never taken a partner, detesting the Serpent's tendency to suppress their gentlewomen.

"Your Rankil will win." She smoothed the hair escaping her own uncovered braid. "She has a true heart on her side. Leonor is greedy, trying to replace a mate who barely tolerated her in the first place."

"Mother pray you're right." Myrla gripped Wikkib's hand.

In the circle, Rankil and Leonor exchanged words, Rankil's calm and curse free, Leonor's vile, personal and disjointed.

"Bitch child! Insignificant waste of the Mother's time!" Leonor kicked up sand as she paced. "No scar-faced baby is going to cheat me out of what's mine!"

"She's not a belonging." Rankil remained still, watching her opponent's movements, the slight paralysis that slowed her left arm, the manner in which she kept reaching for her absent weapons. Leonor was reliant on her arsenal, as was Rankil, giving neither the advantage in this fisticuff.

"Myrla has freely chosen me." She eyed the other woman's punch-ready hands. "Why not give her what she wishes? If you cared you'd listen."

"I'll have none of your conspiracy! What's mine is mine!" Leonor spanned the distance between them in a single stride, delivering a heavy downward blow Rankil avoided. She returned the strike with a solid uppercut that stumbled her adversary back a pace. Leonor shook her head a few times then lunged again, this time landing a punch to Rankil's jaw. Rankil remained toe to toe with her, returning Leonor's well-placed hits until Leonor dropped, one leg sweeping out to knock her off-balance. The move proved successful, and Leonor took the lead, kicking Rankil's legs from beneath her when she attempted to rise.

"Blasted, annoying little misplaced bitch!" Leonor spat in her face. "I've yet to lose a battle!"

"There's a first time for everything." Rankil grabbed Leonor's leg, twisting as she pulled to flip her onto her stomach.

"Yes!" Myrla's cheer prompted a fierce glare from Recca. "You forced me to choose my champion," Myrla called to her. "You'll not deny me the right to cheer her on!"

Recca took a step toward her then turned, distracted by the fight. Leonor was in trouble, her head in a lock that could easily snap her neck. As it was, Rankil was choking her into unconsciousness. When she fell limp, Rankil released her hold and stood. "To the winner go the spoils. Myrla is mine."

"I cannot deny you victory." Recca's disappointment repeated throughout the Serpents. Leonor was a valiant fighter, the trainer of warriors. For her to lose was a blow to Serpent integrity, shaking their dwindling numbers to the core. But when Recca turned to retrieve Myrla, a small movement caught her eye. Leonor's open palm closed, gathering a fistful of sand. Recca, smiling ever so slightly, extended her hand to Myrla whose round eyes saw nothing but Rankil. Rankil's eyes were transfixed as well, until Leonor threw the handful of sand into them. Rankil dropped to her knees, and Leonor launched into her, striking her so hard she fell prone upon the circle. Myrla ran onto the sands, but Recca caught her about the waist.

"A challenge is not finished until the victor has hold of her prize. Rankil doesn't have you." She glanced at Leonor's vicious assault on her disabled foe. "And she never will."

"Unfair!" cried Genevic, charging onto the circle. "No weapons!"

"Sand is not a weapon," Recca replied with referee's decisiveness. "It is the ground beneath our feet—or in our eyes. Rankil made the mistake of assuming Leonor was incapacitated, a decision she is paying dearly for. I suggest you leave, trooper, and explain to your superiors why one of their own won't be returning."

"This is a murder!" Guards forced Genevic from the Serpent fireside. She could see Rankil, one arm covering her stinging eyes, trying to fight back. But what good were such moves when one couldn't see and the enemy moved so quickly? Leonor bounced from one side of Rankil to the other, hitting then bounding away, laughing at Rankil's feeble retaliations until one succeeded, throwing her from the circle.

"Enough play!" Leonor grasped Rankil by the shoulder, throwing her beside the fire. "Feel the heat, girl?" The hairs on Rankil's head singed. "Feel your death?" Leonor cracked the back of Rankil's head repeatedly against the firestones. The observers cried shock, the majority turning away from the sight. Rankil convulsed then collapsed, her blood soaking the sands beneath her head as her chest ceased to rise.

Myrla sobbed when it ended, falling hard against Recca in her own wish to die. The watch held down Genevic, who bellowed for Rankil to keep fighting.

"Bring my winnings." Leonor extended her hand to Myrla.

Recca looked at Myrla, whose breath sounds were ragged and shallow. "She's in no condition. I'm giving her to Wikkib."

"But I'm the victor!" relented Leonor, stepping to the edge of the sands. "Give her to me, Recca. I'm to have her this night."

"Not this night." Wikkib called two others to assist her as everyone else retreated to the living cavern and their beds. "It's late, Leonor." Wikkib placed some of Myrla's weight onto the women who aided her. "Myrla's ill. I'll care for her."

"But she's mine!" Leonor shook her head. "I defeated a challenger to get her. Nothing has changed. She's still mine."

"You killed her heart's desire," said Wikkib with a sympathetic stroke of Myrla's head. She turned from Leonor, blocking her reach. "Besides, you've a body to prepare for the death rights. We can't return it to the Tekkroon looking like it does. It would further the unfavorable light you've cast on the Serpents tonight."

"Recca?" said Leonor in a beseeching tone. "What of my rights?"

"Clean the body," Recca turned toward the cavern. "Then, go to bed. Alone. We'll finalize our arrangement when Myrla rises from her stupor."

"Let my objection be known, but I will abide by the clan leader's wishes. Wake me if she comes to before dawn. Her place is with me." Disappointed Leonor, her skull aching, several of her ribs quite possibly broken, stood over her victim while she watched the others drift toward the cavern.

"It's not fair." She dropped to one knee to inspect her handiwork. "This one's a waste of shrouding. And where is the shrouding, anyway?" She looked up. "Hey, where is—"

Her query slid from a cry of surprise into an ear-piercing scream. Rankil, despite the blood and sand blocking her sight, had grasped Leonor by the belt and flipped her forward, into the fire.

"Can you feel the heat, girl?" She rose to watch her opponent's dying gyrations. "Can you feel your death?" Leonor shrieked her answer, fully engulfed in flames as she rolled from the coals.

Recca called for water, but Leonor was gone before it could be brought.

Wikkib and the two others brought Myrla to Rankil, placing them together.

"The challenge is over when the victor holds her prize." Wikkib placed Rankil's arm around Myrla and stepped away. Rankil's knees buckled with the weight, and she fell back with Myrla, thudding against Recca who lowered them to the sands.

"I'm sorry." Rankil began drifting into unconsciousness. "Leonor was—"

"No match for a Barrier trooper with a misplaced sister's beginnings." Recca's pinched her nose against the stench rising from

233

Leonor's doused remains. She called for the watch to bring Genevic, then handed the pair off as something near mourning clouded her eyes.

"Perhaps it is time for the Serpents to petition the Tekkroon for full membership. We'd be a small colony, strict in our ways but a fighting one nonetheless. Maybe then I'd cease losing my best warriors." Recca turned to Wikkib.

"You're too flaming independent to be a Serpent. Assist the young lovers home then find a place within the Tekkroon depths, preferably with someone who understands your liberated rationale."

"Thank you." Wikkib helped Genevic load Myrla and Rankil into the small, nassie-drawn cart Recca called for, then, Rankil's head cradled in her lap, she rode toward the Gretchencliff colony, reciting an unusual verse she'd once heard, the words of which had never had meaning until that night.

"Note the winds of change for you never know what shores they'll send you toward."

Chapter Nineteen

Endings make for beginnings.

—*Myrla Rankils*

———————

Rankil remained bedridden for two moon cycles then, much to her dismay, the next cycle's movements were limited to short jaunts down the infirmary halls. "With assistance," stressed Augustus. "And be slow about it. We cannot risk reopening those cracks in your skull. They are knitting exceptionally well." Rankil would have ignored the restrictions had it not been for Myrla. Garrziko had successfully jarred her from her catatonia and since that point she had served as Rankil's nurse, leaving only when Archell, Genevic or occasionally Dawn coaxed her out for exercise.

On the day of Rankil's discharge from the infirmary, Archell arranged for a cart to carry them home. As they rode, he commented on the dreary atmosphere in the grotto appointed them.

"It's a new complex, Rankil Roo. It's sparse but it will do." He shrugged and squinted in what those who loved him knew as a signal of serious conversation. "It's first level, too, since Augustus said you weren't to walk far."

"Or do much else," murmured Rankil with a longing glance to Myrla. "Personally, I believe she's being overcautious." The cart's right wheel caught on a rock as she spoke, rattling her tender noggin until she winced. "But maybe she does have a point."

"Poor Rankil." Myrla extended her arm across the back of the driver's bench, creating a cushion Rankil could rest against. Rankil settled back and kept her eyes closed the remainder of the short trip, meditating away the discomfort.

"We're here." Archell announced their arrival in an excited tone he lowered when he looked back at his cousin's face. "Sorry, Rankil dankle."

"I'm glad to be home, too, Archie," she said in a quiet laugh. "Help Myrla out first. I'll be along in a moment."

"He'll do no such thing." Myrla slid from the cart and extended her arm again. "I've been caring for most all your needs for four cycles now so it's my arm you should lean on. This is, after all, our homecoming."

"So it is." Rankil knew Myrla well enough not to object, besides, Archell didn't seem to mind. He was already to the grotto's door, pulling the latch. He was seldom excited about anything, but this day he seemed ecstatic, one might say deviously so. Rankil wondered what he was hiding.

"Wait." Rankil paused just outside the threshold to catch her breath.

"You all right?" Myrla looked up. Rankil smiled back at her then with a sudden burst of energy, tossed her walking cane to the side, scooped Myrla into her arms, and stepped across the threshold. "Rankil!" shrieked Myrla, still in the air, "Augustus said—"

"No more healer's talk, My. We're home." Rankil placed her on her feet, and then looked about their new home.

"Dreary?" Delighted, she settled into the cushioned chair

Archell pushed her toward. "You lied to us, Archie. How unlike you."

"A little clever lie," he said with a grin. "If we'd asked you would have denied."

"Who's we?" inquired Myrla, fingering the curtains hanging over the grotto's glass window. The home was far from sparsely furnished. In fact, it was lavishly appointed, every inch of floor covered by a fluffy rug of some sort. And the walls! The typical dark stone walls had been whitewashed, highlighting the delicate landscapes painted on them. There was a bedroom and a spacious main room with a kitchen, complete with table and chairs. The sitting area they were in was at the room's opposite end, and it was plushest of all, furnished with a pair of large chairs flanked by a small table, a lounger of rich red velvet, and a set of shelves stacked high with precious hide scrolls. There were dozens, no, hundreds of scrolls! And there were blank hides for writing and delicate porcelain knickknacks. But most importantly, Kaelan and Jewel's image which Rankil had saved during her separation from Myrla had been framed and placed eyelevel on the shelves.

"Archie?" Myrla turned to him with tears in her eyes. "Who did all this? Who is *we*?"

"*We* would be the lot of us." Harlis stood in the doorway. Medrabbi and Elreese peeked over her shoulder and Genevic stood behind them, waving her arms. "You, my young friends," Harlis took a seat on the lounger, "You have become quite the celebrities."

"Celebrities?" Myrla stood behind Rankil's chair, one hand on her lover's shoulder.

"Yes, celebrities. Your romance has become the stuff of Tekkroon legend as well as trooper Rankil's discovery of the downed spacecraft," Harlis chuckled. "Why that little find has advanced us by centuries."

"You mean you've figured out all those thingamabobs?" Rankil tilted her head with interest.

"Me?" Harlis laughed merrily. "Not me. I'm far too cranky and close-minded for such modish thinking. I leave such doings for others." A small, throat-clearing sound turned Harlis's gaze toward the door. Wikkib had pushed to the front of the crowded doorway and was standing, one hand on her hip, looking expectantly at the Tekkroon clan leader. Her hair was short, all but as short as Harlis's and she wore hide leggings, which perfectly matched the low-cut Tekkroon top she wore.

"Rankil just came from the infirmary. For the Mother's sake, give her some space."

"You both know Wikkib." The grin never left Harlis's face. "Come sit a moment, my love, I'm just finishing up."

"That's good to hear, considering the wait outside." Wikkib pushed the door closed, then shared the lounger with Harlis, placing one hand upon her knee when she sat. "You were saying?"

"I was going to say a word or two about their new home. Plush, isn't it?"

"Very much so," agreed Wikkib. "But, as I have discovered, much of the Tekkroon live in luxury that I, until recently, had only dreamed of."

"It's the utmost in Tekkroon housing, running hot and cold water with drainage, two steam elements for cooking, lanterns that burn piped-in fuel, and best of all," Harlis pointed to the small door at the rear of the main room's kitchen area, "something I believe to be the greatest Tekkroon, quite possibly the greatest Taelach achievement ever—an indoor privy."

Archell laughed at the young couple's astonishment. "Augustus doesn't want Rankil walking too much."

"Are we the only ones with such luxuries?" Rankil felt unworthy her new accommodations.

"No," said Harlis, "but you are among the first. Currently only new constructions have such advantages, but with a quadrupling in the building rate there'll soon be many living as you are."

"Quadrupled building rate?" exclaimed Rankil. "I know the Tekkroon population is growing but—"

"You were incapacitated in the infirmary for over three moon cycles." Myrla reminded her. "A lot happened in that time."

238

"That much?"

"And more," said Wikkib. "The clans are converging, becoming one force, but Myrla will update you in due time, I am sure. Harlis, I say we leave the updating to others and say our good-byes."

"But—"

"Your dinner is waiting at home."

"Oh, then perhaps we should go." Harlis, her eyes lit with clear amusement, followed Wikkib to the door. She helped Wikkib with her cloak, then on the threshold with one hand low on Wikkib's hip, turned. "If anyone had ever told me Serpent gentlewomen were such delightful hotheads I would have encouraged Recca to join the Tekks long ago. Seems we both have our hands full, trooper Rankil."

"I know just what you mean." Rankil kissed the hand Myrla rested upon her shoulder then greeted their next visitors, Medrabbi and Elreese.

Elreese held out two loaves of black bread to them. "May your home always be filled with Tekkroon bounty," she said, and then motioned to Medrabbi, who produced a crystal of aged Gretchencliff wine from her cloak.

"And may your life be overflowing with the Mother's spirit." Medrabbi placed the crystal and bread on the dining table. "We won't monopolize your time. We only wished to see you settled."

"We are overwhelmed by the generosity," said Rankil. "Thank you."

"Yes," added Myrla. "Thank you ever so much."

"You're quite welcome." Elreese took Myrla by the arm. "Have you seen the bedroom yet?"

"I haven't had the opportunity."

"Well, take a moment now." Elreese whisked her into the bedroom and pulled the divider curtain. "Is your shoulder healing okay?" she whispered.

Myrla pulled back her collar to show the new inking. "It hardly hurts at all."

"I don't see any places I missed. What does Rankil think of it?"

"She hasn't seen it." Myrla took a second to peer about the room. It was a pleasant space, and she looked forward to the night.

"She hasn't seen it?" remarked Elreese in surprise. "Has the new already worn off?"

"No," said Myrla with a faint blush. "But there's little privacy in the infirmary."

"Say no more. Medrabbi spent more than enough time there herself when we were young." Elreese glanced about. "It is a nice space. Big enough for a cradle should you take a notion."

"Maybe someday. I think Rankil and I need time to ourselves first." Myrla smoothed the double bedroll over the sleeping platform.

"How different things would be had the Serpents not reclaimed you when they did." Elreese tossed the new hull pillows to the head of the platform.

"Hestra has good raisers now," replied Myrla with a bit of sorrow in her tone. "She doesn't remember either of us." Rankil's soft chuckle rose from the next room, lifting her spirits. "I suppose it's for the best."

"You say that in a most reflective, resigned manner," Elreese allowed, resting her backside against the clothing box. "There will be other children should you want them."

"We know."

"Reesie?" Medrabbi poked her head through the curtain. "You ready to go? I've a meeting at dusk."

"And I suppose you'll be wanting your dinner first?" Elreese jerked her thumb toward Medrabbi and rolled her eyes. "Broadbacks are walking stomachs, aren't they?"

"Taelachs are a large breed." Medrabbi tapped her chest. "Some bigger than others."

"Or at least we think we are," teased Elreese. "Come on, we'll eat in the common mess tonight."

"But, Reesie," whined Medrabbi, "I'm never sure what I'm eating there."

"Like you take the time to taste." Elreese gave Myrla's hand a squeeze then followed her partner out the door, waving farewell to Archell and Rankil as she went. Genevic appeared before the door could close.

"Up to a couple more visitors?" she asked in a happy voice.

"What took you so long?" Rankil beckoned her friend inside. "Haven't seen hide or hair of you in the last cycle. What's up? Single life got you down?"

"Who's single?" Genevic stepped inside, pulling along quiet Isabella. "I couldn't let my junior bunkmate beat me to the draw." She held a box in her other hand which she dropped in Rankil's lap. "A get well gift from your squadron."

"Very funny." Rankil held the contents, a helmet, up for the others to see. "Whose bright idea was this?"

"I dunno." But Genevic's smile revealed her own doings.

Rankil couldn't help but laugh. "I suppose I could wear it during mounted maneuvers."

"You, nassieback, with your head?" Commander Stiles's voice called through the cracked doorway. "Mind if I come in?"

"Please." Myrla pushed Rankil back into her chair when she attempted to emulate Genevic's attentive salute.

"Sit down." Stiles pointed to her splotched tunic and leggings. "It's my off day and Annya is having me fade out our grotto's walls. Seems to be all the rage." She glanced at the new apartment. "It does create a nice effect though. One might call it airy. But enough of me, how is my fissure-headed trooper doing these days? I had heard you got home. Thought I'd check in on you."

"I'm much improved, Commander Stiles." Rankil drummed her fingers over the helmet. "Was the gift your doing or Genevic's?"

"Not mine. Wish it had been though." Stiles snorted her amusement. "Pretty damned hilarious, unneeded though, considering what I came to tell you."

Rankil frowned. "Now I know I'm down for a while, Commander, but Healer Augustus assured me that I'll be the image of health in a few more cycles. Please don't—"

"Your place among the Barrier is secure," blurted Stiles before

Rankil could finish the plea. "In fact, I've come to deliver your transfer orders."

"Transfer orders?" Rankil's hand flattened against the helmet. "But—"

"But nothing, junior." Stiles's eyes flickered with mischief as she handed Rankil a scroll. "As soon as Augustus releases you for the lightest of duty you are to report to Technician Maeminya aboard the star craft. Seems she wants you to try and fly the thing."

"Me?" Rankil sat a little taller in her seat.

"You and one other." Stiles produced a second scroll from her cloak and passed it to Genevic. "Seems Rankil's reputation is well-known. Maeminya insisted on a copilot who could tolerate the pilot."

"Now that's a tall order, Commander." Genevic winked at Myrla then grinned at Rankil. "But I suppose I am up to the job."

"And it will keep you both from the battlefield." Stiles added. "Your women will appreciate that."

"To think," Myrla whispered in Rankil's ear. "You'll be flying."

"Who'd have thought?" Rankil tried to stifle a yawn, but it escaped anyway, alerting all present to her fatigue.

"Visiting is finished," said Myrla in a tone that no one dared argue with. "Rankil needs her rest."

"Time we were going anyway." Genevic drew Isabella to her feet. "Well, partner," she clasped Rankil's hand. "I'll be seeing you soon."

"For new training," said Rankil with a light sigh.

"Never ends, does it?" Genevic drew Isabella to the door, taking her to the home they could now without fear of separation enjoy as a couple.

Stiles glanced at the dwindling daylight when the door opened. "Annya should be expecting me for dinner about now," she said almost absently. "Try not to rattle that head of yours, Rankil." Then her face changed to full military decorum. "And, junior, don't go running off on any more challenges. They're bad for your constitution."

"I'll keep that in mind. Goodbye, Commander Stiles."

"Later, j—So long, Rankil." Stiles closed the door behind her.

"You have many good friends, Rankil dankle." Archell made his way to the kitchen. "Myrla, if you can get her to the bed, I'll fix a tray so she can be fed." He squinted. "Dawn brought some cheeses yesterday and Abbyegale dropped by with a pot of soup just before I left to get you."

"You're a blessing, Archie." Myrla followed Rankil's slow walk to the bedroom and helped her undress, assisting with her boots and leggings. Then, with her love safely in a nightshirt and between the blankets, she permitted herself a trip to the new privy. She had once used an experimental flushing privy near the Gretchencliff colony square, but had never dreamed the technology could be used on a wide-scale basis. The idea delighted her so much she had to pull the water release chain a second time, laughing aloud at the sound. She emerged from the water closet, washed her hands in the kitchen basin then returned to the bedroom. A dinner tray was waiting on her bedside table. "Where's Archell?"

"Gone home," replied Rankil through her mouthful of dark bread. "Said he'd stop by tomorrow after choral practice."

"Then we're finally alone?" Myrla dropped to the bed and removed her boots.

"Hello, what's this?" Rankil pushed her tray to the side and stared hopefully at her love's back.

"Your dinner will get cold." Myrla loosened her hair from its binder. "Rankil?"

"Huh?"

"Eat."

"How can I when—" Rankil sighed when Myrla stepped behind the dressing screen. "Prude."

"Am I now?" Myrla peeked around the screen, exposing the shoulder bearing her tattoo.

"Hey! You had my symbol inked!"

"Yes, and you'll have mine as soon as you're healed." Myrla stepped from behind the screen with a frumpy winter shirt hiding her curves. "Ready for sleep?"

"No," mumbled Rankil when Myrla sat on the side of the bed and began eating. "You know what I am ready for."

"Oh yeah?" Myrla pushed a phase that almost made Rankil drop her tray. *So, I'm a prude?*

I could be wrong.

Damn right you are. Myrla dropped her phase and began to eat. "Now, finish your dinner."

"Aw, My."

"Eat."

Tease.

Myrla rolled her eyes. *That's all I'll ever be if you don't eat.*

Rankil wolfed down her dinner then set the tray on Myrla's knees. "Finished."

"Well, I'm not."

"Then hurry up."

"Don't rush me."

"Myrla, come on."

"Why are you in such a hurry? Augustus said we're not to do that until you're better healed. No jarring motions, remember?"

"Please?"

"Would it be easier if I slept on the lounger?"

"You want me to beg?"

"Of course not." Myrla finished her meal then stacked their trays beside the bed. "Turn down the lantern."

"Might as well since you won't let me do what I want."

"Don't be hateful."

"Hmph." Rankil dimmed the light then lay with her back to Myrla. "Goodnight."

"Turn over." Myrla touched her shoulder.

"I'm comfortable as I am."

"I'm not, so please turn over." Myrla pushed up on one elbow.

"Geez, My. Can you be any more impossible?" When Rankil brushed Myrla's life braid from her face, Myrla grabbed her hand, placing it in a spot that would show her intentions.

"What?" Rankil rolled over.

"Don't you know?" Myrla moved Rankil's hand to her thigh. "What about this?"

"Myrla Rankils, you're naked under that shirt!"

244

"As the day I was claimed."

"But you just quoted Augustus' orders. What gives?"

Nothing gives, my beloved. Myrla threw back the covers to straddle her lover, pulling off the shirt as she encouraged Rankil to explore her. *Augustus said you weren't to jar yourself. I am much gentler than that.*

Is this some of that gentlewoman equality I've heard Wikkib talking about? There were no inhibitions between them now, no uneasiness, only desire to find what they both ached for.

You have a problem with the concept?

Definitely not. Rankil pushed Myrla down, drawing them together with the gentle swirl of her hips, deepening the contact with an arousing phase. Myrla clutched at Rankil's pillow then arched back, moaning as white-hot pleasure shot through her body.

Yes! Rankil's pulse quickened as Myrla pressed harder, grinding them into complete oneness. *Yes, My. Yes.*

Positively yes, panted Myrla in their mutual link. *More.*

Much more. Rankil pulled Myrla up until her breast touched her mouth, taking nips timed with the urgent pursuit of her fingers. She caressed the folds surrounding Myrla's clitoris, sliding between them then back, careful but persistent as she pushed against the final barrier between them. It soon gave way with a small shudder that remained lost in the pleasure and Rankil sank one then two fingers into her lover, relishing the wet that greeted her. *Much, much more.*

So continued the conversation until Myrla collapsed, quite tired and fulfilled, across Rankil's sweating body. "That was stunning." She ran her fingers up Rankil's stomach, stopping to run quick circles around her breasts. "Thank you."

"They say first impressions are the lasting ones. Did I say everything right?"

"And then some." Myrla slid back to Rankil's side, leaving their legs entangled as she placed her head against her lover's shoulder.

"My turn," she whispered and slid her hand between Rankil's legs.

"But—" Rankil's eyes rolled back, every objection concerning broadbacks not needing fading from her mind as Myrla began stroking her, deepening her phase, delivering a quivering peak that she repeated until Rankil lay a hand to her face.

"My head, we'd best—"

Myrla immediately dropped her phase and pulled back, her face awash with concern. "Did I hurt you?"

"No," assured Rankil with a smile. "I'm surprisingly pain free at present. We were just beginning to move too much."

"Oh." Myrla rested again on her chest. "Then I suppose it was best that we quit."

"I suppose." Rankil remained quiet for a moment then became troubled, worried by her lack of experience and the time they'd spent apart. "Was the phase all right? I never, I mean, didn't—"

"It was perfect. Thanks for saving it for me."

They lay in silence a while longer, Myrla reliving the pleasure in her thoughts as Rankil drifted in and out of sleep.

"Rankil?" Myrla's whisper roused Rankil from the depths of her contentedness.

"Yes?"

"Next time I believe you should wear the helmet. A little jarring might be fun." Myrla ran her leg up Rankil's, pausing at the rise of her hip before trailing back down.

"You know," replied Rankil. "It just might at that." She lay awake long after Myrla fell asleep against her, reliving the events that had brought them together then tore them apart just to bring them together again. This time would be enduring, Rankil was certain. They were respected members of a community, a community whose numbers were growing exponentially, a community on the brink of phenomenal change.

"Well, Rankil dankle," Rankil whispered to herself as healing sleep finally took hold. "You're one misplaced sister who won't be lost again." She kissed the top of Myrla's head. "You're pretty damn lucky, pretty damn lucky indeed."

Taelach Words, Clans and Slang Defined

Adner Colony. Small colony in the Tekkroon clan named for Andrea Adner, an early Tekkroon clan leader.

Aut. Taelach slang for Autlach.

Autlach. Indigenous species to Saria II, the second planet orbiting Sixty-One Cygni, short and stocky humanoid species with dark features.

battle braid. Taelach marker of battle victories and military rank worn in the hair.

birther. A Taelach trained in assisting Autlach women in giving birth to a Taelach child, slang term used to indicate an Autlach woman giving birth to a Taelach child.

blood marking. Tekkroon commitment ceremony (nuptials).

Bowriver Colony. Small colony in the Tekkroon clan named after the Bow River, the underground river which surfaces in the Tekkroon lands.

broadback. Woman who pursues a more masculine role in Taelach society.

gentlewoman. Woman who pursues a more feminine role in Taelach society.

Gretchencliff Colony. Largest of the Tekkroon clan colonies, named after Gretchen Taelakowski, founder of the Tekkroon clan.

grotto. Small cave or cavern used by Taelachs as a private residence.

ground mat. Small cloth and grass rugs used by the Taelach for sitting.

hopper. Rabbit-like creature hunted for its meat and fur.

Hunt. An organized pursuit and capture of Taelachs by Autlachs.

inking. A tattoo.

isolation cavern. Large caves used by the Tekkroon to temporarily quarantine Taelachs seeking asylum or membership within the clan.

knee skirt. Garment worn by Taelachs too young to choose broadback or gentlewoman status.

letcher bear. Large mammal indigenous to Saria II known for its soft fur and nauseating stench.

life braid. Taelach marker of family and clan affiliation worn in the hair.

mate challenge. Taelach custom where one may object to or defend a claim for another's affections using strict protocol.

McDougal Colony. Tekkroon clan colony named after Zuli.

McDougal a human refuge on Saria II and early supporter of the Taelach.

milker. Nassie used to provide milk.

Mother Maker. Taelach religious figure, comparable to Gaia.

nassie. Three-toed llama-like mammals used by the Taelach and Autlach for meat, wool, riding and as beasts of burden.

phase. Telepathic process used by the Taelach.

pilta. Sarian tobacco-like plant with a slight narcotic effect.

The Pit. Tekkroon clan psychiatric facilities.

Powder Barrier. Elite of Tekkroon clan military forces, named for the black powder long-rifles they carry.

Raskhallak. Popular Autlach deity that openly condemns the Taelach.

recognition. Tekkroon clan ceremony that establishes a woman as a broadback.

Saria II. Second planet orbiting Sixty-One Cygni.

sister. Term of endearment and/or respect used by Taelachs when addressing other Taelachs.

Serpents. A small Taelach clan known for its fighting skills and stringent moral doctrine.

Sixty-One Cygni. A yellow dwarf star in the Milky Way thought to be similar to Earth's sun.

Taelach. A subspecies of the Autlach who are all are born female, pale-skinned, willowy in build, sterile and telepathic.

Tekkroon. The largest and technologically superior of the Taelach clans.

whitehair. Autlach derogatory slang for the Taelach.

winnolla. An Autlach male or female, generally of rare musical or artistic talent, who lives among the Taelach.

THE KILLING ROOM by Gerri Hill. 392 pp. How can two women forget and go their separate ways?   1-59493-050-3 $12.95

PASSIONATE KISSES by Megan Carter. 240 pp. Will two old friends run from love?
                                                                                1-59493-051-1 $12.95

ALWAYS AND FOREVER by Lyn Denison. 224 pp. The girl next door turns Shannon's world upside down.   1-59493-049-X $12.95

BACK TALK by Saxon Bennett. 200 pp. Can a talk show host find love after heartbreak?
                                                                                1-59493-028-7 $12.95

THE PERFECT VALENTINE: EROTIC LESBIAN VALENTINE STORIES edited by Barbara Johnson and Therese Szymanski—from Bella After Dark. 328 pp. Stories from the hottest writers around.   1-59493-061-9 $14.95

MURDER AT RANDOM by Claire McNab. 200 pp. The Sixth Denise Cleever Thriller. Denise realizes the fate of thousands is in her hands.   1-59493-047-3 $12.95

THE TIDES OF PASSION by Diana Tremain Braund. 240 pp. Will Susan be able to hold it all together and find the one woman who touches her soul?   1-59493-048-1 $12.95

JUST LIKE THAT by Karin Kallmaker. 240 pp. Disliking each other—and everything they stand for—even before they meet, Toni and Syrah find feelings can change, just like that.
1-59493-025-2 $12.95

WHEN FIRST WE PRACTICE by Therese Szymanski. 200 pp. Brett and Allie are once again caught in the middle of murder and intrigue.   1-59493-045-7 $12.95

REUNION by Jane Frances. 240 pp. Cathy Braithwaite seems to have it all: good looks, money and a thriving accounting practice . . .   1-59493-046-5 $12.95

BELL, BOOK & DYKE: NEW EXPLOITS OF MAGICAL LESBIANS by Kallmaker, Watts, Johnson and Szymanski. 360 pp. Reluctant witches, tempting spells, and skyclad beauties—delve into the mysteries of love, lust and power in this quartet of novellas.
                                                                                1-59493-023-6 $14.95

ARTIST'S DREAM by Gerri Hill. 320 pp.When Cassie meets Luke Winston, she can no longer deny her attraction to women . . .   1-59493-042-2 $12.95

NO EVIDENCE by Nancy Sanra. 240 pp. Private Investigator Tally McGinnis once again returns to the horror filled world of a serial killer.   1-59493-043-04 $12.95

WHEN LOVE FINDS A HOME by Megan Carter. 280 pp. What will it take for Anna and Rona to find their way back to each other again?   1-59493-041-4 $12.95

MEMORIES TO DIE FOR by Adrian Gold. 240 pp. Rachel attempts to avoid her attraction to the charms of Anna Sigurdson . . .   1-59493-038-4 $12.95

SILENT HEART by Claire McNab. 280 pp. Exotic lesbian romance.

1-59493-044-9 $12.95

MIDNIGHT RAIN by Peggy J. Herring. 240 pp. Bridget McBee is determined to find the woman who saved her life.   1-59493-021-X $12.95

THE MISSING PAGE A Brenda Strange Mystery by Patty G. Henderson. 240 pp. Brenda investigates her client's murder . . .   1-59493-004-X $12.95

WHISPERS ON THE WIND by Frankie J. Jones. 240 pp. Dixon thinks she and her best friend, Elizabeth Colter, would make the perfect couple . . .   1-59493-037-6 $12.95

CALL OF THE DARK: EROTIC LESBIAN TALES OF THE SUPERNATURAL edited by Therese Szymanski—from Bella After Dark. 320 pp.   1-59493-040-6 $14.95

A TIME TO CAST AWAY A Helen Black Mystery by Pat Welch. 240 pp. Helen stops by Alice's apartment—only to find the woman dead . . .   1-59493-036-8 $12.95

DESERT OF THE HEART by Jane Rule. 224 pp. The book that launched the most popular lesbian movie of all time is back.   1-1-59493-035-X $12.95

THE NEXT WORLD by Ursula Steck. 240 pp. Anna's friend Mido is threatened and eventually disappears . . .   1-59493-024-4 $12.95

CALL SHOTGUN by Jaime Clevenger. 240 pp. Kelly gets pulled back into the world of private investigation . . .   1-59493-016-3 $12.95

52 PICKUP by Bonnie J. Morris and E.B. Casey. 240 pp. 52 hot, romantic tales—one for every Saturday night of the year.   1-59493-026-0 $12.95

GOLD FEVER by Lyn Denison. 240 pp. Kate's first love, Ashley, returns to their home town, where Kate now lives . . .   1-1-59493-039-2 $12.95

RISKY INVESTMENT by Beth Moore. 240 pp. Lynn's best friend and roommate needs her to pretend Chris is his fiancé. But nothing is ever easy.   1-59493-019-8 $12.95

HUNTER'S WAY by Gerri Hill. 240 pp. Homicide detective Tori Hunter is forced to team up with the hot-tempered Samantha Kennedy.   1-59493-018-X $12.95

CAR POOL by Karin Kallmaker. 240 pp. Soft shoulders, merging traffic and slippery when wet . . . Anthea and Shay find love in the car pool.   1-59493-013-9 $12.95

NO SISTER OF MINE by Jeanne G'Fellers. 240 pp. Telepathic women fight to coexist with a patriarchal society that wishes their eradication.   ISBN 1-59493-017-1 $12.95

ON THE WINGS OF LOVE by Megan Carter. 240 pp. Stacie's reporting career is on the rocks. She has to interview bestselling author Cheryl, or else! ISBN 1-59493-027-9 $12.95

WICKED GOOD TIME by Diana Tremain Braund. 224 pp. Does Christina need Miki as a protector . . . or want her as a lover?   ISBN 1-59493-031-7 $12.95

THOSE WHO WAIT by Peggy J. Herring. 240 pp. Two brilliant sisters—in love with the same woman!   ISBN 1-59493-032-5 $12.95

ABBY'S PASSION by Jackie Calhoun. 240 pp. Abby's bipolar sister helps turn her world upside down, so she must decide what's most important.   ISBN 1-59493-014-7 $12.95

PICTURE PERFECT by Jane Vollbrecht. 240 pp. Kate is reintroduced to Casey, the daughter of an old friend. Can they withstand Kate's career? ISBN 1-59493-015-5 $12.95

PAPERBACK ROMANCE by Karin Kallmaker. 240 pp. Carolyn falls for tall, dark and . . . female . . . in this classic lesbian romance. ISBN 1-59493-033-3 $12.95

DAWN OF CHANGE by Gerri Hill. 240 pp. Susan ran away to find peace in remote Kings Canyon—then she met Shawn . . . ISBN 1-59493-011-2 $12.95

DOWN THE RABBIT HOLE by Lynne Jamneck. 240 pp. Is a killer holding a grudge against FBI Agent Samantha Skellar? ISBN 1-59493-012-0 $12.95

SEASONS OF THE HEART by Jackie Calhoun. 240 pp. Overwhelmed, Sara saw only one way out—leaving . . . ISBN 1-59493-030-9 $12.95

TURNING THE TABLES by Jessica Thomas. 240 pp. The 2nd Alex Peres Mystery. *From ghosties and ghoulies and long leggity beasties* . . . ISBN 1-59493-009-0 $12.95

FOR EVERY SEASON by Frankie Jones. 240 pp. Andi, who is investigating a 65-year-old murder, meets Janice, a charming district attorney . . . ISBN 1-59493-010-4 $12.95

LOVE ON THE LINE by Laura DeHart Young. 240 pp. Kay leaves a younger woman behind to go on a mission to Alaska . . . will she regret it? ISBN 1-59493-008-2 $12.95

UNDER THE SOUTHERN CROSS by Claire McNab. 200 pp. Lee, an American travel agent, goes down under and meets Australian Alex, and the sparks fly under the Southern Cross. ISBN 1-59493-029-5 $12.95

SUGAR by Karin Kallmaker. 240 pp. Three women want sugar from Sugar, who can't make up her mind. ISBN 1-59493-001-5 $12.95

FALL GUY by Claire McNab. 200 pp. 16th Detective Inspector Carol Ashton Mystery. ISBN 1-59493-000-7 $12.95

ONE SUMMER NIGHT by Gerri Hill. 232 pp. Johanna swore to never fall in love again—but then she met the charming Kelly . . . ISBN 1-59493-007-4 $12.95

TALK OF THE TOWN TOO by Saxon Bennett. 181 pp. Second in the series about wild and fun loving friends. ISBN 1-931513-77-5 $12.95

LOVE SPEAKS HER NAME by Laura DeHart Young. 170 pp. Love and friendship, desire and intrigue, spark this exciting sequel to *Forever and the Night*. ISBN 1-59493-002-3 $12.95

TO HAVE AND TO HOLD by Peggy J. Herring. 184 pp. By finally letting down her defenses, will Dorian be opening herself to a devastating betrayal? ISBN 1-59493-005-8 $12.95

WILD THINGS by Karin Kallmaker. 228 pp. Dutiful daughter Faith has met the perfect man. There's just one problem: she's in love with his sister. ISBN 1-931513-64-3 $12.95

SHARED WINDS by Kenna White. 216 pp. Can Emma rebuild more than just Lanny's marina? ISBN 1-59493-006-6 $12.95

THE UNKNOWN MILE by Jaime Clevenger. 253 pp. Kelly's world is getting more and more complicated every moment. ISBN 1-931513-57-0 $12.95

TREASURED PAST by Linda Hill. 189 pp. A shared passion for antiques leads to love. ISBN 1-59493-003-1 $12.95

SIERRA CITY by Gerri Hill. 284 pp. Chris and Jesse cannot deny their growing attraction . . . ISBN 1-931513-98-8 $12.95

ALL THE WRONG PLACES by Karin Kallmaker. 174 pp. Sex and the single girl—Brandy is looking for love and usually she finds it. Karin Kallmaker's first *After Dark* erotic novel.
ISBN 1-931513-76-7 $12.95

WHEN THE CORPSE LIES A Motor City Thriller by Therese Szymanski. 328 pp. Butch bad-girl Brett Higgins is used to waking up next to beautiful women she hardly knows. Problem is, this one's dead.
ISBN 1-931513-74-0 $12.95

GUARDED HEARTS by Hannah Rickard. 240 pp. Someone's reminding Alyssa about her secret past, and then she becomes the suspect in a series of burglaries.
ISBN 1-931513-99-6 $12.95

ONCE MORE WITH FEELING by Peggy J. Herring. 184 pp. Lighthearted, loving, romantic adventure.
ISBN 1-931513-60-0 $12.95

TANGLED AND DARK A Brenda Strange Mystery by Patty G. Henderson. 240 pp. When investigating a local death, Brenda finds two possible killers—one diagnosed with Multiple Personality Disorder.
ISBN 1-931513-75-9 $12.95

WHITE LACE AND PROMISES by Peggy J. Herring. 240 pp. Maxine and Betina realize sex may not be the most important thing in their lives.
ISBN 1-931513-73-2 $12.95

UNFORGETTABLE by Karin Kallmaker. 288 pp. Can Rett find love with the cheerleader who broke her heart so many years ago?
ISBN 1-931513-63-5 $12.95

HIGHER GROUND by Saxon Bennett. 280 pp. A delightfully complex reflection of the successful, high society lives of a small group of women.
ISBN 1-931513-69-4 $12.95

LAST CALL A Detective Franco Mystery by Baxter Clare. 240 pp. Frank overlooks all else to try to solve a cold case of two murdered children . . .
ISBN 1-931513-70-8 $12.95

ONCE UPON A DYKE: NEW EXPLOITS OF FAIRY-TALE LESBIANS by Karin Kallmaker, Julia Watts, Barbara Johnson & Therese Szymanski. 320 pp. You've never read fairy tales like these before! From Bella After Dark.
ISBN 1-931513-71-6 $14.95

FINEST KIND OF LOVE by Diana Tremain Braund. 224 pp. Can Molly and Carolyn stop clashing long enough to see beyond their differences?
ISBN 1-931513-68-6 $12.95

DREAM LOVER by Lyn Denison. 188 pp. A soft, sensuous, romantic fantasy.
ISBN 1-931513-96-1 $12.95

NEVER SAY NEVER by Linda Hill. 224 pp. A classic love story . . . where rules aren't the only things broken.
ISBN 1-931513-67-8 $12.95

PAINTED MOON by Karin Kallmaker. 214 pp. Stranded together in a snowbound cabin, Jackie and Leah's lives will never be the same.
ISBN 1-931513-53-8 $12.95

WIZARD OF ISIS by Jean Stewart. 240 pp. Fifth in the exciting Isis series.
ISBN 1-931513-71-4 $12.95

WOMAN IN THE MIRROR by Jackie Calhoun. 216 pp. Josey learns to love again, while her niece is learning to love women for the first time.
ISBN 1-931513-78-3 $12.95

SUBSTITUTE FOR LOVE by Karin Kallmaker. 200 pp. When Holly and Reyna meet the combination adds up to pure passion. But what about tomorrow?
ISBN 1-931513-62-7 $12.95

GULF BREEZE by Gerri Hill. 288 pp. Could Carly really be the woman Pat has always been searching for?
ISBN 1-931513-97-X $12.95

THE TOMSTOWN INCIDENT by Penny Hayes. 184 pp. Caught between two worlds, Eloise must make a decision that will change her life forever. ISBN 1-931513-56-2 $12.95

MAKING UP FOR LOST TIME by Karin Kallmaker. 240 pp. Discover delicious recipes for romance by the undisputed mistress. ISBN 1-931513-61-9 $12.95

THE WAY LIFE SHOULD BE by Diana Tremain Braund. 173 pp. With which woman will Jennifer find the true meaning of love? ISBN 1-931513-66-X $12.95

BACK TO BASICS: A BUTCH/FEMME ANTHOLOGY edited by Therese Szymanski—from Bella After Dark. 324 pp. ISBN 1-931513-35-X $14.95

SURVIVAL OF LOVE by Frankie J. Jones. 236 pp. What will Jody do when she falls in love with her best friend's daughter? ISBN 1-931513-55-4 $12.95

LESSONS IN MURDER by Claire McNab. 184 pp. 1st Detective Inspector Carol Ashton Mystery. ISBN 1-931513-65-1 $12.95

DEATH BY DEATH by Claire McNab. 167 pp. 5th Denise Cleever Thriller.
ISBN 1-931513-34-1 $12.95

CAUGHT IN THE NET by Jessica Thomas. 188 pp. A wickedly observant story of mystery, danger, and love in Provincetown. ISBN 1-931513-54-6 $12.95

DREAMS FOUND by Lyn Denison. Australian Riley embarks on a journey to meet her birth mother . . . and gains not just a family, but the love of her life. ISBN 1-931513-58-9 $12.95

A MOMENT'S INDISCRETION by Peggy J. Herring. 154 pp. Jackie is torn between her better judgment and the overwhelming attraction she feels for Valerie.
ISBN 1-931513-59-7 $12.95

IN EVERY PORT by Karin Kallmaker. 224 pp. Jessica has a woman in every port. Will meeting Cat change all that? ISBN 1-931513-36-8 $12.95

TOUCHWOOD by Karin Kallmaker. 240 pp. Rayann loves Louisa. Louisa loves Rayann. Can the decades between their ages keep them apart? ISBN 1-931513-37-6 $12.95

WATERMARK by Karin Kallmaker. 248 pp. Teresa wants a future with a woman whose heart has been frozen by loss. Sequel to *Touchwood*. ISBN 1-931513-38-4 $12.95

EMBRACE IN MOTION by Karin Kallmaker. 240 pp. Has Sarah found lust or love?
ISBN 1-931513-39-2 $12.95

ONE DEGREE OF SEPARATION by Karin Kallmaker. 232 pp. Sizzling small town romance between Marian, the town librarian, and the new girl from the big city.
ISBN 1-931513-30-9 $12.95

CRY HAVOC A Detective Franco Mystery by Baxter Clare. 240 pp. A dead hustler with a headless rooster in his lap sends Lt. L.A. Franco headfirst against Mother Love.
ISBN 1-931513931-7 $12.95

DISTANT THUNDER by Peggy J. Herring. 294 pp. Bankrobbing drifter Cordy awakens strange new feelings in Leo in this romantic tale set in the Old West.
ISBN 1-931513-28-7 $12.95

MAYBE NEXT TIME by Karin Kallmaker. 256 pp. Sabrina has everything she ever wanted—except Jorie. ISBN 1-931513-26-0 $12.95

WHEN GOOD GIRLS GO BAD: A Motor City Thriller by Therese Szymanski. 230 pp. Brett, Randi, and Allie join forces to stop a serial killer. ISBN 1-931513-11-2 $12.95

A DAY TOO LONG: A Helen Black Mystery by Pat Welch. 328 pp. This time Helen's fate is in her own hands. ISBN 1-931513-22-8 $12.95